That's My Baby!

Tom's first thought when he entered his living room was that he didn't remember leaving the lights on when he'd left.

His second thought was that he was *certain* he hadn't left a baby on his coffee table!

Slowly Tom glanced from the rosy-cheeked infant to the one on the Valentine's Day card he'd just received from his mother.

Cupid, he thought blankly.

A sound from the hallway brought his head up. Just as he'd started to deal with his amazement at finding a baby in his living room, he was slammed by another, even more paralyzing shock.

Leslie Harden smiled at him.

"Hello, Goose," she said lightly. As casually as if it hadn't been eighteen months since she'd walked out of his life.

Tom rubbed a hand over his eyes. All the times he'd fantasized about Leslie coming back to him, he'd never imagined it happening anything like *this....*

Dear Reader,

In celebration of Valentine's Day, we have a Special Edition lineup filled with love and romance!

Cupid reignites passion between two former lovebirds in this month's THAT'S MY BABY! title. *Valentine Baby* by Gina Wilkins is about a fallen firefighter who returns home on Valentine's Day to find a baby—and his former sweetheart offering a shocking marriage proposal!

Since so many of you adored Silhouette's MONTANA MAVERICKS series, we have a special treat in store for you over the next few months in Special Edition. Jackie Merritt launches the MONTANA MAVERICKS: RETURN TO WHITEHORN series with a memorable story about a lovelorn cowboy and the woman who makes his life complete, in *Letter to a Lonesome Cowboy*. And coming up are three more books in the series as well as a delightful collection of short stories and an enthralling Harlequin Historical title.

These next three books showcase how children can bond people together in the most miraculous ways. In *Wildcatter's Kid*, by Penny Richards, a young lad reunites his parents. This is the final installment of the SWITCHED AT BIRTH miniseries. Next, *Natural Born Trouble*, by veteran author Sherryl Woods—the second book in her AND BABY MAKES THREE: THE NEXT GENERATION miniseries—is an uplifting story about a reserved heroine who falls for the charms of rambunctious twin boys...and their sexy father! And a sweet seven-year-old inspires a former rebel to reclaim his family, in *Daddy's Home*, by Pat Warren.

Finally, Celeste Hamilton unfolds an endearing tale about two childhood pals who make all their romantic dreams come true, in *Honeymoon Ranch*.

I hope you enjoy this book and each and every title to come!

Sincerely,

Tara Gavin,
Senior Editor and Editorial Coordinator

Please address questions and book requests to:
Silhouette Reader Service
U.S.: 3010 Walden Ave., P.O. Box 1325, Buffalo, NY 14269
Canadian: P.O. Box 609, Fort Erie, Ont. L2A 5X3

GINA WILKINS
VALENTINE BABY

Published by Silhouette Books
America's Publisher of Contemporary Romance

My thanks to Pete Reagan of the Fayetteville, Arkansas,
Fire Department, who patiently answered questions for
this book and the one preceding it.

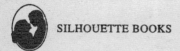 SILHOUETTE BOOKS

ISBN 0-373-24153-4

VALENTINE BABY

Copyright © 1998 by Gina Wilkins

Books by Gina Wilkins

Silhouette Special Edition

The Father Next Door #1082
*It Could Happen To You #1119
Valentine Baby #1153

*From Bud to Blossom

Previously published as Gina Ferris

Silhouette Special Edition

Healing Sympathy #496
Lady Beware #549
In From the Rain #677
Prodigal Father #711
†*Full of Grace* #793
†*Hardworking Man* #806
†*Fair and Wise* #819
†*Far To Go* #862
†*Loving and Giving* #879
Babies on Board #913

†Family Found

Previously published as Gina Ferris Wilkins

Silhouette Special Edition

‡*A Man for Mom* #955
‡*A Match for Celia* #967
‡*A Home for Adam* #980
‡*Cody's Fiancée* #1006

‡The Family Way

Silhouette Books

Mother's Day Collection 1995
Three Mothers and a Cradle
"Beginnings"

GINA WILKINS

declares that she is Southern by birth and by choice, and she has chosen to set many of her books in the South, where she finds a rich treasury of characters and settings. She particularly loves the Ozark mountain region of northern Arkansas and southern Missouri, and the proudly unique people who reside there. She and her husband, John, live in Arkansas, with their three children, Courtney, Kerry and David.

Dear Reader,

There's just something about a baby....

All I have to do is see one, and I melt. I watch babies in restaurants, in stores, in church. I can be entertained for hours, just studying their expressions, and the wonder of exploration in their wide, curious eyes. My husband and I have three children of our own—ages seventeen, fourteen and nine—and we agree that nothing in our lives is more important to us than our kids. Our children have brought us joy, pride, fun—a few gray hairs—but mostly, children bring love.

Babies have a way of changing priorities, as Leslie and Tom discover in this story. Leslie thinks her career is the most important part of her life—until she finds herself responsible for a tiny, totally dependent baby boy. And Tom rediscovers his own strengths through the vulnerability of the baby who unexpectedly enters his life. Their commitment to taking care of Kenny gives them the courage to acknowledge the lasting commitment they have for each other. Their Valentine Baby brings love into their lives—and a few other lives along the way.

There's just something about a baby....

Gina Wilkins

Chapter One

Tom Lowery shook his head as he prepared to turn into the driveway of his Fayetteville, Arkansas, home. Apparently, the high-school cheerleader who lived with her parents next door was having a party again. Cars and pickup trucks—some fairly new, others barely roadworthy—were parked everywhere on the narrow cul-de-sac, hardly leaving enough room for Tom to navigate through them.

At least no one had blocked his driveway, as had happened last time Brandi had thrown a party, though one vehicle was parked right on his curb, two tires on the grass. He lifted his eyebrow when he identified that one as a late-model Lexus. Some parent was being awfully brave to entrust a teenager with that expensive vehicle, he thought as he drove into his carport.

He could hear faint sounds of the party as he climbed out of his own functional, sport utility vehicle. Wondering if Brandi's parents were home, and, if so, how they withstood the constant pounding bass of the music blasting from a stereo, he unlocked his kitchen door. He turned on the light in his kitchen and paused to glance through the day's mail, which he'd retrieved from his mailbox at the curb. There was a bill from the electric company. A you-have-already-been-approved credit-card solicitation. And a bright-red envelope addressed to him in his mother's familiar handwriting. That one he opened, after tossing the others onto the counter.

He chuckled when he saw the card his mother had sent him. On the front was a photograph of a chubby, bald infant wearing nothing but a diaper and holding an enormous red heart—a captivating Cupid with a big, slobbery grin. The words "Happy Valentine's Day, Baby" were printed inside the card, and beneath them Nina had signed, "To my favorite valentine. Love, Mom."

He had a great mom, Tom thought with a fond smile. Always seemed to know when he needed cheering up.

Maybe it was the date that was bothering him. Friday, February 14. Valentine's Day.

Maybe it was just his awareness of the occasion that made being alone seem lonelier than usual tonight. Or maybe it was the fact that he'd spent the past few hours with three couples who'd been so blissfully paired off. Zach and Kim, still practically honeymooners after eight months of marriage. Chris and Burle, happily entangled in a lengthy engagement. And Sherm and Sami, who'd been married for years, were the parents of a month-old daughter and still held hands and sneaked kisses when they thought no one was looking.

They'd all made every effort to keep Tom from feeling the odd man out, but they hadn't been entirely successful. He'd been encouraged to take a date to the dinner party, but there hadn't been anyone in particular whom he'd wanted to invite. So he'd come home early, prepared to spend the rest of the evening guzzling soda and staring at the tube. Hardly high excitement, but it sure beat sitting alone and watching all those couples falling all over each other. Especially since they all insisted on treating him as "poor, brave Tom."

Still holding the valentine, he walked out of the kitchen,

deciding to change into comfortable sweats before crashing into his favorite recliner.

His first thought when he entered his living room was that he didn't remember leaving the lights on when he'd left.

His second thought was that he was certain he hadn't left a baby lying on his coffee table.

The rosy-cheeked infant was strapped into a molded plastic carrier that sat squarely in the center of Tom's large, round oak coffee table. The baby was looking around the room with bright, curious eyes, seemingly perfectly content to be there. Slowly, Tom glanced from the baby on his coffee table to the one pictured on the front of his valentine's day card from his mother.

Cupid, he thought blankly.

A sound from the doorway into his hall brought his head up. Just as he'd started to deal with his surprise at finding a baby in his living room, he was slammed by another, even more paralyzing, shock.

Leslie Harden smiled at him.

"Hello, Goose," she said lightly, as casually as if it hadn't been eighteen months since she'd walked out of his life.

She hadn't changed at all. Her figure was still willowy, graceful. Her dark-auburn hair still waved softly around a face that looked younger than her actual age. There were no lines around her clear blue eyes or her soft, sweetly shaped mouth. She was thirty now, he acknowledged slowly. Less than three months younger than he was.

Two thoughts occurred to him almost simultaneously. He hadn't gotten over Leslie Harden, and the baby in the carrier was obviously too young to be his. He was trying not to analyze his reactions to either observation just yet.

She was still waiting for him to say something. He cleared his throat and tried to speak as casually as she had. "Hello, Leslie. Er, how did you get in?"

She reached in the pocket of the red-and-black-plaid blazer she wore with a red turtleneck and black jeans. "You haven't changed your locks,'' she said as she held up a jingling key ring.

And he hadn't asked for his key back when she'd left. He wondered how that detail had been overlooked—and if it really had been unintentional.

He glanced at the baby, noting that it still lay quietly in its carrier, and that it was staring at Tom as if studying a new life form. It was almost bald, with only a bit of dark fuzz covering its soft scalp, and it was dressed in a soft white romper thing that could have suited either gender. ''Er, is this yours?''

''Sort of,'' Leslie answered with a vague half shrug.

Tom rubbed a hand over his face, half-seriously wondering if he'd fallen asleep in his recliner in front of the TV and was now having a really bizarre dream. All the times he'd fantasized about Leslie's coming back to him, he'd never imagined it happening anything like this.

He wondered if she had any idea what seeing her again did to him.

He cleared his throat. ''I've got to admit that this is a surprise.''

She walked toward him, her expression rueful. ''I know. I suppose you could charge me with breaking and entering, if you like.''

He moved his hand to the back of his neck to massage a muscle that had tightened into a knot. ''When I gave you that key, I told you that you were welcome to use it whenever you liked. That hasn't changed.''

Her lower lip quivered—just for a moment, but he saw it. His stomach clenched in reaction. Tom had always been a sucker for someone in need, and all his instincts told him that Leslie was in trouble.

''I, er...''

She didn't seem to know how to continue, but just stood there, looking at him. Looking lost. Uncharacteristically vulnerable. And his first instinct was to take her in his arms and promise her anything.

Apparently, he'd learned little from the heartache he'd suffered when she'd walked out on him.

"Maybe we'd better sit down," he suggested, waving her toward the couch.

She nodded and perched on the very edge of the boldly striped sofa, her gaze averted as she made a visible effort to pull herself together. Tom glanced at the empty space beside her and quickly decided to sit in one of the two matching recliners, instead. He moved toward it, grimly aware of his limp, aware of Leslie watching him.

An uncomfortable memory flitted through his mind. Leslie's voice echoed through his thoughts, as it had many times during the past year. At least I won't be around to watch you kill yourself, she'd said just before she'd left him. He'd been annoyed then by her implication that he was reckless and irresponsible just because he liked taking a few risks, seeking a few thrills.

He wondered if she would be able to resist the impulse to say "I told you so" when she found out about the accident that had come too damned close to leaving him confined to a wheelchair for the rest of his life.

The baby squirmed in its seat and stuck a finger in its mouth, reclaiming Tom's attention.

"Who is this?" Tom asked, wondering if he really wanted to hear the answer.

Leslie smiled. "This," she said, "is Kenny. My ward."

Ward. Tom digested the word for a moment, trying to analyze his reactions to it—foremost of which seemed to be relief. "Your ward?"

"He's Crystal Pendleton's son."

Tom recognized the name. "Your stepsister."

Looking a bit surprised, Leslie nodded. "I wasn't sure you'd remember. You never met her, and I didn't talk about her much."

"You mentioned her a couple of times." Tom could have added that he remembered almost every word Leslie had said to him during the few spectacular months they'd been together, but he didn't. After all, he still didn't know why she'd come back.

Crystal, he recalled, had been the daughter of a woman Leslie's father had married after divorcing Leslie's mother when Leslie was very young. There had been other wives and other children after that, but Leslie had mentioned Crystal with a warmth in her voice that hadn't been there for the others.

Leslie took a deep breath, then spoke rather flatly. "Crystal died six weeks ago."

Tom looked from the baby to Leslie. "I'm sorry to hear that."

"She had cancer. She discovered it during her pregnancy. She could have had treatment in the early stages, but she refused because she didn't want to harm the baby. By the time Kenny was born, it was already too late to stop the spread of the cancer. She and the baby were living with me when she died in her sleep just after Christmas. She was only thirty-two."

"I'm really sorry, Leslie. I know you were fond of her."

"She was my sister." A quiver ran through her voice, but she steadied it quickly. "She made a will before she died, naming me as the baby's guardian."

"What about the child's father?"

"She never told me his name. She said it didn't matter, that the guy was married to someone else and didn't want anything to do with his son. I have no way of finding out who he is."

Tom looked again at young Kenny, trying to imagine Leslie raising him alone. He was having a little trouble visualizing it. During the time he and Leslie had been together, she'd never expressed any real desire to have children of her own. Not that they'd ever talked about anything that permanent between them, of course.

Career was all that had seemed to matter to her, he thought with a touch of lingering bitterness. It had been her career as an up-and-coming young attorney that he'd blamed for their breakup.

"There was no one else to take him?"

Leslie shook her head. "No. Crystal's mother died years ago, and her only other living family member was an elder brother, Steve. He and Crystal were estranged. They hadn't spoken in a long time when she died."

Tom remembered that name, too. Steve had been several years older than Leslie, and she'd said he intimidated her the few times she'd seen him as a child. She'd described him as an angry teenager who'd detested his stepfather—Leslie's father—and had wanted nothing to do with Leslie.

Tom could remember the night he and Leslie had talked about her childhood. They'd been lying in bed, their bodies limp and sated, her head on his chest. He'd told her a little about growing up as the beloved only child of a woman who'd been an unmarried teenager when he was born. Leslie had talked very briefly about her parents' ugly divorce and the remarriages that had followed for both of them, causing a lot of confusion in her childhood as she'd struggled to adapt to new homes, new families, new situations. He'd felt sorry for her, though he'd had enough sense not to tell her so, and he'd been grateful that his own mother, young as she had been when she'd had him, had never caused him to doubt that she'd loved him above everything else.

So now he knew what she was doing with a baby, but he still couldn't quite understand why she was sitting in his living room. "Leslie—why are you here?"

She twisted her fingers in her lap, something she'd always done when she was nervous—another memory that had remained with him long after she'd gone.

"I have a favor to ask you," she admitted.

Aware of a faint sense of disappointment with her answer, he braced himself. "What can I do for you?"

"I, er, don't think I'm quite ready to ask," she said ruefully, tucking a strand of auburn hair behind her ear. She seemed to search for words, then blurted, "How have you been, Goose?"

It was such an obvious stalling tactic that he had to smile, though the silly nickname that only she had ever called him sent a pang through his heart. "Fine, thanks. What's the favor, Les?"

She avoided answering by asking another question of her own. "I noticed you were limping just now. Have you and Zach been jumping out of planes again?"

Tom didn't quite wince, but it took an effort. "No. Not in a long time."

He fell silent, and she apparently got the message that he wasn't going to explain his limp, at least not yet. So she tried something else to delay the inevitable moment when she would have to explain the favor she wanted of him. Tom was beginning to sense that whatever it was, it was serious. And extremely difficult for her to put into words.

"Zach's doing okay?" she asked.

"He's fine. I spent the evening with him and his wife and a few other friends."

Leslie's blue eyes widened almost comically. "Zach McCain has a *wife?*"

Tom nodded. "They've been married almost a year."

"Wow." She shook her head, looking bemused. "I'll bet that wedding broke some hearts."

Tom took the comment as rhetorical. It was well-known that handsome, dashing Zach McCain had been extremely popular with women, yet believed to be a confirmed bachelor. Zach himself had thought so until he'd met Kim.

Leslie seemed to take a sudden interest in a loose thread on the sleeve of her jacket. Avoiding Tom's eyes, she plucked at it as she asked a bit too casually, "What about you? Thinking about following Zach's example any time soon?"

An uncomfortable silence fell between them as Tom tried to decide what, exactly, she was asking. If he was involved with anyone else? He wasn't, and hadn't been since she'd left him, for various reasons, foremost of which was that he hadn't been able to find anyone who appealed to him the way that she had.

Was she trying to find out if he was interested in getting

back together? He didn't quite know how to answer that, even to himself.

Sure, he'd fantasized about it. Dreamed about it, occasionally. But she'd hurt him when she'd left, though he'd made sure that neither she nor anyone else knew just how hard her desertion had hit him. He wasn't sure he wanted to open himself up to that sort of pain again. Not without some sort of assurance this time that she wouldn't just walk away again.

He tried to speak as lightly as she had. "Hardly. I'm not even dating anyone in particular at the moment."

An expression that seemed to be an odd mixture of relief and anxiety crossed her face. She started to speak, then stopped, tugging industriously at the loose thread as she seemed to be working up her nerve to ask whatever favor she'd come for. The room grew quiet, the tension thick.

His patience wearing thin, Tom cleared his throat. The rough sound startled Kenny, who had been lying so patiently in the carrier during the conversation. The baby jumped and squawked in protest, his face creasing, his tiny mouth opening to cry.

Leslie hurriedly released the baby from the safety straps that held him in the carrier and took him into her arms. Rocking him against her shoulder, she patted his back and crooned reassuringly to him. The child quieted, snuggling contentedly against her shoulder.

"He's tired," she explained, looking more than a little weary herself. "We've been on the road all day."

Tom stared at them with mixed emotions, still finding it hard to believe that Leslie had simply reappeared in his house after so long, that they'd been having this polite, detached discussion after the heated words they'd exchanged the last time they'd been together.

He'd regretted some of the words he'd spoken ever since. But he'd regretted even more some of the words he hadn't been able to say.

"Why are you here?" he asked, unable to bear the suspense any longer.

She looked straight into his eyes. "There's something I have to ask you," she repeated. "It isn't going to be easy for me. But I want you to know in advance that I'll understand completely if your answer is no. In fact, I wouldn't blame you a bit. It's just that—well, I didn't know where else to turn...but don't let that influence you, okay? I'll work it out...somehow...if you can't help me. I don't want you to feel any obligation or any..."

"Leslie," he broke in impatiently, "for God's sake, just ask the question."

She moistened her lips and patted Kenny's back. Her request came out in a nervous rush. "Tom—could you possibly consider marrying me?"

It took Tom maybe thirty seconds of stunned immobility to decide that he couldn't possibly have heard her correctly. "Would you repeat that?"

Leslie's expression held a jumble of emotions. Embarrassment. Nerves. Apology. A plea for understanding. Tom saw all of that and more in the minute or so it took her to work up the courage to say it again.

"I asked if you would marry me."

Which was exactly what he'd thought she'd said the first time. He just hadn't believed it.

He looked from her colorless face to the child now dozing peacefully in her arms. It seemed obvious to him that there was some connection between the baby and the unexpected marriage proposal, but he couldn't quite figure out what it was.

He'd bet that Leslie the attorney would have effectively argued that there was no reason at all that a woman needed a man to help her raise a child. She made plenty of money—certainly more than Tom ever had—and could pay for any assistance she required. So what was making her so desperate that she'd abandoned her considerable pride and taken the potentially humiliating risk of asking her ex-lover, a man she hadn't even seen in more than a year, to marry her?

Seeming to hear the questions in his silence, Leslie drew a deep breath.

"I'm sorry. I'm not usually so blunt and clumsy."

"No." She did, after all, make her living with cleverly phrased questions and carefully chosen words.

"It's just that...I didn't know where else to go. And you said that if there was anything I ever needed from you, anything at all—"

"All you had to do was ask," he finished with a rueful nod. Even as she'd walked out on him, he'd made one last attempt to keep the door open behind her. He'd fallen back on the only thing he'd had to offer—his help, if she ever needed rescuing for any reason.

Apparently, Leslie had no idea that Tom's rescue days were long behind him now. If she was looking for a hero, she'd come to the wrong place.

"What kind of trouble have you gotten yourself into, Les?" he asked warily.

"I've lost my job and my home. I'm almost broke. I'm solely responsible for a four-month-old infant. And now I'm being taken to court," she recited flatly, her blue eyes glittering with chagrin and with tears she was too proud to shed. "Would you say any of that qualifies as trouble?"

"Whoa." Trying to comprehend the magnitude of her plight, he put up a hand to rub his forehead, which was beginning to ache. "Maybe you'd better start from the beginning."

"The beginning?" Leslie shook her head wearily. "I'm not even sure when that would be."

"Just start talking. If I get confused, I'll ask questions."

She began further in the past than he'd expected. "My parents divorced when I was six," she said.

Tom nodded to show that he remembered.

"My father remarried only weeks after the divorce was final. He'd been having an affair with the woman, who was also married when they met. She was the mother of two children—Steve, who was almost fourteen, and Crystal, who was eight. Crystal and I were two bewildered little girls whose homes had just been ripped apart. We were shuttled between battling parents and stepparents, and in our mutual pain and confusion, we became sisters.''

"And Steve?''

"Hated my father. Hated me,'' Leslie answered simply. "His father was devastated by the divorce and blamed mine, of course. It was very ugly. It didn't help that my father dumped Steve's mother for yet another woman four years later. By that time, my mother had remarried—also a man with children of his own—and it was getting very complex just keeping the families sorted out. Since we all continued to live in the same little south Arkansas town, Crystal and I went to the same schools and remained friends.''

Again, she wasn't telling him anything he hadn't heard before. "Go on.''

"Neither of my parents had any more biological children, so I never had a true sibling, only a series of stepsiblings. Crystal was the only one who ever felt like family to me. She and I both grew up with too many scandals, too little security, too many people who thought they had a right to tell us what to do, too few who put our needs ahead of their own.''

Leslie stroked Kenny's downy head, her eyes focused somewhere in the past. "Crystal's emotional damage came out in her rebellious behavior during her teen years. Boys. Booze. Drugs. I thought she was bold and gutsy and incredibly cool. I probably would have followed right in her footsteps, had my mother been more lenient. As it was, she kept a close eye on me, limiting my contact with Crystal, giving me few opportunities to get into trouble. Of course, she couldn't watch me every minute, and the few times I was around Crystal, I always ended up getting into mischief with her. People began to whisper that I was just like her. Steve was very angry with her for causing him so much embarrassment, and he resented the bond she and I had, no matter what happened within our dysfunctional families.''

Tom only nodded again, silently encouraging her to continue.

"As soon as she was old enough, Crystal left small-town

life and gossip behind and moved away. She sent me postcards and little gifts from the most exciting places. New York. L.A. London. Rome. She was beautiful—tall, brunette, well built—and she made her living modeling. Sometimes with her clothes on, more often with them off. As I grew older and a bit wiser, I stopped wanting to emulate her, but I never stopped loving her. We'd been through too much together.''

Despite the less-than-flattering picture he was getting of Crystal, Tom could still identify with the friendship between her and Leslie. There'd been a time when he and Zach McCain had been closer than brothers, their kinship formed through experience and affinity rather than blood. Despite their natural differences, they had uniquely understood each other.

Losing that bond with Zach had hurt Tom almost as much as Leslie's earlier desertion. He'd felt very much alone during the past months. If it hadn't been for his headstrong and sweetly relentless mother, he might well have given in to the depression that had threatened during the months of pain and therapy following the accident.

"Anyway," Leslie went on flatly, breaking into Tom's musing, "as you know, I entered the university here in Fayetteville when I was eighteen, right out of high school. Earned my degree, then got accepted into law school. I chose the law because it interested me, because I was good at it and because I saw a chance to make enough money to be truly independent. I thought I could find the security, the respect and the control of my own life that I'd lacked as a child.''

All of which confirmed Tom's suspicions that her aversion to serious commitment was directly connected to her unstable upbringing. She'd been working in a law firm in nearby Springdale when he'd met her, and though he'd fallen hard and fast, he hadn't pushed for more than she'd wanted to give, had allowed her all the time and freedom he'd thought she needed. Even when she'd gotten the job offer from a prestigious firm in Chicago—a once-in-a-lifetime opportunity for her—he hadn't said much. He had told her he would miss her, but he hadn't begged her to stay, as he'd been tempted to do.

He clearly remembered the day she'd told him about the offer. She'd been glowing with satisfaction and excitement, but there had been a hesitation in her manner, as if she wasn't sure exactly how he would react. He remembered his sense that she'd been waiting for something from him, and he'd wondered if she'd expected a scene, but he'd merely congratulated her and told her to make the decision that seemed right to her. He'd been a firefighter then, overworked and underpaid and loving every minute of it, and he'd had little to offer in comparison with the very advantageous offer from the law firm.

She'd taken the job.

Things had become strained between them during those last few weeks as she'd prepared to move. Tempers and patience had gotten short; words had been exchanged. She'd accused him of being reckless and irresponsible, risking his life for fun on a regular basis with his thrill-seeking buddies from the fire department, inconsiderate of those who cared for him and worried about him. She claimed to be thinking only of his mother, who would, she insisted, be devastated if anything happened to her sole child. In return, Tom had accused Leslie of being a control freak, so obsessed with her career and her security that she took no risks at all.

"I still don't understand—" he began, only to be interrupted by a loud, hard knocking on his door.

Tom looked curiously at his watch. It was almost 9 p.m., and he wasn't expecting company this evening.

He shoved a hand through his hair. "Let me see who that is and then we'll finish this."

Leslie nodded and cradled the sleeping baby in her arms. Acutely aware of his limp, which was always worse at night when he was tired, Tom crossed the room to open the door. He knew he'd have to explain his physical limitations to Leslie eventually, but he wasn't looking forward to it.

The man on Tom's doorstep was a stranger. Tall. Dark haired. Dark eyed. Somewhere in his late thirties. He looked angry.

"May I help you?" Tom inquired.

"I'm looking for Leslie Harden. I understand she's here."

There was an audible gasp from behind Tom's left shoulder. He turned to find Leslie standing there, the baby in her arms, her eyes wide. Instinctively, Tom moved between her and the stranger. "Who are you?" he demanded. "What do you want with Leslie?"

"How did you find me here?" Leslie demanded before the guy could answer. "How on earth did you know where to look?"

"I had you followed," the man replied, and there was a touch of smugness in his voice, as if he were quite pleased with his own cleverness. "I figured you would try something like this. There's been someone parked out on the street watching this place since you let yourself in. I've been an hour and a half behind you, ever since you sneaked out of your apartment in Chicago."

"I did not sneak out of my apartment. I moved out. I don't have to report my whereabouts to you, Steve."

Steve Pendleton, Tom thought. Crystal's brother. Leslie's one-time stepbrother, who'd never liked her.

"You do as long as you've got my nephew," Pendleton growled, moving as though to take the baby away from Leslie, who shrank back, cradling the infant to her chest.

Tom planted himself more firmly between Leslie and Pendleton. "This is my house," he said flatly. "You haven't been invited inside."

Dark eyes glittering, Pendleton glared at Tom. "Stay out of this," he ordered curtly. "It doesn't concern you."

"Yes, as a matter of fact, it does," Tom corrected him coolly, reaching out to wrap an arm around Leslie's waist.

His frown deepening, Pendleton looked from that protective, possessive arm to Tom's carefully expressionless face. "Who the hell are you?"

Tom felt Leslie stiffen, but he kept his attention on Pendleton's face as he answered with a touch of the old recklessness, "The name's Tom Lowery. I'm Leslie's fiancé. And just who the hell are *you?*"

Chapter Two

Tom watched the instant suspicion cross Pendleton's face. And then he glanced sideways at Leslie. Whatever her thoughts were about Tom's impulsive announcement, she kept them hidden, showing no surprise at hearing that she was engaged.

Pendleton, too, was looking at Leslie now. "Is this true?" he demanded. "You're marrying this guy?"

"Yes." Her reply was firm, cool, utterly convincing.

Pendleton made no effort to hide his skepticism. "Since when? No one mentioned a fiancé before."

Leslie shrugged. "I guess your so-called investigators weren't as good as you thought. I hope you didn't pay them too much. I hate to see anyone, even you, taken for a ride by sharp operators."

Tom chuckled and tightened his arm around her waist, admiring her spirit despite her obvious distress at Pendleton's presence.

Leslie wasn't finished. "You wasted your time chasing after

me, Steve. As you can see, Kenny is just fine, but it's late and I need to get him into bed. And by the way, if you don't stop having me followed, I'm charging you with harassment, is that clear?"

"If you think I'm going to disappear from your life just because you've ordered me to, you're wrong," he snapped. "I—"

A musical voice from the open doorway interrupted Pendleton's threat, startling all of them.

"Goodness, there are a lot of cars parked out here. Tommy? What's going on?"

The woman in the doorway was tiny, no more than five feet tall. Her eyes were green, her hair ash-blond and cut into a soft bob that framed a pretty, oval face. Her unlined skin gave little indication of her age. She was dressed in a bright-blue pantsuit and she held a covered pie plate in front of her.

"Who's this?" Pendleton asked sarcastically, looking from the woman in the doorway to Tom. "Another fiancée?"

"This," Tom answered with some satisfaction, "is my mother."

This time Pendleton's expression was openly disbelieving. "Yeah, right."

Leslie smiled, though she looked a bit worried. "Hello, Nina. It's good to see you."

"Leslie!" Nina's face brightened with pleasure as she moved around Steve Pendleton to greet Leslie as warmly as if it hadn't been over a year since she'd last seen Tom's ex-girlfriend. "And look at this little angel," she crooned, admiring the baby still sleeping in Leslie's arms.

"Leslie and her nephew just got into town, Mom," Tom said, sending her frantic mental messages. "I know you've been looking forward to seeing this baby I've been telling you about."

"Of course," Nina replied promptly, with only one searching glance Tom's way. "You and Leslie know how much I love babies."

"He is not her nephew," Pendleton, growing frustrated

again, almost shouted. "He's *mine*. And I'm the one who's going to make sure he is properly raised. I don't know what you're planning with this guy, Leslie, but I'm not giving up. I'm filing for custody of my nephew, and if you think I'm just going to let you get away with—"

"Crystal left this baby in my care," Leslie broke in heatedly. "Her will made it very clear how she felt about that. You don't care about Kenny. You just can't stand it that I'm the one Crystal trusted to raise him."

Pendleton opened his mouth to argue, but before he could speak, Nina handed Tom the pie plate and moved toward Pendleton with a smile and an outstretched hand. "Forgive me. I've been terribly rude by not introducing myself. I'm Nina Lowery. And you are…?"

Tom wasn't surprised when Pendleton closed his mouth, cleared his throat, then took Nina's hand and managed a fairly polite expression. Nina had a way of slipping past any guy's guard.

"I'm Steve Pendleton," he answered just a bit stiffly. "Kenny's uncle. I'm sorry I raised my voice, Mrs. Lowery, but that baby is my late sister's child and I have a responsibility to make sure that he will be brought up in the right environment. I don't know anything about this sudden engagement between Leslie and your son, but it's going to take more than that to make me just go away and forget about my nephew."

"Sudden engagement?" Nina repeated.

Tom stiffened, as did Leslie at his side.

Nina laughed. "I would hardly call it sudden," she went on smoothly. "My Tommy's been head over heels for Leslie for almost two years now. They make such an attractive couple, don't they?"

"Er—"

Nina patted Pendleton's arm. "And of course you're concerned about your little nephew. I think it's admirable that you care so much about his welfare, and I'm sure Leslie and Tom understand how you must feel. Perhaps tomorrow, after everyone's had a good night's rest, you can all sit down and talk about what would be best for little Kenny's future. Do you have a place to stay tonight, Mr. Pendleton?''

"No, I, um—''

"There are several excellent inns not far from here. I'll be passing one of them on my way home. Would you like to follow me in your car? That's much easier than trying to give directions.''

"Well, I—''

The baby stirred and began to fret.

"He's hungry,'' Leslie said. "He wants his bottle and bed.''

"Of course he does, poor little darling,'' Nina cooed, stroking the baby's flailing fist. "We'll leave you to take care of him now.''

She moved toward Pendleton, who was staring at her as if trying to decide whether she was putting him on. And then she stopped and clapped her hands.

"Why don't you all come to my apartment for lunch tomorrow?'' she asked as though on impulse. "We'll have a nice long talk so we can all get to know one another better.''

"Oh, no, we can't—'' Leslie began.

"But I—'' Pendleton blurted at the same time.

"That's a great idea, Mom,'' Tom said, overriding both of them. "We'll enjoy your cooking and talk about Kenny's future.''

"Fine.'' Smiling almost smugly, Nina nodded. "I'll give Mr. Pendleton directions to my place on the way to our cars. Shall we say twelve-thirty?''

"We'll be there,'' Tom agreed, holding the pie plate in his left hand and sliding his right arm possessively around Leslie's shoulders.

Giving each other glowering looks, Leslie and Pendleton nodded reluctantly, apparently conceding defeat. For the moment.

Nina sent Tom a glance that spoke volumes. "Good night, dear. We'll talk tomorrow.''

They certainly would. Tom could already hear the dozens

of questions she was going to have for him at the first opportunity. "Good night, Mom. Thanks for the pie." And everything else, he added silently.

"You're welcome. I made one for my bridge club tonight, and I decided to make an extra pie for you while I was baking. I had planned to bring it to you earlier, but I ran out of time. You share it with Leslie, you hear? And happy Valentine's Day to you both, by the way," she added.

Looking as though he wasn't quite sure what had happened during the past few minutes, Pendleton allowed Nina, still chattering brightly, to usher him out the door. Tom and Leslie were left alone with the now crying baby.

Leslie patted Kenny's back ineffectually. She had to raise her voice slightly to be heard above his wails. "Tom, I—"

The telephone rang, adding to the din.

Tom massaged his aching forehead and nodded toward the kitchen. "You feed the baby. I'll answer that. We'll talk later."

With a faint exhale, Leslie turned to comply. Tom set the pie on the coffee table and picked up the phone, wondering what could possibly happen next. "Hello?"

"Tom, it's Chris. Are you okay?"

He winced. Great. Just what he needed. "I'm fine, Chris. Why do you ask?"

"Well, you left the party so early. Everyone was sort of worried about you. Your back isn't hurting or anything, is it?"

No more than usual, he could have told her, but he simply replied, "No, really. I'm fine. Just a bit tired. Long day at the office."

"Ton of paperwork, huh?" she asked, commiserating.

She knew that Tom would rather walk across hot coals than do paperwork, but since his injuries had permanently sidelined him from active fire-fighting duty, paperwork had become a necessary evil for him. Sometimes he thought the fire marshal's office had been created specifically to generate more paperwork.

"Yeah."

"You're sure you're feeling okay?"

Only his awareness that Chris was genuinely concerned about him kept Tom from snapping his answer. "I'm fine. Thank you."

"Good. Listen, some of us are getting together at Lou's Grill tomorrow night. I've got a girlfriend coming I'd love for you to meet. Her name's Pam, and I think the two of you would really hit it off. I was going to tell you about her at the party, but you took off before I had a chance. I've already told her about you and she can't wait to meet you. What do you say?"

"Chris." He almost groaned her name. What would it take to convince this woman that he did not want her introducing him to every single woman in northwest Arkansas?

"You'll like her, Tom. She's very pretty," Chris said enticingly.

Tom heard Leslie moving around in the kitchen. "Thanks, but I already have a date for tomorrow evening."

"A date?" Chris sounded skeptical. "With a girl?"

"No, with a horse," he retorted curtly.

"Someone new?" she persisted, unperturbed by his acerbity and oblivious, as usual, to hints that this was none of her business.

"No. Someone I've known a long time. Look, Chris, I—"

"Did I mention that Pam's a classic-car buff?" Chris broke in breezily. "Loves antique imports. I know she would have loved that MG you used to have. You and she have a lot in common."

She wasn't going to give up. Chris Patton, bless her matchmaking little heart, never gave up. "Chris, I'm involved with someone. Seriously involved," he said impulsively. "So there's really no need for you to keep trying to fix me up, okay? I'm not available."

She laughed. "Sure, Lowery. Nice try. Did I tell you that Pam—"

"Chris. Forget it. There's someone else. As a matter of fact, she's here now, so if you'll excuse me..."

Chris didn't sound convinced. "What's her name?"

"Leslie."

"Leslie? Didn't you once date someone named Leslie? I'm sure the guys at the station mentioned that name."

"Right. Same one. We were apart for a while, but we've reconciled. And I'd like to get back to her now. So, thank you for calling and good night."

"Wow. Wait'll everyone hears about this! This is great, Tom. I can't wait to meet her."

His head was beginning to pound in earnest now. He didn't know what had gotten into him. Why had he told Chris he was back with Leslie? By this time tomorrow, everyone in town would have heard about it. He hadn't been thinking clearly since he'd come home to find her waiting for him. Since then, everything seemed to have spun out of control.

If he wasn't careful, he was going to find himself married to Leslie Harden before he knew what hit him. And he certainly didn't want that to happen...

Did he?

He said good-night again and hung up the phone while Chris was still sputtering questions. And then he looked toward the kitchen, squared his shoulders and started walking in that direction. Might as well get this over with, he thought. And besides, he kept the headache tablets in the kitchen pantry.

Something told him this headache was going to get worse before the night was over.

Leslie had the baby propped against her shoulder for a burp when Tom entered the kitchen. She noted the lines of strain around his eyes and mouth and regretted that she'd put them there.

Darn Steve for showing up tonight before she'd finished her explanations to Tom. Actually, everything was Steve's fault. Had he not decided to cause such problems for her after his sister's death, Leslie would not have been forced to turn to Tom at all.

She refused to even consider that Steve's actions had only provided her an excuse to justify what she'd wanted to do all along.

Tom rummaged in the pantry, found a small plastic bottle and popped the lid. He swallowed two capsules dry, replaced the pill container in the pantry, then opened the refrigerator. "Want anything to drink?" he asked. "I have soda or juice."

"No, thank you."

He nodded and pulled out a canned soda for himself, popped the top and tipped his head back for a long drink.

Leslie watched him, emotions swirling inside her. He'd changed since she'd last seen him, but she wasn't exactly sure how to define the difference. It wasn't so much in appearance. His dark-blond hair was still full and thick and habitually tousled. He was slim and fit, his shoulders broad beneath a cable-knit oatmeal-colored sweater, narrow hips and long legs snugly encased in denim. She hadn't forgotten the rich, deep green of his eyes, but the faint lines around them had been carved since she'd left.

So much had happened to her since she'd moved away, and she assumed that there had been changes in his life, as well. And yet, some things hadn't changed at all. The way her heart quivered when he smiled at her, for example. The way her breath caught in her throat when he turned those all-too-perceptive green eyes her way.

Tom had always had a tendency to conceal his thoughts behind a smile and a deceptively open-looking expression. She had never known exactly how he'd felt about her leaving eighteen months ago, and she didn't know how he really felt about her reappearance now.

She'd really made a mess of this evening. She'd been so relieved to learn from a telephone directory in a nearby convenience store that Tom's address was still the same. When he hadn't answered the doorbell, she'd deliberated for several long minutes about trying the key she'd carried like a good-luck charm on her key ring ever since she'd gone away. But it had been cold out and Kenny had been tired and fussy and she hadn't known what else to do. It had been a great relief to find that the key still worked.

She hadn't been there long before Tom returned. She'd left the living room only to wash her hands in the bathroom, where she'd been when Tom had come into the living room and first spotted Kenny. She had been somewhat relieved to see no immediate evidence that another woman spent much time in his house. When she and Tom had been together, her things had somehow gotten scattered all over. It had taken her an entire day to gather them all. She remembered that day as being a particularly difficult one, with Tom concealing his thoughts more than usual behind jokes and repartee, and her trying very hard not to show her own convoluted emotions.

He'd said he wasn't even seeing anyone now. The relief she'd felt had been immediate and powerful. She had more than half expected to find some other woman's belongings scattered through his house, some other woman sharing his life and his bed. She hadn't really known what she would have done had that been the case.

"Looks like he's asleep again."

In response to Tom's comment, Leslie turned her attention to Kenny, who'd fallen asleep on her shoulder. "Poor thing, he's worn out," she murmured. "It's been a long day—for both of us."

"Where do you want to put him while we talk? Will he be okay on my bed, or will he roll off?"

"He rolls," she answered. "I'll strap him back in his carrier for now."

Tom frowned. "Not the most comfortable place for him to sleep."

"I have a portable crib in my car, but—"

Tom nodded. "I'll get it."

She thought of the limp she'd noticed earlier, and she wondered how badly he'd hurt himself this time. During the months she'd spent with him, he'd been perpetually covered in bumps and bruises from his active and daring life-style. She'd lived in constant fear that his recklessness would one day result in more than minor aches and pains, but he'd laughed off her warnings. Tom and his buddy Zach had seemed to believe they were invulnerable, practically immortal. They'd laughed at danger, if they'd ever even acknowledged its existence. They'd spent their working hours rescuing other people, yet hadn't hesitated to place themselves in danger, either for work or fun.

"You aren't feeling well," she said, glancing at the pantry to remind him that she'd just watched him take the painkillers. "I'll get it."

"Leslie."

The set of his jaw told her that he had just about reached the limits of his patience that evening.

"Give me your keys."

She reached in her pocket and pulled out the keys. "It's the black Lexus at your curb," she said. "The crib's in the back seat."

"What else should I bring in? Do you have everything you need for the baby for now?"

She nodded. "I brought his bag in earlier." She'd left her own in the car. She hadn't been quite bold enough to take for granted that she would be spending the night here.

"I'll be right back," Tom said.

When he left the room his limp was even more noticeable than it had been earlier.

Feeling worried, weary and guilty, Leslie carried the baby into the living room, where she changed his diaper and refastened his warm sleeper without even rousing him. She'd gotten pretty good at things like that during the past four months. She'd been wholly responsible for this baby since his birth. Crystal had been in no shape to care for him by the time he'd been delivered by cesarean section as soon as he had developed enough to survive. He'd been small, less than five pounds, but healthy, and he'd thrived in Leslie's care. Just watching her baby had given Crystal a great deal of joy in her last few painful weeks of life, and Leslie would never regret anything she'd done, anything she'd sacrificed for the woman who'd been her sister in spirit.

She wasn't letting Steve take Kenny away from her. No matter what she had to do to stop him, she thought with renewed determination. Which was why she'd come to Tom. She'd known deep inside that he was the only one who could help her. And somehow she'd known, as well, that he wouldn't turn her away.

The baby was tucked into the portable crib in the spare bedroom, sleeping soundly, and Tom and Leslie sat at the kitchen table behind cups of coffee and slices of chocolate pie. Tom toyed unenthusiastically with his dessert, and noticed that Leslie wasn't eating with much more interest, which was, he thought glumly, a terrible waste of a great chocolate pie.

He hadn't said much after he'd come back in with the crib. Mostly, he'd sat quietly, listening to Leslie as she'd explained how Crystal had shown up sick and five months pregnant on her doorstep in Chicago. Leslie had taken her friend in without question and had then cared for her through the remainder of the pregnancy as cancer had slowly eaten away at Crystal's body. Leslie had sacrificed her private life and neglected her career during those months and the ones that followed Kenny's delivery. Crystal had made Leslie promise that she would raise Kenny with love and tolerance and the security that Crystal and Leslie had never had as children.

Shifting in his chair in an effort to relieve the dull ache of his back, Tom asked, "And when did Steve enter the picture?"

"Not long after Crystal died. She wouldn't let me contact him during her illness. They'd had a terrible fight a couple of years earlier and hadn't spoken since. Steve didn't approve of Crystal's life-style—her nude modeling or her lack of judgment or restraint when it came to men, her refusal to plan for the future or worry about the consequences of her actions. Steve and Crystal reacted very differently to the vagaries of their childhood. Steve became as careful and conservative as Crystal was rebellious and reckless."

"And yet Crystal refused medical treatment for the sake of her baby."

Leslie's eyes softened. "Yes. She said it was the first time in her life anyone ever really needed her for anything, and she couldn't fail him."

"Could her life have been saved?" he asked. "If she'd risked the baby, I mean."

Leslie sighed. "I don't know. Maybe...but she made her choice. And she died believing she made the right one."

Tom shifted in his seat again.

Rousing herself from her thoughts, Leslie went on. "Steve was notified of Crystal's death, of course. I called him myself. Crystal hadn't even wanted me to tell Steve about Kenny, but I thought he had a right to know he had a nephew. I thought maybe he would like to be a part of Kenny's life—you know, visit occasionally, exchange birthday and Christmas cards. But I never expected..."

"That Steve would try to take Kenny away from you?" Tom finished when Leslie let the words trail off.

She nodded unhappily. "I hadn't realized how much anger he still harbored toward my father...and, indirectly, toward me. He said Kenny was his flesh and blood, not mine, and he didn't want his nephew being raised by Ben Harden's daughter. He said I'd never tried to save Crystal from her own actions. Steve knew I'd sent Crystal money a few times when she got into trouble, and he said that had only encouraged her."

"So Steve filed for custody of Kenny."

"He hasn't actually filed suit yet, but he insists that he's going to. The will was valid, of course. I made sure it was legal and correct. But custody battles are tricky. Judges don't always take the mother's wishes into consideration, especially when the mother...well, when the mother was like Crystal."

"But you're an attorney, with an impeccable reputation," Tom protested.

"Now," she agreed. "But I told you I did a few foolish things in my youth, usually in Crystal's company. Nothing serious, but Steve could produce enough evidence to make me look somewhat less than spotless. And losing my job didn't help my case."

"What happened?"

"I just couldn't keep up," she admitted. "It was a high-powered firm. There wasn't a lot of tolerance for personal problems. Too many people standing in line to take my place. Looking after Crystal took a lot of my time, and then after Kenny was born, small and a bit sickly at first, it was all I could do to get in to the office a few hours a day. I finally made a mistake in a case—nothing major, just a small error—but it was the excuse the partners had been looking for. They let me go with polite regrets and insincere best wishes for my future. I have no hope that I'll be given a glowing recommendation when they are contacted by future potential employers."

Tom shook his head in sympathy. "You've had a hell of a year, haven't you?"

She nodded fervently. "It's wiped me out," she said flatly.

Tom knew she'd made a lot of money for the firm, and that she wasn't one to live lavishly. Which left him only one conclusion. "You paid Crystal's medical bills?"

"As much as I could," she acknowledged. "They were astronomical. And so were the bills for Kenny's delivery and the week he spent in the newborn intensive care unit until he weighed enough to come home. Crystal had no insurance, of course, but I was afraid to ask for too much assistance for fear that it wouldn't look good when I applied for full guardianship of Kenny. Most of the bills are paid now, but I have almost nothing left. Only the Lexus, and I plan to sell that as soon as I can."

She was looking directly into Tom's eyes, and he had the impression that she was giving him a clear picture of her situation so that he couldn't claim to have been misled in any way. She really was in a bind, he mused. And she'd asked him for help, even though he'd always considered Leslie Harden to be the proudest, most stubbornly independent woman he'd ever known, with the exception of his mother.

It couldn't have been easy for her to come to him. It was a measure of her love for little Kenny, and her fear of losing him, that she had.

"What do you want me to do, Leslie?" he asked finally, simply.

She drew a deep breath. "Steve is a single male, but he has a good job and the financial means to hire help if he wins custody of the baby. I'm without a job or immediate prospects, as I'm sure he'll point out, and he's also made it clear that he doesn't believe a single woman can do an adequate job of raising a boy."

Tom scowled. His mother, no doubt, would have a few things to say about that.

"There's a chance," Leslie continued doggedly, "that I could win the case alone. I have Crystal's will on my side, and it's no longer generally believed that a single woman can't be an effective parent. And yet..."

Again, Tom sensed what she wanted to say. "You're afraid to take the risk."

She nodded, her lower lip quivering just faintly. "I can't lose him, Tom. He's all I have left."

He stifled a renewed impulse to take her into his arms and comfort her. There were still things that needed to be said, decisions that had to be made. "You decided it would help your case to be married," he prompted.

"An attorney I consulted suggested it and asked if I was involved with anyone who would be willing to help me out. I immediately said no, of course, but then I thought of you. And I wondered..."

"Why didn't you call me?"

"I didn't know how to talk to you about this over the telephone. For all I knew, you had moved or gotten married or involved with someone. How could I just call you up out of the blue and propose to you?" she asked ruefully.

Tom wasn't sure it would have been any more awkward than his finding her unexpectedly in his living room, but he kept quiet.

"Steve seemed so determined, so confident that he would take Kenny away from me. I thought I could buy some time by disappearing for a little while. I came straight here because I didn't know where else to go. I had no idea, of course, that Steve was having me watched," she added scornfully.

"What, exactly, does Steve do?"

"He's in business for himself. Some sort of distribution business, I think. He makes good money, but Crystal said he doesn't seem to take much pleasure in it. He wanted her to settle down and work for him, but she said there were too many strings attached. She refused. I think that was when they had their big quarrel and stopped speaking."

"He probably thought he was doing her a favor. Offering her a chance to make a living in a respectable job."

"He probably did," Leslie agreed with a sigh. "But he suggested it so arrogantly that she wouldn't even consider it. Maybe he thought he was trying to save her, but in her eyes, he was trying to control her. And Crystal couldn't accept that."

Leslie sounded as if she fully understood Crystal's sentiments in that respect, at least.

Tom finally asked the question that had been hovering at the back of his mind during the entire conversation. "Leslie...why me?"

She gave him a look of apology and said, "Partly because you were the last man I was involved with. The first one who came to mind when my associate mentioned a, er, marriage of convenience."

Tom nodded grimly.

"And I kept remembering what you'd said to me the day I left—about being here for me if I ever needed you. We were both grumpy that day, said a few words we probably shouldn't have, but...well, I knew your offer was genuine. You weren't just trying to be polite, or to say something nice to see me on my way. You meant it.''

He nodded again. ''I meant it.''

''We were good friends, weren't we, Goose?'' she asked softly.

''We were more than that,'' he reminded her.

''Yes.''

She looked a bit uncomfortable that she was taking such blatant advantage of the relationship they'd had. The relationship that she had ended, he couldn't help remembering with a sting that was still as fresh as it had been eighteen months earlier.

He sighed, pushed his plate away and glanced at his watch. ''It's getting late,'' he said, having noted the lines of weariness around her mouth. ''You've been on the road most of the day. You must be tired.''

She nodded without meeting his eyes.

''You can take the bed in the spare room, if you don't mind rooming with Kenny. Or you can take my room, leave the baby where he is, and I'll bunk on the couch.''

She looked up then. ''I'll sleep in the spare room with Kenny. I didn't come here to throw you out of your bed.''

He didn't think she'd come to share it with him, either. His mouth twisted, but he said only, ''Fine.''

Leslie cleared her throat. ''You, um, haven't given me an answer. To my, er, proposal.''

He nodded. ''I know. Let's take it a day at a time for now, okay? After all, we're meeting with Steve tomorrow. There's always a chance he'll see reason and drop his case.''

''Which would mean you'd be off the hook,'' Leslie remarked with a forced smile.

''As would you,'' he noted.

''There's always a chance,'' she murmured, though she didn't sound particularly optimistic.

''Mmm.'' He didn't even try to read her expression, just as he was deliberately not analyzing his own feelings at the moment. "You'll need your bags. Tell me which ones to bring in and I'll get them for you."

"No," she said, her chin firming again. "I'll get my own bags. You've done enough tonight."

She sounded prepared to argue. Tom just wasn't in the mood. "Fine," he said. "I'll clear out of the bathroom so it'll be free when you need it."

Blinking a little in surprise at his quick capitulation, Leslie gathered her plate and glass and carried them to the dishwasher, then left to collect her bags. Tom limped into the bathroom, his head still pounding, his pulse still jumping from the shock of having Leslie Harden back in his life.

Tom didn't sleep particularly well that night. He couldn't blame Kenny, though he did hear the baby cry out once during the early hours, immediately followed by the sounds of Leslie moving around and speaking in soft, shushing tones. But the baby's cry hadn't awakened him. Tom had been lying awake for hours, pondering what his answer would be if Leslie asked him again to marry her.

By the time daylight crept through the slats of the blinds in his bedroom window, he was no closer to an answer than he had been when he'd gone to bed.

Chapter Three

Leslie felt as though she'd been dragged over a gravel road by a pickup truck when she awoke Saturday morning, after managing maybe two hours of sleep. Kenny hadn't slept well, probably because of his unfamiliar surroundings and the overstimulation of a full day of car travel, but Leslie didn't blame the baby for her sleeplessness.

She'd spent most of the night wondering what was different about Tom. She hadn't exactly expected an open-arm welcome, of course, especially since they'd parted coolly. She wouldn't have been at all surprised to find him involved with another woman, maybe to the point of cohabiting. He was, after all, an attractive and intriguing man who'd always been popular with the local women. But she hadn't expected him to be almost a stranger to her.

He'd looked tired...and not the kind of tired that follows a hard day's work. The kind of tired that seeped all the way through to the soul.

Crystal had looked that kind of tired when she'd shown up on Leslie's doorstep, broke, sick, pregnant, defeated.

Tom had always been animated, even after a strenuous, twenty-four-hour stint at the fire station. Even after rescuing stranded hikers or kayakers or climbers from next-to-impossible predicaments. Even after boldly risking his own life to save a stranger. There'd been a flame inside him that had burned hot, bright, reckless. Leslie had seen it gleaming in his eyes the first time she'd met him. She'd worried even then that she would get burned by it.

That flame had been dampened since she'd left eighteen months ago—if not completely extinguished.

She didn't try to delude herself that her departure had affected him that deeply. They hadn't had that sort of relationship, had never spoken any words of commitment. She'd never expected more from him than what he'd given her—a few months of excitement and exhilaration, fun, laughs, passion. Things that had been sadly absent from her life before he'd swept into it.

Leslie had never stopped missing those feelings—missing Tom.

She brushed her hair and pulled the top back into a barrette. Her face looked pale, so she put on just a touch of makeup, chiding herself for her vanity even as she applied it.

Wearing the red fleece shirt and black fleece pants she'd slept in, she carried Kenny into the kitchen for his morning bottle. She'd stashed a couple in the refrigerator last night; all she had to do was take one out and warm it in the microwave. Kenny liked his formula at approximately room temperature, she'd discovered through trial and error. In his own wordless manner, he was able to express his tastes quite clearly, she thought with a fond smile.

After carrying baby and bottle into the living room, she settled on one end of the couch and cradled Kenny in the crook of her left arm as she popped the nipple into his open mouth. He began to nurse noisily. Leslie kissed his forehead, then glanced toward the still-closed door to Tom's bedroom. She wasn't surprised that he hadn't made an appearance yet this morning.

It was still early—not quite 7 a.m. Kenny was an early riser. Fortunately, he was a very good baby. He rarely cried, and then only when he was hungry, wet or overly tired. Thankfully, he'd never had colic or anything more serious than minor sniffles. Leslie wasn't sure how she would have coped with those complications on top of Crystal's illness, but she supposed somehow she would have managed. What choice would she have had?

After draining the bottle, Kenny wanted to play. He lay on his back on her thighs, kicking his feet and gazing up at her as he babbled and chortled, pleased with his full tummy and her undivided attention. Leslie crooned to him and chuckled at the funny faces he made. His smiles were sweet, damp, innocent. Utterly trusting. And she loved him so much it hurt.

She wasn't handing this baby over to Steve without one hell of a fight.

Tom's door opened and he came into the living room, his sandy hair tumbled around his unshaven face, his eyes a bit glazed. He wore a gray sweat suit with the Fayetteville fire department logo on the chest, and white socks on his feet.

He didn't look as though he'd slept any better than she had. She certainly understood. She couldn't imagine how he must have felt at having her show up without warning and propose to him. He'd probably spent at least part of the night wondering how to gracefully get rid of her, she thought with a swallowed sigh. She'd have to find a way to convince him that elaborate measures wouldn't be necessary. If he chose not to participate in her fight for Kenny, whatever the reason, she wouldn't cause problems. She could disappear as quickly as she'd arrived.

She would get by without his help. Somehow.

"Have you had breakfast?" he asked, looking toward the kitchen.

"No. Kenny wanted his first."

Tom glanced at the baby, then at Leslie. "I'll make coffee."

She nodded, beginning to frown. Who *was* this somber, distant stranger? And what had he done with Tom Lowery, the laid-back, happy-go-lucky, irreverent joker she'd known before?

She didn't think Tom had cracked a joke since she'd arrived last night. Was he still this angry with her for leaving the way she had—or was it something else?

He was limping again as he moved toward the kitchen. She wondered if he was in pain, if that would explain the way he'd been acting. "Tom?"

He looked over his shoulder. "Yeah?"

"I noticed you're still favoring your right leg. Have you seen a doctor?"

"Yes."

He went into the kitchen without elaborating.

Leslie blinked and gazed at the baby in her lap, stung by the abruptness of Tom's answer. "Well, Kenny," she murmured with a sigh, "looks like we won't be staying here very long."

Tom certainly hadn't welcomed her with open arms.

Tom wanted to blame his less-than-gracious behavior on lack of sleep. That might have accounted for part of it, but he knew there was a lot more to it than that. The sight of Leslie Harden, sitting completely relaxed on his sofa, cooing down at the smiling baby in her lap, had hit him hard that morning.

Damn it, he didn't want to get hurt again. How many blows was a guy supposed to take before he was allowed to throw in the towel?

Partly as an apology for his surly behavior, he cooked breakfast. He remembered that Leslie had a weakness for thick slabs of French toast with powdered sugar and maple syrup. He'd made it for her several times while they'd been together. She'd always fussed at him for tempting her with so many calories, and then had cleaned her plate with an enthusiasm he'd enjoyed.

"That smells heavenly," she said from the doorway, just

as he set the two plates on the kitchen table. She held the baby, who was clinging to her shirt with one chubby hand and had the other crammed into his mouth.

"I hope you're hungry," Tom said, nodding toward her well-filled plate.

"Starved."

"Coffee? Orange juice?"

"Both, please."

He nodded. "I'll get them for you. You want me to bring the carrier in here for the baby? You can't eat and hold him, can you?"

"Actually, I can," she answered with a smile that bespoke experience. "But I'll get the carrier while you pour our drinks."

She set the plastic seat on the table within her reach, strapped Kenny in, and handed him a colorful teething toy, which went immediately into the baby's mouth. "He's getting a tooth, I think," Leslie explained, reaching for her fork.

Tom concentrated on his breakfast. For some reason, he found himself avoiding looking at the baby. He couldn't explain it, exactly, but something about little Kenny made him uncomfortable.

He usually liked babies, enjoyed watching their funny faces, their wide-eyed fascination with everything around them, their innocence and candor. But this baby...well, for some reason it almost scared him. And that was ridiculous, of course. What harm could a tiny infant cause him?

Suddenly aware of the silence between him and Leslie, he cleared his throat and tried to think of something to say. Even he was aware of how strangely he was acting. Leslie must be wondering what on earth was wrong with him. *Quiet* was not an adjective that had been applied to him very often.

"Mom came through pretty well last night, didn't she?" he asked. "Didn't even look surprised to see you here."

"I've always said your mother was a treasure," Leslie remarked. "But I'm very sorry that we—that I put her in such an awkward position."

"Knowing Mom, she's just itching to find out what's going on. I'm surprised she hasn't already called. She'll want to know what to say to Steve during lunch, of course."

Abruptly, Leslie put down her fork. Her face was troubled, her eyes shadowed.

"This isn't going to work," she said flatly. "It was a really stupid idea, a foolishly impulsive mistake on my part. It was just that...well, I panicked in Chicago and I ran, and somehow I ended up here. I should never have done this to you or to your mother, and I can't expect you to get involved in my problems, so as soon as I've showered and dressed, Kenny and I will be leaving. Just forget what I asked, okay? And please accept my apology for intruding on you the way I did."

Keeping his voice very calm to counteract the mounting distress in hers, Tom asked politely, "And just where will you go?"

As he'd expected, she had no immediate answer.

Tom had already figured out that she'd literally had no one else to turn to when she'd come to him. And, while it wasn't exactly flattering that she'd seen him as a last resort, he had no intention of sending her away without doing whatever he could to help her.

Even had there not been a complex history between them, even if the feelings he'd had for her had died—which they had not—even if she were a total stranger, for that matter, it simply wasn't in his nature to turn away someone who needed him. Maybe he was out of the rescue business these days, but old habits died hard. And it felt good to be needed again.

"We'll go to my mother's place for the meeting with Steve," he said before Leslie could come up with another plan. "If we see that it's necessary to let him go on thinking we're engaged, then that's what we'll do for now. If nothing else, it will let him know that you aren't alone in this, that it won't be as easy as he'd thought for him to take Kenny away from you."

Leslie looked at the quietly babbling baby. "For the past few months, Kenny's been my whole life. He brought such joy to Crystal in her last weeks, and such comfort to me after her death. I never thought it was possible to feel this way about a child, but I love him so much it hurts.''

Tom felt his brows dip into a frown, and he immediately blanked his expression. So that was part of the problem, he thought with a flash of rueful self-analysis. He was more than a little jealous of the baby.

Leslie was prepared to do anything to keep Kenny. Yet she'd been all too willing to walk away from Tom eighteen months ago.

Annoyed with himself for his pettiness, he nodded a bit curtly. ''You're not going to lose him, Les. After all you've done for him and his mother, no judge in his right mind would call you an unfit guardian. Steve doesn't have a leg to stand on. He and his sister weren't even speaking.''

''He has a home. A successful business. Money. Influential friends.''

Tom refused to let the fear in her eyes shake his confident tone. ''You have friends, too,'' he said, holding her gaze with his own. ''And we're going to help you.''

He watched her take a deep breath, watched the fear recede, though he knew it hadn't entirely disappeared. She blinked rapidly a few times, obviously fighting tears, then swallowed.

''Thank you,'' she said finally, her voice not entirely steady.

''I haven't done anything yet,'' he said with a faint smile.

''You've done more than you know,'' she answered, entirely serious.

He didn't want her gratitude. He frowned and changed the subject. ''Who gets the first shower?''

He tried not to think of the times they'd showered together. Or to wonder if they would ever do so again. He told himself that it was totally inappropriate for him to be thinking along those lines this morning. Leslie didn't need a lover now; she needed a friend. So that was what he would be.

''You go ahead,'' Leslie urged, her expression unreadable. ''I'll clean up the kitchen, then give Kenny a bath in the sink. He usually takes a nap after his bath, so I can shower then.''

"Fine. I won't take long. Er, if Mom calls..."

"I'll talk to her," Leslie said. "I'll tell her the entire story, and if she has any hesitation about being a part of this, I'll track Steve down and set up a private meeting with him somewhere else."

"That won't be necessary," Tom predicted with a wry smile. "Mom won't have a qualm about helping us out."

In fact, he thought as he headed for the shower, his mother was probably going to throw herself into this battle with full steam. For one thing, she was as bad as Tom about not being able to turn away anyone in trouble. For another, she'd always been fond of Leslie, and had made no secret of her disappointment when Tom and Leslie had gone their separate ways. She was probably delighted with the engagement announcement, even though she surely suspected that it wasn't authentic. Tom wouldn't be at all surprised if she was eagerly hoping that it would become a fact.

The telephone rang less than five minutes after Leslie heard the shower start running. She had just finished cleaning the kitchen and had been gathering towels, diapers and clean clothing for Kenny. Setting the bath supplies aside, she took a deep breath and reached for the telephone, anticipating her embarrassment when she had to explain to Tom's mother that she'd arrived out of the blue on Tom's doorstep and practically begged him to marry her.

She was painfully aware that Tom still hadn't given her an answer.

"Hello," she said, lifting the telephone receiver to her ear.

There was a pause of sorts, and then a man said, "Oh, sorry. I guess I have the wrong number."

"Zach?" Leslie asked tentatively, thinking she recognized the voice.

"Yeah?" He sounded surprised to hear his name.

"Hi. It's Leslie. Leslie Harden."

There was a definite pause this time. "Leslie?" he asked finally. "This is a surprise."

She'd bet it was. Actually, Zach had never seemed all that fond of her. But, then, the coolness had been mutual. She'd thought Zach somewhat cocky, a bit conceited, and all too reckless with his life and Tom's when they'd encouraged each other to pursue ever more dangerous challenges. Rock climbing, rafting, parachuting, car racing, bungee jumping—Zach and Tom had tried them all just in the few months Leslie and Tom were together. And Leslie had worried every time, though she'd tried to hide her fears, knowing that Tom and Zach would only laugh them off.

She'd never tried to come between Tom and Zach, of course. She'd had no right. And besides, her own bond with Crystal had made her fully understand what a special, closer-than-kin friendship was worth.

"How long have you been in town?" Zach asked.

"I arrived last night."

"Tom didn't mention that he was expecting you."

"Didn't he?" She left it at that, deciding that Tom could explain her presence to his friends in his own way.

"So, how have you been?"

"Fine, thanks. Oh, and congratulations. Tom said you're married."

"Yeah. Kim and I have been married for eight months now."

Leslie couldn't help wondering about the woman who'd captured the heart of former local heartbreaker Zach McCain.

"Er, is Tom there?"

"He's in the shower. Would you like for me to take a message?"

"Just tell him I called, okay? I'll talk to him later."

"I'll tell him."

"Thanks."

She was preparing to hang up the phone, when Zach said, "Leslie?"

She brought the phone back to her ear. "Yes?"

"The last year's been pretty hard on Tom. I'd hate to see him hurt again."

The words were uttered in a half-embarrassed growl. Leslie wouldn't have been more startled if he'd shouted them at her.

What was going on around here? What had happened to take the laughter out of Tom, to make Zach act so worried and protective? Neither of them was behaving at all as Leslie had known them.

Zach hung up before she could think of anything to say in response to his less-than-subtle warning.

Thoughtful and more than a little concerned, Leslie hung up the phone, noted that Zach had called, then turned to gather the baby's bath things again. It was obvious that she wasn't the only one who'd had problems since she and Tom had separated, she mused. If only she knew what had gone wrong for Tom.

Leaving the baby sleeping in his portable crib, Leslie took her time in the shower. The hot water felt wonderful against the tension knots in her neck. And maybe she was using the time to avoid Tom for a while.

When she could delay no longer, she dried and styled her hair and reapplied her makeup, then spent a few minutes trying to decide what to wear for this luncheon-showdown at Nina's apartment. She finally decided on a not-too-dressy, not-too-casual ensemble, a peacock-blue tunic sweater over black slacks, accessorized with a simple gold chain and the diamond stud earrings she habitually wore.

When she emerged from the guest bedroom, Tom was on the telephone in the living room, his back turned toward her, so that he wasn't immediately aware of her entrance.

"No, Mom, I haven't told her yet," he was saying as she entered. "I don't know why, but it just hasn't seemed like the right time. There's no need to go into it at lunch, okay? Let's just concentrate on what's best for the baby for now."

Leslie frowned, wondering what he was hiding from her.

Was it something to do with another woman? she asked herself in sudden dismay. Had Tom fallen in love with someone after Leslie had moved away? Maybe he'd had his heart broken. Maybe that was what Zach had meant when he'd said that Tom had been hurt enough. Maybe Tom was still in love with that someone else.

Still unaware of her presence behind him, Tom hung up the phone and crossed the room to pick up the coffee mug he'd left on an end table. Watching him walk, focusing on that uncomfortable-looking limp, Leslie bit her lip. She'd assumed that he'd simply twisted an ankle or something, that the injury had been recent, but the limp looked no better today than it had last night. Just when *had* he hurt himself? And how badly? She realized that he'd been notably evasive each time she'd mentioned it.

She wished she had the nerve to just come out and ask him what was wrong, but she supposed she'd infringed on his privacy enough during the past twenty-four hours. ''That was your mom?'' she asked, instead.

Tom jerked, almost spilling his coffee, and swore beneath his breath.

''I'm sorry,'' Leslie said, taking a quick step toward him. ''I didn't mean to startle you.'' She hadn't realized he'd been so deeply lost in his thoughts.

He swiped at his gray-, white-, and maroon-striped shirt with one hand, checked to make sure no coffee stains spotted his gray chinos, then shrugged. ''No harm done. Guess I was daydreaming. And yeah, that was Mom.''

''You explained everything?''

He nodded. ''She said to tell you that you did the right thing to come to us for help. She'll back us up with whatever we choose to say to Pendleton. I told you she would want to help.''

Leslie was touched. ''That's very kind of her.''

''She always liked you.'' Tom set his mug down. ''She told us to come on over whenever we're ready. If we get there before Pendleton, we'll have a chance to get our stories straight before he shows up.''

Leslie glanced at her watch. ''Kenny should be waking from his nap soon.''

"We'll leave when he wakes up, then. Would you like some coffee or anything?"

She shook her head, hating the stilted politeness they'd fallen into. "I'm fine, thank you."

Tom took a seat on the couch. Leslie perched on a chair, trying to think of some way to break the silence without prying.

"What's Zach's wife like?" she asked finally, seizing on what seemed to be a safe enough topic. "Do you like her?"

"Kim? Yes, I like her," Tom replied with a smile that seemed genuine. "You'd probably be surprised to meet her. She's a bit shy, even a little timid, but a lot of fun once you get to know her. Just passed her CPA exam a few months ago. She's working for a firm downtown now. Seems to really enjoy it."

"Zach McCain married a shy, timid accountant?" Leslie repeated blankly, wondering if Tom was putting her on.

He chuckled, looking more like the man Leslie remembered so well. "It's true," he assured her. "Kim's not nearly as timid as she used to be, but she's still no daredevil. Zach's been trying for ages to get her to go skydiving, but she keeps telling him hell will freeze over first. It's an interesting battle of wills, but my money's on Kim. Once she really sets her mind to something, not even Zach can change it."

"I would have expected Zach to end up with someone just like him," Leslie admitted. "Someone fearless and adventurous. And drop-dead gorgeous, of course, to match him."

Tom's smile was wry. "Kim's very pretty, but I'm not sure she'd qualify as 'drop-dead gorgeous.' Zach's crazy about her. He never worked as hard at anything in his life as he did when he was trying to persuade Kim to give him a chance with her. She thought they were too different to make it work, but he finally convinced her otherwise."

Leslie mused ruefully that she'd bet it was the first time in his life Zach had been forced to work for *any* woman's attention. Women had been chasing after him since he'd reached puberty. It must have been good for his slightly overinflated ego to encounter one who hadn't been so eagerly available.

"Obviously you and Zach are still close," she commented, remembering that Tom had said he'd spent last evening with Zach and Kim and thinking that it was nice for Tom's sake that Zach's marriage hadn't interfered with the longtime friendship.

Tom's hesitation was just long enough for Leslie to notice. "Yeah," he said, not quite meeting her eyes. "We're still good friends."

Taken aback, she tried to read his expression, but he'd shuttered it again. Something was definitely wrong here. Something that had affected Tom's personality, and even his friendship with Zach. And she was growing increasingly concerned.

For the first time in months, Leslie found herself worrying more about someone else's problems than her own.

Nina Lowery held little Kenny in her lap while her son and Leslie explained all the details of the custody battle and the reasons Leslie had come to Tom for help.

"You poor dear," Nina said to Leslie. "I can't imagine how difficult these past months have been for you."

Leslie's throat tightened around a sudden lump. She hadn't realized until now quite how lonely she'd been during the past months. She hadn't made many friends in Chicago, and had had little time for any social life after Crystal had moved in with her, needing so much time and attention. The law firm where she'd worked had been fast-track and cutthroat, co-workers seen as competition rather than allies. It was an attitude that had been encouraged by the senior partners and accepted within the lower ranks. Leslie had known almost from the beginning that she'd made a mistake taking the position there, but she'd desperately needed her salary during Crystal's illness.

No one there had looked at her as Nina was now, and expressed genuine sympathy. No one had unquestioningly offered any help she needed, as Tom had when he'd opened his home to her and Kenny.

When she'd had nowhere else to go, no one else to turn to, it had seemed utterly natural for her to come here. And now she fully understood why.

Kenny babbled and kicked his feet, instantly reclaiming Nina's attention. "What a little darling you are," she crooned, tickling the baby's tummy through his one-piece, blue-and-white-striped playsuit. "A perfect little angel, aren't you?"

Tom chuckled. "Just show Mom a baby and she turns to mush," he commented fondly.

"I'm crazy about babies," Nina agreed, and kissed Kenny's bobbing head. She glanced at Leslie. "And I can see that you love this child very much."

Leslie nodded. "I've taken care of him since he came home from the hospital, a week after he was born. I don't think I could love him more if he were my own."

"Then we'll have to make sure he stays with you, won't we?" Nina looked at Tom as she spoke, her resolution to help clear.

Tom nodded. "We'll do whatever we can."

Even marriage? Leslie couldn't help wondering. Would Tom really sacrifice that much to help her? And if he did, how could she ever repay him?

"I simply don't understand why Steve Pendleton is causing such problems," Nina fretted. "Surely he can see that this baby is healthy and happy and perfectly well cared for."

Leslie repeated her explanation about Steve's resentment toward her because of the old, painful debacle between her father and his mother.

Nina shook her head. "That has nothing to do with this. It isn't your father who's taking care of the child. It's you."

"Ben Harden's daughter," Leslie said with a touch of bitterness. "Steve would hate me for that alone, but he also resents my friendship with his sister, who was estranged from him for so long. And he knows that I have no job now and no immediate prospects."

Nina shook her head. "That shouldn't be such an issue. You'll find another job. Other single women with fewer job skills than you have managed to raise children," she added, glancing meaningfully at her own son.

On that long-ago night when Tom and Leslie had shared stories of their childhood, Tom had explained that Nina had become pregnant at sixteen, had been abandoned by Tom's father and only grudgingly supported by her disapproving family. Tom had alluded to how hard his mother had worked to provide him a home and a secure childhood. He'd expressed some guilt that Nina had devoted herself so totally to him that she'd never married or even dated more than a few rare times during his childhood.

At forty-seven, Nina was still petite and youthful looking, her face barely lined, her green eyes clear and bright, her smiles frequent and contagious. She seemed content with her nice apartment and the profitable florist shop she owned and managed in historic downtown Fayetteville. She made no secret that she adored her son, but Leslie had never considered Nina an interfering or demanding mother. In fact, Leslie had often envied Tom and Nina their relationship. Her mother had been more involved in her own problems than in her only daughter's life.

As if she'd read Leslie's thoughts, Nina asked delicately, "You have no family to help you, dear?"

Leslie shook her head. "My mother lives in Florida with her third husband. We aren't particularly close. My father moves around a lot. He's just divorced wife number four, and I think he's hanging around Vegas, trolling for his next ex-wife. I hear from him sometimes, when he remembers my existence."

She'd tried to speak with her usual wry humor in regard to her parents, having learned years earlier that it was better to laugh about them than to cry over them. This time her humor fell sadly flat.

Nina's eyes grew even more sympathetic, and Leslie shifted uncomfortably in her seat. Sympathy she could accept, but pity was difficult for her to take. She cleared her throat and spoke brusquely. "Isn't there anything I can do to help you prepare for lunch?"

Nina shook her head. "The ham is in the oven, the green beans are simmering and the cold side dishes are prepared and waiting in the refrigerator. All I have to do is brown the rolls, which will only take a few minutes and can be done after Mr. Pendleton arrives."

Tom lifted an eyebrow. "You went to a lot of trouble for this, didn't you?"

Nina's smile was impish. "I've learned that a well-fed man tends to be a more reasonable man. We'll make sure Mr. Pendleton has a nice meal before we discuss business."

Leslie couldn't help smiling. To be honest, she didn't know if Steve was more approachable after eating or not, since she had seen him only a handful of times in the past twenty years, but if anyone could soften him, she would bet that Nina Lowery was the one.

The doorbell rang. Leslie's pulse jumped, and she saw the sudden tension that gripped Tom. Both of them rose, feet planted as if prepared for battle. Only Nina seemed completely calm about the impending confrontation. She kissed the baby again, stood and placed him in her son's arms.

"You hold the baby. I'll get the door," she said, smoothing her hands over her trim navy pantsuit.

Tom looked surprised to find himself suddenly holding the baby, and Leslie realized that it was the first time he'd done so. There was an odd expression on Tom's face when he looked down at the baby, who was eyeing him. Kenny suddenly broke into a smile and clutched Tom's shirt with damp fingers. Tom couldn't seem to help returning the smile, though there was still an expression in his eyes that Leslie couldn't quite interpret.

"Here, I'll take him," she offered, moving toward them.

Tom shook his head and adjusted the baby more securely against his chest. "He's fine."

Before Leslie could reply, Nina came back into the room,

Steve Pendleton following closely behind her. Leslie was wryly amused at Steve's expression as he was practically towed along in Nina's wake. Nina was chattering as comfortably as if she'd known him forever, treating him as an honored guest in her home, nothing in her manner implying that there was even a possibility of unpleasantness or conflict. Leslie tried to read Steve's expression, but his sternly cut, reasonably attractive face had always been closed to her.

She saw reminders of Crystal in Steve—the dark hair and eyes, the shape of his mouth, the slight cleft in his chin. But even at the lowest point of her illness, Crystal had never been as grim and somber as Steve habitually appeared. Maybe Crystal had made some bad choices in her life—actually, there was no doubt of that—but she hadn't deserved her brother's disapproval or anger.

It was that thought that brought Leslie's chin up, so that the first expression Steve saw when he looked at her was defiance. She watched his eyes narrow in immediate reaction.

As though sensing the unspoken challenge, Nina stepped between them. "I hope everyone's hungry. Lunch is almost ready."

Steve hesitated a moment, then reached into the pocket of his conservatively cut gray sport coat. He pulled out a small cardboard rectangle. "Actually," he said, "I only came today to bring this to Leslie."

He held the card out to her, and she took it instinctively. "What is it?"

"That's the name of my attorney," he replied, his gray eyes hard. "A custody suit on my behalf is being filed here in Washington County first thing Monday morning. If you run with the baby again before a ruling is made, you're going to find yourself facing legal action."

Chapter Four

Leslie heard Tom growl a curse, heard a small, distressed sound from Nina, but she kept her attention focused on Steve. Trying to hide the surge of panic she felt, she spoke coolly. "I told you that I didn't run from Chicago with the baby, Steve. I simply moved back here to marry the man who is going to help me raise Kenny."

As if in affirmation, the baby grinned around the fingers he'd crammed into his mouth. He rested his head trustingly on Tom's broad shoulder. Tom patted Kenny's back, looking utterly at ease with the child.

Leslie noted that Steve was watching Tom and Kenny with narrowed eyes. She thought she saw the faintest hint of concern in Steve's expression. Was he thinking that some judges would tend to give preference to a married couple rather than to a single man when it came to deciding the best home for a child? Even if the man was the child's biological uncle, Leslie reminded herself with mentally crossed fingers. Especially since the child's mother had expressed a definite preference about whom she wanted to raise her child.

"Mr. Pendleton," Nina said softly. "Won't you reconsider this course of action? Surely you can see that Leslie loves your nephew very much and has taken excellent care of him. He's obviously happy and healthy."

"He is my sister's child," Steve argued stubbornly. "He should be raised by his own family. And I think I can provide the best home for him. I don't for a minute believe in this convenient engagement. There wasn't a hint of any involvement between your son and Leslie before I told her that I intended to file for custody of my nephew. Which means that you're asking me to turn Kenny over to a single woman who has no home, no job—you do know she was fired by the legal firm in Chicago, don't you?"

"Yes," Nina replied calmly, interrupting when Leslie would have answered much more heatedly. "She told me about that. When she had to make a choice between her job and taking care of little Kenny, she chose Kenny and was penalized for it. It sounds to me as though she takes her responsibilities to this child very seriously. I understand her employers were also annoyed with her for spending so much time taking care of your sister during her illness."

Steve's face hardened. "I would have taken care of Crystal, had anyone bothered to notify me that she was ill."

Leslie wondered if that was part of the reason Steve was pursuing this custody battle. Was he trying to punish her for keeping him from Crystal during those last months? Did he blame her for not contacting him? She wanted to tell him that she'd tried repeatedly to talk Crystal into calling her brother before her death, but Crystal had refused. In fact, Crystal had begged Leslie not to call Steve.

Leslie opened her mouth to tell him, but found that she couldn't. It simply seemed too cruel—unless, of course, he left her with no other option.

"The engagement," Tom cut in smoothly, taking a step closer to Leslie, "is real. If you want proof that Leslie and I have known each other as long as we said, I'll give you names and phone numbers of people who knew us as a couple before Leslie moved to Chicago. Sure we split up for a while. But we're back together now. And Kenny is very much a part of our family. We're not letting you take him away from us.''

Us. The word hung meaningfully in the air. Tom was making it very clear that Leslie was no longer facing this conflict on her own. She had reinforcements now, and they were fully prepared to do battle on her behalf.

"Maybe we'd better let a court decide that," Steve challenged, throwing an angry look at Leslie. "And all of you had better be prepared—I'll use any evidence I can find to support my claim that I will be the better guardian for my nephew."

Leslie felt Tom go very still. "Is that a threat?" he asked slowly.

"Take it however you want."

Nina wrung her hands. "Please, can't we just sit down and discuss this over lunch? I'm sure we can work something out. Something that doesn't involve an ugly court battle. Leslie and Tom aren't trying to keep you from seeing your nephew, Mr. Pendleton. They only want—"

"I'm not interested in visitation rights," he snapped, then looked at Nina and sighed faintly.

"I'm sorry," he said more quietly. "I know you're only trying to help your son and his…friend. And it was very kind of you to invite me to lunch, but under the circumstances, I think I'll decline."

"You won't win this, Steve," Leslie said, trying to speak with utter confidence. "You're only going to be out a great deal of effort and expense for nothing. I have Crystal's will on my side, and you have absolutely nothing to use against me in court."

"You're the lawyer," Steve noted with a curl of his lip that made the word almost obscene. "You know better than most that justice in this country is for sale to the highest bidder. Well, I'm prepared to invest everything I have in this battle, if that's what it takes. Are you willing to do the same?"

"I've already invested everything I have in Kenny," Leslie answered frankly. "And I'm not letting you have him."

As if sensing the tension in the room, the baby began to fret. Leslie reached for him. "He's getting hungry," she said. "Maybe you'd better go now, Steve, so the rest of us can enjoy our lunch."

He flushed at her deliberately curt, dismissive tone, but he nodded tautly. "Fine. You'll be hearing from my attorney."

Leslie looked at him over Kenny's head. "As you will from mine."

Steve turned abruptly to Nina. "I'm sorry," he said to her. "I'm sure you went to a great deal of trouble to prepare a nice lunch. But I really must go now."

She nodded regretfully. "I suppose so. I wish it didn't have to be this way."

"So do I," he assured her. "But I can't see that I have any choice."

With one last, challenging look at Leslie and Tom, he departed without waiting for an escort to the door. He left a strained silence behind him, broken only by Kenny's increasingly demanding whimpers.

"I'll go warm his bottle," Leslie murmured, turning toward the kitchen with the baby held tightly in her arms. She found herself suddenly reluctant to meet the others' eyes. She was embarrassed that Steve had just illustrated so cruelly exactly how alone and vulnerable Leslie would be without Tom and Nina. For someone who'd taken such pride in her independence and self-sufficiency, that admission was very difficult to make, even to herself.

Nina didn't immediately follow Leslie to the kitchen. She was looking at her son, searching his face with too-perceptive eyes. "You didn't say much," she commented.

Tom shrugged. "There wasn't much to say. Pendleton made his position clear. He's going to cause trouble for Leslie any way he can. All I wanted him to know about me at this point is that I'm prepared to fight back on her behalf."

"And how far are you prepared to take this fight?"

He didn't hesitate before he answered. "As far as I have to."

He couldn't quite read his mother's expression, but he thought he saw approval deep in her eyes. "Leslie's lucky to have a friend like you," was all she said.

Friend. Tom mulled over the word for a moment, decided he didn't particularly like the sound of it, but nodded anyway. "That's what friends are for, right?" he asked, knowing the words came out more flippantly than he'd intended.

Nina only smiled.

Nina watched Tom and Leslie during lunch. They were so very polite to each other, she observed thoughtfully. Like two friendly acquaintances rather than a couple with an intimate history between them.

Tom had never actually talked to his mother about his feelings after Leslie had taken the job in Chicago and moved away, but Nina knew her son had been hurt more than he'd let on. Nina had liked Leslie, and had been disappointed when the relationship fell apart. She'd always wondered if Tom had ever expressed his real feelings to Leslie. Her son had never been comfortable verbalizing emotions, and camouflaged them, instead, with perpetual jokes and wisecracks.

Or at least that was the way he'd been before the accident, she mused a bit sadly. Since then, he'd become rather quiet. Subdued. It was obvious to everyone who knew him that he had changed. It was that thought that made her ask, "What's Zach up to this weekend, Tommy?"

"He and some of the guys were going rock climbing today, since the weather's turned so nice," Tom answered offhandedly. "He called this morning to ask if I wanted to join them later to watch the basketball game at his house. I told him I had other plans," he added with a glance at Leslie.

Leslie frowned. "Don't skip the game on my account. I don't need to be entertained. I'm sorry you had to miss rock climbing with the guys this morning. I know how much you love that sort of thing."

Nina saw the spasm that crossed her son's face, but she wasn't sure that Leslie did. Nina's heart ached. She knew how Leslie's innocent words must have hurt Tom, but again he hid whatever he felt behind a casual shrug. "No big deal," he said. "There'll be other climbs."

But probably not for Tom, Nina thought sadly. She wondered when he was going to tell Leslie.

Leslie apparently missed the undercurrents beneath Tom's nonchalant reply. "Really," she said a bit too brightly. "Go watch the game with your friends, if you like. Kenny and I will be fine at your place—if you don't mind us staying there awhile longer," she added somewhat hesitantly, glancing at the baby, who dozed in his plastic carrier, his newly filled tummy making him drowsy.

"Don't be ridiculous. You're welcome to stay as long as you need to."

Tom's reply was a bit impatient, making Nina frown in disapproval at the way he was acting. She had definitely taught him better manners than that.

"As for the game," Tom added, "I've already told Zach I won't be there. I told him you and I have some catching up to do. He understood."

Nina suspected that Tom would have made an excuse to Zach even if Leslie hadn't been there. He'd been doing that more and more lately. Avoiding his friends—particularly Zach. She thought she understood Tom's behavior, but she knew Zach didn't. She hated to see them all hurting so badly.

Leslie was toying with her food, trying to look appreciative of Nina's efforts, but the unhappiness in her eyes was unmistakable.

"Try not to worry so much, Leslie," Nina felt compelled to say. "I can't imagine that any judge would take Kenny away from you. Not after all you've done for him."

Leslie bit her lip, looked at the baby, then glanced at Nina. "I hope you're right. But Steve's obviously prepared to fight dirty."

Nina frowned. "I don't understand why he's being so hard about this. He doesn't seem like a cruel man."

He had, in fact, been nothing but polite to Nina. Her first impression of him had been positive—tall, attractive, courteous. His coffee-brown eyes had seemed kind to her. And then they had hardened when he'd looked at Leslie, and she'd seen the darker side of him.

"Steve has an impeccable reputation," Leslie admitted. "He's successful in his business, an honest, upright, straitlaced citizen. He's never been in trouble with the law, pays his taxes regularly, sings tenor in a church choir and is a member of an expensive Little Rock country club, where he plays golf and tennis."

Tom raised an eyebrow. "Sounds as if you've done your homework."

Leslie's mouth twisted. "I like to know my enemies."

"No matter how successful he is in his business or his social life, it's still foolish of him to blame you because he and his sister were estranged," Nina insisted loyally. "You were the one who felt obligated to contact him after Crystal's death, the one who very generously invited him to be a part of his nephew's future. He's being terribly unfair to you."

"Thank you," Leslie murmured, her genuine gratitude for Nina's moral support evident in her voice.

Nina reflected that Leslie must have felt very much alone during the past few months. She wasn't alone now, Nina thought in satisfaction as Tom scowled and spoke.

"I don't care if Pendleton regularly plays golf with the president. He isn't taking Kenny away from you, Leslie. He doesn't have a leg to stand on in court."

"Doesn't he?" Lines of strain etched themselves around Leslie's mouth. "You heard what he's going to use against me."

Tom snorted. "The blood relationship? His own sister didn't want him to have the baby. You have her will on your side. Your dismissal from the law firm in Chicago? You can prove that you were released because of your dedication to

Kenny—which only confirms the depth of your commitment to him. No judge will condemn you for that. He said you have no home. That's not true. You have a home with me. You can find another job here if you want—we have enough local strings to pull to arrange that—or you can take some time off to take care of the baby, if you want. I might not make as much as you did in Chicago, but my salary will support a wife and baby.''

Wife. Nina watched surreptitiously as the word drained all the color from Leslie's face. Nina herself was affected by it. Her son was talking marriage, and he was grimly serious about it. A bit too grim, actually.

''You, er, said that might not be necessary,'' Leslie reminded Tom.

''No, you were right. Being married gives you an advantage Pendleton doesn't have. Actually, the sooner we take care of it, the better.''

Without looking away from her son's face, Nina narrowed her eyes thoughtfully. ''How soon did you have in mind?''

Tom looked from his mother to Leslie. ''How does tomorrow afternoon sound?''

Nina blinked. Tom certainly wasn't wasting any time, she mused, her mouth twitching with the beginnings of a smile.

She was starting to suspect that chivalry wasn't the only reason her son was so willing to marry Leslie Harden. She wondered if he even suspected that there was much more to it than that.

Leslie parked her car in the driveway of Tom's house later that evening, but didn't immediately get out. She studied the lights in the windows of the neat, brick-and-cream-sided house, thinking that it looked cozy and welcoming.

Tom had grown up in this house. His mother bought it when Tom was a little boy, because she'd wanted to raise him in a nice, family neighborhood with a safe, fenced yard. She'd held two jobs to make the mortgage payment. She'd spent her days working for the florist shop she now owned. In the evenings, she'd worked long into the night doing typing and other pre-computer clerical work out of her home so she could be with her son.

Several years ago, Nina had decided to move into an apartment closer to her business, and Tom had bought the house from her. He'd told Leslie that he'd never cared much for apartment living, preferring the space and privacy a house provided. And the upkeep gave him something to do with his spare time to keep him out of trouble, he'd added with a grin.

Tom and his mother seemed to have a very special relationship—independent, yet fully supportive; loving, yet tolerant. It was the kind of relationship Leslie wished she'd had with her parents. The kind she hoped to have with Kenny, whom she already regarded as her own son.

She reached over the back of the seat for the bag of diapers and canned baby formula she'd just purchased. Tom had offered to go after the items, but when Leslie had pointed out that he didn't know what brands or sizes to buy, he'd offered to baby-sit, instead. Leslie had hesitated, but Kenny had been peacefully sleeping, so she'd taken Tom up on his offer.

To be honest, she'd needed the time to herself.

She was still reeling from Tom's calm announcement that they would be married tomorrow.

"To-tomorrow?" she'd stammered when he'd dropped the bombshell at lunch. "We can't possibly be married tomorrow."

"Why not?" he'd asked reasonably.

"Well, because—we need a license and we have to make arrangements and...well, we just can't," she'd protested almost incoherently, looking to Nina for support.

Nina, however, had agreed with Tom. "Steve said his attorney is filing the custody suit first thing Monday morning. If you and Tom are married tomorrow, you can beat him to the punch, so to speak."

"But—"

"You haven't changed your mind about this, have you?" Tom had asked.

And there'd been a challenge in his green eyes she couldn't quite interpret.

"I haven't changed my mind about being willing to do anything necessary to keep Kenny," she'd answered flatly. "But we don't really know yet that this is necessary."

"It would definitely be a benefit to you," Nina had argued. "Any judge is going to look at a nice couple like you and Tom and know that you'll be wonderful parents. And my Tommy knows a lot of people in this town, enough to pull the right strings to have the ceremony performed tomorrow. Everyone knows what a wonderful man he is, and there are any number of witnesses who'll testify to his character. There's no way Steve Pendleton can claim that my son won't provide an excellent home for you and Kenny."

Leslie had been forced to swallow her instinctive protest that she didn't need Tom to provide a home for her. That she didn't need anyone's help. That she was perfectly capable of taking care of herself and Kenny. She'd swallowed the words only because she knew they weren't entirely true. She *did* need help, if only temporarily. But she still wasn't entirely sure that what she needed was a husband.

Now she sat in her car outside Tom's house, diapers and formula clutched in her arms, and wondered if she'd made a terrible mistake coming to Fayetteville. She had no right to involve Tom in her problems, particularly after the way they'd parted. She had no right to ask him to sacrifice his freedom for her or for the child of a stranger to him.

She had to find a way to convince him that he didn't have to go through with this. That she and Kenny would get by, somehow, without him. Maybe.

And then she walked into Tom's house and found him playing with the baby. Tom was sitting on the couch, supporting Kenny between his large, strong hands as the baby bounced on Tom's knees, tiny bare feet flailing. Kenny was squealing in delight at the attention, and Tom was laughing.

Leslie realized that it was the first time she'd heard Tom really laugh since she'd come back.

Kenny, she realized with a faint pang, had finally been able to reach Tom in a way that she had not since she'd arrived on his doorstep.

Tom waited until Leslie had fed the baby and put him to bed before telling her, "I called Judge Haverty while you were out. It's all settled. He'll marry us tomorrow afternoon."

"Judge Haverty," she repeated, her fingers twisting nervously in front of her. "Didn't you save his mother from a burning house a few years ago?"

Tom winced at the mention of his former career, but managed to shrug lightly enough. "Never hurts to have friends in high places," he murmured.

Now, he urged himself. *Tell her now.*

And yet he remained silent.

"You're not on duty tomorrow?" Leslie asked, as if reminded of a firefighter's twenty-four-hour-on, forty-eight-hour-off schedule.

"No." *Damn it, Lowery, tell her.*

Her fingers were twisted so tightly by now that her knuckles had to ache. "Goose," she said, trying to smile. "You really don't have to go through with this, you know. Maybe we should talk about it more, consider our options. Speak to a lawyer."

"You are a lawyer," he reminded her with his own pathetic attempt at a smile. "Will this marriage help you in court or not?"

"Well, yes, perhaps, but..."

"So we get married," he said with a shrug. "I don't have anything better to do tomorrow anyway."

Her hands stilled in her lap as she studied his face with a frown. "What's happened to you, Tom?"

He cleared his throat, looked down at his feet. "What do you mean?"

"You've changed. You're...different."

"I'm older."

She made an impatient gesture. "Eighteen months. Big deal."

It felt longer. Much longer. Tom shoved a hand through his hair and turned away. "Do you still have an apartment in Chicago?"

"No. It was a furnished apartment, so there wasn't much to do to clear out. I kept meaning to buy my own furniture, but then Crystal came and I…" She bit her lip, then continued. "Anyway, when I decided to leave Chicago, I packed some of my stuff in the car, left the rest in storage and drove away the next morning. Unaware, of course, that I was being followed."

He nodded. "We'll have your things shipped here. We'll make the arrangements Monday."

"So I'm moving in?" She wrapped her arms around her upper body, gripping her forearms as if against a sudden chill.

"Of course. You and Kenny," he added, reminding them both of her reason for being here.

"You're sure you know what you're getting into? Having a baby in the house…well, it changes things. A lot," she warned.

He nodded. "I know. We'll manage."

She took a step toward him, put a hand on his arm. She waited until he looked at her before she asked, her voice strained, "Why are you doing this? Why would you…?"

His hand rose as though it had a mind of its own. Cupped her cheek. He felt the iciness of her skin against the warmth of his own. "You need me," he said simply.

"I can take care of myself," she felt compelled to point out. "If you don't want to do this, I'll get by. I'll fight for Kenny in court, and the chances are good that I'll win."

"The chances are better if I fight with you."

She didn't try to argue with that. "If you—if we do this, I'll do everything I can to make it easier for you. I'm not asking you to support us. I'll find a job. I'll take care of the baby. I won't make any demands on your time. I won't expect you to change your life for me. And when the time is right, I'll give you your freedom.''

Everything about that noble little speech annoyed him. His hand dropped to his side. His voice came out more curtly than he'd intended. "I've already told you that there's no rush for you to find a job. I'll help you with the baby when you need help. And I refuse to talk about the end of a marriage that hasn't even begun yet. Now, since I think that covers everything, I'm going to call my mother and invite her to our wedding.''

He was aware that he left Leslie gaping after him as he limped irritably from the room.

Chapter Five

They were married in the judge's office on Sunday afternoon, with only Tom's mother and the judge's wife for witnesses. Wearing a flattering blue silk dress, Nina held Kenny during the brief ceremony. Dressed in his best sailor-styled white suit, the baby watched the proceedings with apparent fascination.

At the appropriate time, Tom surprised Leslie by producing a set of matching gold rings. He'd left his house an hour earlier than Leslie, telling her he had a few errands to run and instructing her to meet him at the judge's office. Nina had picked Leslie and Kenny up and brought them to the judge's office so that Tom and Leslie wouldn't have two vehicles to deal with afterward.

Tom had arrived carrying a small bouquet of red and white roses for Leslie to hold during the ceremony. They were perfect for the winter-white suit that had been the only appropriate outfit she'd brought with her.

"A wedding doesn't seem right without flowers," he'd said

when she'd tried to tell him how much the gesture touched her.

Now she knew what else he'd bought during that hour on his own.

"A wedding wouldn't have been right without rings, either," he murmured when he slipped the smaller band on her finger.

She stared up at him, struck by the gravity of that simple gesture. "Tom," she whispered, knowing that he was the only one who could hear her. "Are you absolutely sure you want to go through with this?"

He merely smiled and raised her left hand to his lips. Mrs. Haverty sighed audibly in response to the romantic gesture.

Leslie's hands were shaking when she placed her ring's mate on Tom's finger. She wondered if he'd bought it to reassure her that he was taking this commitment seriously. Or maybe, she thought, the rings were intended to convince Steve that the marriage was real.

Either way, it was a nice touch, just as the flowers had been. But there was still a hollow feeling inside her as she tilted her head upward so Tom could give her the customary kiss when the judge completed the ceremony.

His lips covered hers, and she realized with a slight start that it was the first time he'd kissed her since she'd come back to town. She'd been so preoccupied with the baby and with worrying about Steve and with her doubts about coming to Tom for help that she simply hadn't realized how little personal contact there'd been between them.

Standing there in front of the judge and their witnesses, Leslie suddenly became aware of exactly what she had done.

She had married Tom Lowery.

He lifted his head slowly and looked down at her with a slightly questioning expression. He must have been aware of the sudden tension that had gripped her when he kissed her.

She swallowed painfully and forced a smile that she knew was too bright. Tom opened his mouth as if to say something, but then, to Leslie's relief, was interrupted by Judge Haverty.

"Congratulations, Tom," he said, slapping Tom lightly on the shoulder. "You've got yourself a beautiful bride here."

Tom smiled and nodded, while Leslie tried to look flattered. "Yes, I know," Tom said. "Thank you for going to this trouble for us, Judge. This means more to us than you can possibly know."

The judge's broad, florid face grew serious. "I haven't forgotten the way you risked your life to save my mother, Tom. I'll never be able to repay you for that."

Tom cleared his throat, muttered something incoherent and turned to accept Mrs. Haverty's warm kiss on his cheek.

Nina approached Leslie first. Her green eyes were a bit too bright, hinting at unshed tears. Leslie hoped Nina was just being sentimental, and not regretful. Leslie doubted that this was the way Nina had envisioned her only son's being married.

If Nina had misgivings, she hid them well. Her smile was sweet and unshadowed as she rose on tiptoe to kiss Leslie's cheek. "Welcome to the family, dear," she murmured, Kenny held securely in her arms.

Kenny made a grab for the bouquet of roses. Leslie smiled and held them away. "You were a very good boy, but you can't have my flowers," she said, leaning over to kiss his soft cheek.

He promptly reached out to her. Nina handed him over, helping Leslie get the baby settled on her hip. And then Nina dug in her large purse and pulled out a small point-and-shoot camera. "Tommy, come here," she said imperiously. "I want pictures."

Tom groaned and rolled his eyes. "I should have known Mom would bring the camera."

"I always take pictures when my little boy does something special," Nina teased, making the others laugh as Tom's cheeks darkened.

"I'm a thirty-year-old married man," he reminded her in a fake grumble. "You're going to have to stop calling me your 'little boy' now."

Nina lowered the camera for a moment, her smile soft. "When you are sixty, you will still be my little boy."

Mrs. Haverty, who had three strapping sons of her own, murmured agreement. Leslie smiled when it was obvious that Tom had nothing to say in response to that maternal observation.

Leslie stood self-consciously at Tom's side while Nina snapped pictures of them with Kenny and then with the Havertys. Mrs. Haverty insisted on taking the camera so that Nina could be included in some of the shots. The atmosphere was quite festive, Leslie mused, faking one smile after another. Like a real wedding. Of course, the Havertys had no reason to believe that it was not, and Nina and Tom were certainly playing their parts.

She had married Tom Lowery. The thought kept replaying itself in her mind, each time making her ask herself what on earth she'd been thinking when she'd come up with this crazy plan. Or where on earth she'd found the nerve to propose to Tom. Or why he had so readily agreed.

She slanted a sideways glance at him. He looked relaxed and faintly pleased with himself, which was probably the way the others would expect him to look on his wedding day. His dark-blond hair was neatly brushed, and he was dressed in a dark suit that emphasized his firm, slender build. His bright-green eyes, so like his mother's, gleamed when he looked at her. The Havertys probably thought he was anticipating the wedding night. Leslie couldn't begin to guess what he was thinking. His handsome face was completely unreadable to her today.

It was a beautiful afternoon when they finally stepped outside the judge's office. Unseasonably warm and sunny, the air crisp and clear. The hills surrounding downtown Fayetteville were still winter-nude, but would soon don their spring greens. The town square, which had been given a multi-million-dollar face-lift during the past two decades, was busy with people taking advantage of the nice weather to browse through the eclectic assortment of shops. At the center of the square stood the historical old brick post office, now home to a popular restaurant, surrounded by gardens that would be breathtaking in the spring and summer.

Leslie had loved Fayetteville from the time she'd first come here as a student at the University of Arkansas, and had eagerly accepted a job with a local law firm upon her graduation from law school. She deeply regretted now that she'd allowed her head to be turned by the enticements of the bigger and more prosperous firm in Chicago. She winced as she remembered the way the people there, influenced by the hard-nosed senior partners, had treated her during her family crisis. She strongly suspected that everything would have been different had she remained with the small, laid-back firm here.

Leaving here was only one of the many mistakes she'd made in the past eighteen months.

Turning to his mother after the Havertys drove away, Tom said, "Well, since we're all dressed up, there's no need to rush home. Why don't we go out for a wedding dinner?"

Nina smiled and shook her head. "Thank you, dear, but I have things I must do this evening."

Tom nodded and glanced at Leslie with a faint smile. "Looks like it'll be just the three of us, then."

Leslie pulled Kenny's exploring fingers out of the neckline of her suit jacket. "Better pick a place that's baby-friendly," she warned lightly. "Kenny's not quite ready for quiet elegance."

A smile lighting his eyes, Tom wrinkled his nose, and for a moment he looked exactly as Leslie had remembered him. Her heart twisted at the reminder of how much he had changed.

"I'm not really into quiet elegance myself," he commented. "I think Kenny and I will be able to choose a place we both like."

To Leslie's surprise, he reached out and took the baby from her arms. "Come on, kid, I'll strap you into your seat," Tom said to the baby. "Guess I'd better get some practice at this sort of thing."

Judging from his dimpled grin, Kenny seemed perfectly content to be practiced upon by Tom.

"He's going to be such a good father," Nina murmured, stepping to Leslie's side as they watched Tom carefully deposit Kenny in the car seat he'd transferred from Nina's car to his own vehicle.

Leslie's breath hitched.

Nina patted Leslie's hand. "I know I've said this before, but you made the right decision to come to Tom for help, Leslie. I have a very good feeling about this custody battle. I know you'll win, especially now that you have my Tommy on your side."

"Tom's been very kind," Leslie said, just a bit stiffly. "I'll never be able to repay him for helping me this way. And I'm grateful to you, as well. You've been so supportive, and it must have been difficult for you to watch Tom make this sacrifice."

"Sacrifice?" Nina glanced from Leslie to Tom, who was laughing as Kenny kicked happily in his seat, hampering Tom's efforts to strap him in. "I don't think you realize that Tom needs you and Kenny every bit as badly as the two of you need him now," she murmured. "Trust me, dear, I am pleased with this marriage for many reasons."

Leslie turned impulsively to face Nina. "What's happened to Tom?" she asked quietly, urgently. "Why has he changed so much since I left?"

"You'll have to ask him that."

"But I'm not imagining things, am I? He *has* changed."

Nina shook her head sadly. "No, you aren't imagining things. He hasn't been the same since..."

She bit her lip, then brightened when Tom's laughter drifted their way again. "But everything's different now. He has you and Kenny, and I can see that he's taking this commitment very seriously. He needs you, Leslie," she repeated. "That's how you can repay him. Just be there for him, as he has been for you."

Leslie wanted to reply that she didn't know how she could

help Tom when she didn't even know what had happened to him. But before she could speak, Tom rejoined them, making a production of breathing heavily and wiping his brow. "Wow. That was like trying to stuff an octopus into a leotard," he said. "Takes quick reflexes, doesn't it?"

Leslie laughed at his analogy, thinking that it, too, sounded like something the "old Tom" would have said. Maybe Nina was right, she thought. Maybe Tom did need Kenny to bring the joy back into his life. Kenny had certainly brought joy to Leslie.

Whether Tom needed *her*—well, that remained to be seen.

Nina had to stop at a service station on her way home to fill the tank of her little economy car. Truth was, she had nothing pressing to do that evening, but she'd thought Tom and Leslie should spend some time alone after their wedding.

Their wedding. Nina sighed and shook her head, her ash-blond bob brushing softly against her cheeks. Hard to believe her son was a married man now.

Nina wished, of course, that the wedding had taken place under different circumstances. That she could be certain Tom had found true love and happiness. And yet, something told her that this marriage was right. That Leslie and Kenny would be good for Tom. That they would be able to slip through the cracks in that protective, invisible wall Tom had built around himself. He'd allowed Nina inside only briefly during the past months, and she believed she was the only one who'd had that privilege. She suspected that all Tom's friends—even Zach—had been politely, but firmly, shut out.

She unscrewed the cap from her gas tank, then fumbled with the nozzle of the hose. She truly disliked filling her tank, but years of necessary economizing had left her almost incapable of being frivolous with her money. She simply refused to pay extra to have someone do something she was perfectly capable of doing for herself.

She had just slid the nozzle into place in her tank, when a man spoke from behind her.

"Would you like some help with that?"

Looking over her shoulder, she saw Steve Pendleton watching her, a bit uncertain of her reaction to his offer.

"I just filled my own tank," he explained, waving toward a luxury car parked out of the way of the other customers. "I was about to drive away, when I recognized you."

"Oh. Well, thank you for your offer, but I can handle this. I do it all the time." She squeezed the handle to start the flow of gasoline. The fumes rose around her, making her sneeze. "I always sneeze when I smell gasoline," she said ruefully.

Steve smiled. "It's not my favorite odor, either."

Studying that very attractive smile, Nina swallowed a sigh. He seemed like such a nice man. But Nina couldn't help remembering the fear in Leslie's eyes when she'd worried that she might lose the baby she'd come to love as her own. Steve Pendleton had driven Leslie into a desperate marriage of convenience—which meant that Leslie was Nina's daughter-in-law now, and Nina's full allegiance was with her.

"Mrs. Lowery—"

She didn't bother to correct him about her marital status. "Yes?"

"I wonder if I might buy you a cup of coffee."

Her fingers fumbled on the handle. She kept her eyes on what she was doing as she asked, "When?"

"Now. If it's a convenient time for you, of course. I notice there's a little diner just down the road. It looks like a decent place."

Nina glanced down the street toward the Red Hog Diner, a popular hangout for the firefighters who worked at the station nearby—the station to which her son had once been assigned. The owner and most of the customers knew Nina there. She wasn't at all sure she wanted them watching her have coffee with a man they didn't know.

The gas pump clicked to signal that the tank was full, and she took her time replacing the nozzle and the gas cap.

Only then did she turn to look up at Steve Pendleton. Way up. He was a full foot taller than her own five feet, and while she wasn't physically intimidated by him, she felt a definite disadvantage. "Why would you want to have coffee with me, Mr. Pendleton?"

"'Steve,'" he corrected her. "And I just want to talk."

"Talk about what?" she asked suspiciously.

He shrugged, looking a bit lost. "Your son claims that he's going to marry the woman who has my nephew. I guess I just want to know that little Kenny is in good hands for now."

"I think you should know that Tom and Leslie were married this afternoon," she informed him. "I've just come from the wedding."

She watched as some of the color drained from his face. "They're married?"

"Yes. A judge who is a close friend of my son's performed the ceremony."

Steve's mouth twisted, his expression bitter. "I suppose your son has a lot of close friends in the legal system here."

"A few," she agreed evenly. "But your custody dispute will be a fair one, Mr. Pendleton. Tom and Leslie will have no trouble convincing a judge that they can provide a very good home for Kenny."

He sighed, and there was a dispirited, unhappy look in his eyes that touched her, despite her best intentions. Nina had always been too softhearted for her own good. It was a trait she acknowledged, and occasionally regretted, but it was definitely interfering now. She should be sending Steve Pendleton on his way, refusing to have anything to do with the man who was causing Leslie so much stress and anxiety. But he looked so lonely...

Maybe, she thought, knowing she was reaching for rationalizations, she could actually be of help to Leslie and Tom if she had coffee with Steve. Perhaps he would listen to her and consider dropping the custody case. Maybe this entire situation could be settled amicably.

Nina bit her lip, considered that angle for a moment, then slowly nodded. "All right, Mr. Pendleton. Steve," she corrected herself when he frowned. "I'll have coffee with you.

We need to talk. But not at the diner. I know too many people there and we wouldn't be able to speak without interruptions.''

"I'll go anywhere you want," he said, sounding a bit weary. "Just give me directions. I don't know this town very well."

"You can just follow me," she answered, taking her courage in both hands. "We'll have coffee at my place. There are quite a few things I want to say to you."

Tom and Leslie chose a popular Italian chain restaurant on busy Highway 71 for their wedding dinner. It was early for the dinner crowd, so they didn't have to wait long for a table. A perky young college student brought an infant high chair for Kenny, and commented that they certainly had a beautiful baby. Tom merely smiled and thanked her, then picked up his menu.

A portly man in a police officer's uniform passed the table, paused and greeted Tom. "Hey, Tom."

Tom glanced up and smiled. "Hey, Bill. How's it going?"

"Can't complain. What about you? You look good. Feeling okay?"

Leslie was a bit surprised at the solicitousness in the older man's voice, but Tom only shrugged.

"Doing great. Thanks," he said.

The officer glanced at Leslie, open curiosity in his faded blue eyes, then nodded. "I've got to be going. Enjoy your meal."

Tom made no effort to detain the man or to introduce Leslie. As she pretended to study her menu, she wondered how he would act when they ran into someone who knew them both. Tom had lived in Fayetteville all his life, knew an amazing number of people here. She'd met many of them when they'd dated. What would Tom say to those who would be surprised to see them together again? How would he possibly explain?

"What about you, Les?"

Hearing him say her name, she lowered her menu. "I'm sorry, what did you say?"

He gave her a look that chided her for her inattention. "I said the lasagna sounds good to me tonight. What would you like?"

"Oh. The cannelloni, I think."

"You seem very far away. Second thoughts?"

He spoke lightly, but she knew he meant the question seriously. She glanced at Kenny, who was dozing in his seat, his pacifier in his mouth. "No," she said. "No second thoughts."

"Good." He set his menu aside. "Did I mention that you look beautiful today?"

She surprised herself with a blush. "No. And thank you."

"I should have said it earlier."

The young server came to take their orders. She smiled at Kenny and said, "Is your baby always this good?"

"Yes," Tom said.

"Not always," Leslie answered at the same time.

Their server laughed and walked away.

"You haven't seen Kenny on one of his bad days yet," Leslie informed Tom. "He can be a real little grouch."

Tom shrugged. "How difficult can a little guy like this be?"

Leslie winced. Tom had a lot to learn about babies yet. She'd learned quite a bit herself during the past four months.

"Tell me about your life in Chicago," Tom said when their meals were in front of them.

Leslie tilted her head in question. "What do you want to know?"

"Everything," he said simply.

She laughed, then realized he was serious. She began tentatively, not wanting to bore him with minor details...but it quickly became obvious that he wanted even those, for some reason. So she told him about her early, insecure days at the law firm. How difficult it had been to make friends in a tense and competitive atmosphere. The teasing—some good-natured, some cruel—about her Southern accent. She told him about the time she got lost in a particularly bad neighborhood of Chicago and worried about getting out alive. And she told him some of the good things—the very nice people she'd encountered away from the office, the museums, the food. Pizza and chocolates.

With his encouragement, she talked more about Crystal's illness. About the hours spent in medical waiting rooms. About the long nights she'd stayed awake to talk to Crystal to distract her from her pain and fear, and had then tried to work the next day on less than four hours' sleep. She talked about Kenny's birth and the concern that he would be too small or that something would be wrong with him. About the first time she'd held him in her arms, and had tumbled hopelessly into love. About the night he'd come home from the hospital and had cried all night, until finally Leslie and Crystal had cried with him. About his first smile.

And then she described Crystal's last days. The pleasure Crystal had taken in having her tiny son nearby, even though she'd been too weak to even hold him for more than a few minutes at a time. Her last words had been to Leslie. "Take care of Kenny."

Because Tom listened with interest and understanding, Leslie was able to tell the story without tears. She was even able to smile when she talked about her panic at the staggering moment of awareness that she was suddenly wholly responsible for a tiny baby. Her smile died when she talked about Steve Pendleton's arrival in Chicago only two weeks after Crystal's death, and his cold demand that Leslie turn over his nephew immediately.

"You, of course, told him to go to hell," Tom remarked with a slight smile.

"Among other things."

"And then you thought of me."

She drew a deep breath. "Then I thought of you."

Tom swirled the last drop of wine in the bottom of his glass. "For the first time since you left here?"

Leslie dropped her hands to her lap and twisted her fingers tightly together. "No."

A taut silence stretched between them for a moment, and

then Kenny began to squirm in his seat. The pacifier fell out of his mouth, and he puckered to fuss. Avoiding Tom's eyes, Leslie reached for the baby. "He's probably getting hungry."

"Do you have a bottle with you?"

"Yes, in the diaper bag." She lifted the baby from the high chair and set him in her lap. Tom dug in the small blue vinyl bag Leslie carried everywhere and pulled out a disposable bottle. He removed the sanitary plastic covering from the nipple before handing the bottle to Leslie. Kenny spotted the bottle, gave a demanding squawk and reached out with chubby little hands.

"You're so impatient," Leslie chided playfully as she poked the nipple into the baby's mouth. His hands closed around the bottle, which Leslie supported for him as he began to nurse with noisy enthusiasm.

"When will he start to eat real food?" Tom asked, watching the process from across the table.

"He should start with some cereal pretty soon. He seems to be getting hungrier between bottles."

"We'll have to find him a pediatrician here," Tom said. "I'll ask Sherm to recommend someone. He and Sami checked out dozens of them before their baby was born last month."

Leslie looked up in surprise. "Sherm and Sami have a baby?"

"Yeah. A little girl. Katiya. Katie, for short."

"Sherm must be very proud."

"Oh, yeah. He—"

"Tom?" A young woman who'd been passing the table behind a hostess practically skidded to a stop. "Hi. I didn't expect to see you here tonight."

During the months Leslie had dated Tom, she'd grown accustomed to having women pay a great deal of attention to him. Tom and Zach had been the local golden boys, very eligible bachelors. This woman, who was probably in her mid-twenties, wasn't as stunning or glamorous as some of the ones Leslie had seen come on to Tom before, but she was pretty in a wholesome, girl-next-door way. Her brown hair tumbled softly around a heart-shaped face dominated by big brown eyes, and her mouth was full and curved into an engaging smile. Leslie could see how Tom could be attracted to the woman.

She glanced surreptitiously across the table, and fought a frown when she saw that Tom was smiling at the woman in a way that told Leslie that this was someone special to him. She told herself that it was ridiculous to be jealous. It wasn't as if their marriage was a traditional union. She had fought jealousy the entire time she'd been with Tom before, probably due to the insecurity she'd felt because he had never really shared his feelings with her.

She looked down at Kenny, though her attention was focused on Tom and this woman.

Tom seemed to have frozen for a moment. And then he started to rise. "Hello, Kim."

"Don't get up," she urged him quickly, waving him back down. "I won't interrupt your dinner." Her voice rose just a bit at the end of the sentence, changing it into a subtle question.

Tom responded by turning to Leslie. "Leslie, I'd like you to meet Kim McCain. Zach's wife," he added.

Leslie looked at the woman with renewed curiosity. Tom had told her that she would be surprised when she met Zach's wife, and she was. Kim wasn't at all the type of woman Zach had pursued when Leslie knew him. "It's very nice to meet you."

Kim smiled. "It's nice to meet you, too. What a beautiful baby."

"Thank you. His name is Kenny." Leslie didn't bother with further clarifications.

"Where's Zach?" Tom asked.

Kim motioned behind her. "You know Zach. He saw Mark Hackett and the two of them started talking about kayaking. I left them standing in the lobby." She glanced at the hostess. "Which table?"

The young woman pointed to a table for two across the room. "That one."

"Thank you. We'll have a seat as soon as my husband catches up." Having politely dismissed her escort, Kim turned back to Tom and Leslie. "Heaven knows when that will be," she said in resignation. "Once Zach gets to talking about kayaking…"

"Want me to go drag him in here for you?" Tom offered.

Kim smiled. "No, thanks. He'll get hungry eventually."

As if he'd heard them talking about him, Zach rushed up to join his wife. "Sorry, honey," he said. "I couldn't get away. Mark—"

He stopped talking abruptly, staring at Leslie. "Well, look who's here," he said then, breaking into one of his high-intensity smiles. "Lawyer Leslie."

Chapter Six

Leslie smiled in response to the nickname Zach had given her when she'd dated Tom before. "Hi, Maverick," she said, using the name she'd called Zach in return.

Zach McCain, she noted immediately, hadn't changed a bit in the past eighteen months. He was still tanned and fit, dark hair tumbling over bright-blue eyes in a wickedly handsome face. Leslie had heard more than one debate over who was better looking—tall, dark Zach or slightly shorter, sandy-haired Tom. There was no doubt that they were both unusually attractive men, but Leslie had always had a preference for Tom's dark-blond hair and beautiful green eyes.

Of course, she'd been aware of the differences that went much deeper than outward appearance. While both men were high-spirited and adventurous, Zach was more impulsive, impatient, a bit moody. Tom had been somewhat more mellow, open and laughing, well-known for the manners his mother had drilled into him. Tom, for example, would never have forced Leslie to find a table for herself while he lingered with a buddy in the restaurant lobby.

Yet Kim didn't seem to mind her husband's behavior. In fact, she was looking at him with obvious adoration. Leslie was a bit surprised to note that Zach looked at Kim in exactly the same way. Apparently, he'd met his match.

"Cute kid," Zach said, motioning toward Kenny, who'd stopped drinking to stare in fascination at the newcomers. "Yours?" he asked, with typical lack of tact.

"My ward," Leslie replied, thinking that Tom's best friend deserved to hear the whole story. She was somewhat surprised that Tom hadn't already mentioned Kenny. "My stepsister died and left him in my care," she explained.

And as soon as this battle with Steve was settled, she fully intended to adopt Kenny so that she could legitimately call him her son, rather than her ward.

Zach shook his head, looking bemused. "You inherited a baby?"

Kim frowned at her husband, then said to Leslie, "I'm very sorry about your loss. You must have been close to your stepsister for her to leave you her son."

Leslie decided then that she liked Kim McCain. "Yes, we were very close. I miss her."

"Are you moving back to Fayetteville or just visiting?" Zach wanted to know.

"Leslie's here to stay," Tom said, giving her a quick, bracing smile. "I've finally convinced her that this is where she belongs."

Leslie was glad that Zach and Kim were looking at Tom then, since she couldn't stop her eyebrows from shooting up in surprise. Tom made it sound as if he'd asked her to come back, she thought. As if they'd been in contact since she'd left.

Zach looked from Tom to Leslie, searching their expressions. "So you two are seeing each other again?"

"You could say that," Tom replied, sounding a bit smug. "Leslie and I were married this afternoon."

If Tom had hoped for a dramatic reaction to his announcement, he got his wish. Zach froze. Kim blinked in surprise, then broke into a smile. "You aren't pulling our leg, are you, Tom?"

He shook his head and lifted his left hand, displaying the gold band. "You can call my mom if you need confirmation," he added lightly. "She was there."

Kim congratulated them both, seemingly sincere with her astonished pleasure.

Zach's smile didn't quite ring true. "So, how did this come about?" he asked. "I didn't even know the two of you had stayed in touch."

Leslie would have told the truth then. She had never intended for Tom to deceive his friends.

Tom gave her a look that kept her quiet, and said, instead, "You know how I am when I set my mind to something. I don't take no for an answer."

Leslie couldn't help wondering whose pride Tom was protecting by making it sound as though he had done the proposing—hers or his own. She wanted to tell him that he needn't bother on her behalf—especially with Zach. There'd been a time when Tom and Zach had kept nothing from each other.

Yet it was obvious that something about that relationship had changed. So, whatever had happened to Tom had also affected his friendship with Zach, she mused. She felt as if she were trying to put together a jigsaw puzzle with no idea of what it was supposed to look like.

"Let me be one of the first to offer my best wishes." Zach was still smiling when he leaned over to brush a kiss across Leslie's cheek. It was only when he was so close to her that she saw the hurt in his eyes.

"Thank you, Zach," she murmured.

Zach turned to Tom and held out his hand. "Congratulations, Lowery. And welcome to the married men's club."

"Thanks, Zach." Perhaps there was a silent apology in the

look Tom gave his friend. Leslie couldn't be sure, but she thought there was.

Growing bored with the adults, Kenny reached for his bottle again. Leslie tilted him back against her arm and guided the bottle to his mouth. The action brought Zach's attention back to the baby. "Looks like you've got yourself a ready-made family," he commented to Tom.

Tom nodded. "I know. I was just telling Leslie that we're going to have to talk to Sherm and Sami about local pediatricians."

Zach nodded and shoved his hands into the pockets of his slacks. "Yeah, I guess they'd know about that sort of thing."

Kim placed a hand on Zach's arm. "We're starting to get some evil looks from the waiters," she said lightly. "We'd better take our table."

"We've just eaten," Tom said. "We'll be going as soon as Kenny finishes his bottle. We'll all have to get together soon, let Kim and Leslie get to know each other better."

"That would be nice," Kim agreed with a smile that was both shy and warm. "Zach's on duty tomorrow and Thursday, so we have next weekend free, except for Sunday."

"Are you taking some time off for a honeymoon, or will you be going to the office tomorrow?" Zach asked Tom.

Leslie was a bit surprised by the way Zach worded the question. They didn't usually refer to the fire station as "the office."

"No, I have to work," Tom answered, and this time he directed an apologetic look toward Leslie. "I'll try to take some time off later."

"At least you have all your evenings free," Kim said artlessly. "There are some advantages to an eight-to-five, Monday-through-Friday job. It's much easier to schedule around."

Eight to five. Monday through Friday. Since when did Tom work that schedule at the fire department? Obviously, Zach's hours were still the standard twenty-four on, forty-eight off.

"Yeah, well, I'm on call this week, so I may still have to go out some nights." Tom was still looking at Leslie. "The three of us in the fire marshal's office take turns being on call after hours," he said for her benefit. "My week starts tomorrow."

The fire marshal's office. This was the first she'd heard that Tom had changed jobs. It took a massive effort to keep the confusion out of her expression. Zach and Kim probably thought she already knew what Tom's job was—wives were generally expected to know that sort of thing about their mates.

Her new husband, in the words of TV's Ricky Ricardo, had some "'splaining" to do.

Nina Lowery was a good listener. Everyone said so. It wasn't unusual for people who were practically strangers to unburden themselves to her. Steve Pendleton was proving to be no exception.

"Kenny's all I have left of my family," he said, sitting at her kitchen table behind a cup of coffee and an untouched slice of lemon pie. "I can't just forget about him."

"No one's asking you to forget about Kenny," Nina reminded him gently. "The reason Leslie called you was to give you the option to be involved in your nephew's life. She thought you had the right to get to know him. She had no idea you would try to take him away from her."

Steve winced. "You make it sound so cruel."

"From my standpoint, it is cruel. Haven't you seen how much she loves that baby? She's taken such good care of him. She has made so many sacrifices for him—her job, her home in Chicago." Nina didn't mention the hastily arranged marriage to Tom. She had no intention of letting Steve Pendleton know the truth about that marriage.

"And how long will she continue taking such good care of him?" Bitterness coated Steve's words. "Until something more interesting comes along? She's a Harden—trust me, they aren't known for staying around."

Nina couldn't help thinking of the way Leslie had walked out on Tom to take the job in Chicago. Though Nina had never known all the details of that breakup, she knew Tom had been hurt. And yet she couldn't believe that Leslie would ever walk away from Kenny. "You can't blame Leslie for her parents' actions."

Steve ran a hand through his hair. "I don't blame her. I just don't trust her."

"Your sister obviously did."

She watched him flinch as her words struck home. "That's something else I can blame Leslie for," he muttered. "She didn't call me when my sister was dying. I didn't know—until it was too late."

His voice broke, just a little, on the last word.

Nina's heart immediately softened. She didn't want to hurt him further, but she couldn't allow him to continue to blame Leslie for something that hadn't been Leslie's fault. "Your sister asked her not to call you," she said. "Leslie tried repeatedly to change her mind."

Steve sighed and looked down at his hands. "She should have called anyway."

"She couldn't, Steve. Crystal was her friend."

"Yeah, well, she was my *sister!*"

Nina didn't even flinch at the controlled violence in his outburst. She recognized it for what it was. Pain. Frustration. Grief.

"I know what it's like to be estranged from your family," she murmured. "It's very difficult. And when you lose someone without having a chance to make amends, or at least to say goodbye—well, it hurts. Badly."

He searched her face. "You do understand."

"Yes."

"You lost a sibling?"

She shook her head. "My father. He never forgave me for the mistake I made as a teenager. Our relationship was still very strained when he died. I've always regretted that."

"Mistake?"

"I was seventeen and unmarried when my son was born. The father was a college boy who wanted nothing to do with me when I discovered that I was pregnant. So you see, I understand how you feel. And how your sister might have felt. And I'm very sorry for both of you."

"Surely she knew I wouldn't have turned her away. I would have taken care of her. In fact, I would have insisted—" He fell abruptly silent.

"That she make different decisions?" Nina shook her head. "Leslie said that nothing would have changed Crystal's mind about protecting her baby, even at the cost of her own life. Your sister loved her baby more than anything else in the world, Steve. And she wanted Leslie to raise him."

Steve was silent for several long moments, staring glumly at his hands. And then he looked up slowly. "Your son…he'll be a good father to my nephew?"

"My son will be a wonderful father." Nina could make that statement without hesitation.

Steve sighed heavily. "I'm not a cruel man, Mrs., er, Ms.—"

"Nina."

"Thank you." He smiled at her briefly before continuing. "I'm dropping the lawsuit."

She told herself that her heart fluttered only from relief. That it had nothing to do with this younger man's smile. "You're dropping it?"

He nodded. "Yes. It's a fight I probably wouldn't have won anyway, especially now that Leslie has married your son. I just needed to know that Kenny would be well cared for. And—well, I was angry. Hurt."

"I understand that," Nina said warmly. "And I think you're doing the right thing, Steve."

"Yeah, well." He drew a deep breath. "Tell Leslie she'd better take good care of my nephew. I hope she deserves the faith you've shown in her."

Nina frowned. "You'll tell her yourself, when you let her know your decision."

He shook his head. "Maybe it would be best if I just get out of their lives. Leslie and I are hardly friends."

"Then you'll learn to be. For Kenny's sake," Nina said

firmly. "As you've pointed out repeatedly, you are his uncle. You should be a part of his life."

"Tom and Leslie might have something to say about that," Steve answered ruefully. "Especially if they adopt Kenny, which I'm sure they will, once I'm out of the way."

"That will make no difference. Neither of them would deny Kenny the chance to know his only uncle."

"What are you saying? That I should visit? Have dinner with the family? Spend Christmas with them?" He looked at her skeptically as he listed the options.

"Why not?" she asked with a deliberately challenging smile.

"Nina, you weren't listening. Leslie and I don't even get along."

"Why not?" she repeated. "You have things in common. Both of you were hurt by your parents' actions when you were younger. You both loved your sister, each in your own way. You both love Kenny now. If you will allow yourself to get to know Leslie as herself, rather than as her father's daughter, I think you'll like her. I like her very much."

Her smile deepened. "As for my son, he is a wonderful man. Of course I'm biased, but he's kind and loyal and thoughtful and funny. Everyone likes him."

Steve's smile was a bit crooked. He spoke with a touch of indulgence for her maternal pride. "He hasn't exactly been funny when I was around."

"You haven't given him a chance," she reminded him. And then sighed. "But to be honest, he's had a difficult year. Some of the laughter has gone out of him, and it has broken my heart. I'm so hopeful that this marriage will bring the joy back to him."

Steve looked interested, but didn't pry into the details of Tom's problems. He asked only, "So they didn't just marry to keep me from getting Kenny?"

Nina phrased her answer carefully. "Tom and Leslie are meant for each other. They still have some issues to work out between them, but I believe they will have a wonderful marriage.''

He looked concerned by her circumspection, and she knew he was thinking of his nephew.

''They will be good parents, Steve,'' she repeated firmly. ''They'll put Kenny's needs first.''

A sudden, brilliant idea made her bite her lip to hide a smile. ''There is one way you can make sure of that, if it will ease your mind.''

His right eyebrow rose in question. ''And what is that?''

''Eat your pie,'' she said, rising from her chair. ''I'll get you a fresh cup of coffee. And then we'll talk more.''

The baby was asleep by the time Leslie and Tom got home that evening. Without saying anything to Tom, Leslie carried Kenny into the guest bedroom, changed his diaper and slipped him into a one-piece sleeper, then laid him gently on his back in the portable crib and covered him with a light blanket. She knew he wasn't yet down for the night. He'd wake in a few hours for another bottle, maybe stay awake for a little while before going back to sleep. She needed to get him back on the regular schedule that had been disturbed since she'd left Chicago.

She stood for several long minutes just watching Kenny sleep. He was so small. So fragile. So totally dependent. She'd made so many decisions on his behalf in the past weeks. She hoped she hadn't made any serious mistakes.

Taking a deep breath, she went in search of Tom.

He wasn't in the living room or the kitchen. Nor was he in his bedroom. Frowning, she looked down the hallway toward the house's small, third bedroom. Tom had used that one for storage before. The door had remained closed for the past couple of days, so she'd assumed the room was still unused. That door was ajar now, drawing her like an invitation.

The boxes and trunks she'd remembered from before were gone, she noted immediately. The room now resembled a professional gym. Serious-looking workout equipment lined the walls—weight benches, a stationary bike, a treadmill, a stair climber, other machines she didn't recognize. Tom had been into physical fitness when she'd known him before, but not like this. He'd kept in shape then through his very active adventures, not through formal exercise.

Tom sat on a bench in the center of the room, but he wasn't working out. Just sitting there. Watching her.

He'd shed his jacket and tie and had unfastened the top three buttons of his white dress shirt. His sandy hair was disarrayed, as though he'd been running his fingers through it. His eyes were wary.

She looked around the room and waved a hand vaguely toward the equipment. "Very impressive. I thought I spotted a few new muscles."

"They aren't new. I've always had them. They're just somewhat better developed than they were before."

"Well, at least you're cracking jokes again. Sort of." She crossed the room, tested a bar that was fastened to several very heavy weights. "Sometimes I wonder if a stranger has taken over the body of the man I used to know."

He rubbed his right thigh, the gesture seemingly unconscious. "Trust me," he muttered. "No stranger would want this body."

She crossed her arms over her chest, braced herself and turned to face him. "Are you ready to talk now?"

"What would you like to talk about?" he asked, deliberately obtuse.

It was enough to make her want to pull her hair. Or his. "Damn it, Tom, you've been keeping something from me since I arrived. Did you really think I wouldn't know?"

He shrugged. "I didn't think you particularly cared. You accomplished what you came here for. We're married."

He couldn't have hurt her more if he'd slapped her. She took an involuntary step backward, as if recoiling from the impact.

"You make it sound as if I gave you no choice," she protested. "As if I tricked you into it or something. That isn't fair. I told you everything from the beginning. You agreed to help me, and you said this was the best way. I gave you every chance to change your mind."

He exhaled deeply. "I know. I'm sorry, that was out of line."

"If you've had second thoughts…if you want out…" She lifted her chin. "I certainly won't try to hold you. We can get an annulment immediately. I'm sure your friend the judge can arrange that as easily as he arranged the wedding."

"I don't want an annulment. I'm sorry, all right? I didn't mean what I said."

Had she not caught a glimpse of his eyes then, she might well have left the room. But the pain and unhappiness she saw in him drew her toward him. Cautiously, she approached him. She perched on the edge of the bench, facing him, her hands clasped tightly in the lap of her prim winter-white suit.

"The day I left here," she began, choosing her words with care, "we said some cutting things to each other. Later, I decided it was because we were both sad that our relationship was coming to an end, and we sort of took that sadness out on each other."

"You made it look so easy to leave," he murmured, his jaw taut.

"You called me cold. Driven. Career obsessed."

He grimaced, and kneaded his thigh again. "You said I was irresponsible. Reckless. Arrogant."

"Maybe—maybe there was truth in what we said. To an extent. But, Tom…it wasn't easy to leave."

He lifted a hand, touched her hair. "It wasn't easy to let you go."

Her fingers twisted together. Her wedding band felt heavy, unfamiliar. "You're still angry with me for leaving."

It wasn't a question, but he shook his head. "No." And then he corrected himself. "Well, maybe. A little."

"And that's why you've been acting so distant?"

He shook his head. "No. I—well, I didn't know how to tell you."

"Tell me what?" she asked, thoroughly confused. "What happened to you? Why have you changed jobs? What has gone wrong between you and Zach?"

He grimaced. "It's a long story."

She kept her gaze on his face. "I've got nothing but time."

He drew a deep breath, then let it out slowly. "Four months after you left, Zach and I were in an accident. His shoulder was dislocated. My back was broken and my right leg was crushed."

Leslie felt the stiffening go out of her knees, and she was glad that she'd sat down. "My God," she breathed. "What happened?"

"We were riding an ATV. Zach was driving. I was on the back. We collided with another rider who'd spun out of control. My right leg was crushed between the vehicles, and then I was thrown onto a pile of boulders. I landed flat on my back." His voice was emotionless as he recited the facts. "I was brought to Washington Regional Hospital by ambulance, then airlifted to Little Rock for emergency surgery. I've got three rods, five screws and a bone fusion in my back. My leg's held together with rods and pins. I have some paralysis in my foot. It's irreversible."

She thought of his career as a firefighter. His volunteer search-and-rescue work. His joy in climbing and rafting and biking and other physical activities. "Tom, I'm so sorry."

His mouth twisted. "You called me 'Goose,' remember? Zach and Tom—Maverick and Goose, just like the two pilots in the movie *Top Gun*. You thought you were being funny. Best buddies. Partners. Just like the guys in the movie. But there was a plot twist you might have forgotten when you gave me my nickname. Goose died."

"And Maverick went on with his career," she whispered.

"Yeah. Maverick went on."

"That's what wrong between you and Zach? You blame him for the accident?"

"No." The word exploded from him. He shook his head. "No," he repeated more quietly. "It wasn't Zach's fault. If

anyone's, it was the other driver's. But it was really just a senseless accident.''

"Then why—''

"Zach feels sorry for me.'' Tom grimaced as he said the words, his voice coated with distaste. ''I see it in his eyes every time he looks at me. And I hate it.''

"Oh, Tom, no.''

He shook his head. ''I didn't say I hate Zach. I just hate the pity. It's not just Zach. It's everyone. Ever since the accident, they treat me like Saint Tom. Poor Tom. They want to know if I'm okay. If I need anything. If there's anything they can do for me. I'm not…one of them anymore.''

"Could it be that you're imagining some of this?''

He pushed a hand through his hair. ''I wish I were.''

"Well, that's nonsense,'' she said, forcing herself to speak brusquely. ''There's absolutely no reason in the world for anyone to feel sorry for you. You're still ridiculously handsome. You've got a limp, but you're in generally good health, from what I can see. Unless there's something you haven't told me?'' She asked lightly, but with a knot of fear in her chest that eased only when he shook his head.

"Well, then,'' she continued. ''You have a home. A career. A mother who pampers you shamelessly.''

"A beautiful wife,'' he added, his mouth tilting into a slight smile.

Her pulse fluttered. She steadied it with an effort. ''My point is, it's absurd for anyone to feel sorry for you.''

He seemed to relax somewhat. ''That's what I've been trying to tell everyone.''

She wondered if maybe Tom had been feeling a bit sorry for himself. Not that she would have blamed him if he had. She had a feeling that he'd only begun to tell her all he'd lost in that accident. But he wouldn't thank her for bringing it up now.

She touched his arm. ''Just keep telling them until they believe you.'' And until you believe it yourself, she wanted to add.

He looked at her hand, then at her face. The glint in his eyes was still only a pale imitation of the Tom she'd known before...but a definite improvement.

"Ridiculously handsome, hmm?"

She smiled wryly. "I should have known that's the only thing you would hear."

"I heard every word you said," he corrected. "That's the part I liked best."

Leslie couldn't help laughing.

Tom reached out and stroked a finger along her jaw. "I've missed that sound," he murmured.

Nothing could have stopped her pulse from rocketing out of control that time. She couldn't think of a thing to say in response.

He was still wearing that faint, sexy smile when he bent his head toward her. When he brushed his lips over hers.

His smile vanished when she responded. His arms went around her, pulling her closer to him on the narrow, vinyl-covered bench. His mouth opened hungrily over hers. She closed her eyes and kissed him back, surrendering herself to the moment.

His chest felt broader than she remembered. His arms stronger. But the way he kissed her; the way his tongue teased her lips, then thrust between to sweep her mouth; the way his hand cupped the back of her head to hold her against him— all of that was achingly familiar. She'd relived Tom's kisses during too many long, lonely nights in Chicago to have forgotten any detail.

He tilted her back over his arm and deepened the embrace even further. She clung to him, her mind spinning, her body growing warm, malleable. A muffled moan came from deep within his chest, sounding like a mixture of pleasure and pain. She understood that feeling all too well.

His fingers were inches from her breast, when the telephone rang in the other room.

"Ignore it," Tom muttered against her lips when Leslie instinctively stiffened.

"But—"

The telephone rang again. At the same time, they both heard Kenny cry out.

Tom growled a curse. Reluctantly, he released her. "I'll get the phone."

"I'll get the baby." Her voice was decidedly shaky.

Still muttering, he shoved himself to his feet and limped to the doorway. Leslie watched him, her throat tightening. Now she understood what that limp represented—and it broke her heart.

He glanced over his shoulder, saw her expression and frowned. "Don't do that," he warned. "I won't have it from you."

"No," she agreed. "You'll get no sympathy from me."

He nodded curtly. "Good."

And then he disappeared down the hallway.

Kenny cried again, and Leslie rose unsteadily to her feet. It had been, she thought dazedly, quite a day.

Chapter Seven

Carrying the baby against her shoulder, Leslie entered the living room just as Tom hung up the phone. Still somewhat nonplussed from the call he'd just taken, Tom cleared his throat. "That was Pendleton."

Leslie's eyes widened. "Steve? What did he want?"

"He wanted to congratulate us on our marriage."

She looked immediately skeptical. "How did he find out that we—damn it, he's still having me watched, isn't he? I'm going to—"

"Leslie." Tom held up his hands to interrupt her, though the quick temper that flared in her eyes reminded him inevitably of the passion that had flared in his exercise room. "He isn't having you watched. My mother told him. Apparently, they ran into each other at a service station."

Nervously patting Kenny's back, Leslie moistened her lips. "What did he say? More threats?"

Tom shook his head. "He's dropping the custody suit."

Leslie's reaction was much as Tom's had been when Pendleton had quietly told him the decision. "He's *what?*" she asked in disbelief.

"He's dropping it," Tom repeated, beginning to smile. "He said he isn't sure he can win in court now, and he doesn't want to waste time pursuing a lost cause."

Smiling broadly, Leslie hugged the baby. "Did you hear that, Kenny? We can stop worrying now. No one is going to take you away from me."

Kenny babbled in response, the noises he made sounding like a cross between chirps and squeals.

Tom chuckled. "I guess that means he's pleased."

"Of course it does." Leslie's eyes were bright with unshed tears. "Oh, Tom, thank you."

"What are you thanking me for?"

"For everything. If it hadn't been for you, I might have lost Kenny. It's partly because of you that Steve dropped the suit—I'm sure of it. I'll never be able to thank you enough for what you've done for us."

He shook his head, scowling now. He hadn't wanted her pity earlier; he didn't want her gratitude now.

"Now," she said, still giddy with relief, "I can adopt Kenny. I can make a real home for him. I can—"

"It occurs to me," Tom interrupted deliberately, "that you're leaving someone out of this equation."

Still smiling at the baby, she asked almost absently, "Who?"

"Your husband."

That brought her head around. "I, um—"

"I haven't told you everything Pendleton said."

"What do you mean?"

Tom shoved his hands in the pockets of his suit slacks, the satisfaction he'd felt only moments earlier fading fast. "He warned us that he's not going to just quietly disappear. He feels an obligation to make sure his nephew will be well cared for. He said that for the next few months, he wants to visit Kenny regularly and make absolutely sure we're giving him a good home. He said if he sees any evidence that Kenny isn't being given the best of care, he'll go ahead and file the custody suit."

"He's going to monitor our marriage." Leslie spoke slowly as the meaning of Steve's message sank in.

Tom nodded. "I suppose that's the gist of it. You know the law better than I do, but I'm assuming he can sue for custody any time until an adoption is finalized."

"He can sue for custody any time he wants. Whether he would win...well, the only question would be if he could prove that Kenny's health or welfare was in jeopardy. Since Crystal is dead and the biological father unknown, it's hard to guess whether a judge would give any consideration to Steve's blood connection to Kenny. Last week, my position might have been vulnerable. That has changed now."

"Because we were married today."

She nodded with apparent reluctance. "Partly, of course."

"Were you planning to just forget the marriage if Pendleton had folded his tents and gone completely away?"

"I—" She began to rock her upper body, the motion automatic, her hand rhythmically patting Kenny's back.

In her celebration of her apparent victory, she hadn't even thought of their marriage, Tom realized heavily.

Leslie swallowed. "We both know that the marriage took place only because of Steve's threats."

"And it took place today because he said he was going to file suit tomorrow."

"Yes." Leslie gently fended off Kenny's hand as he patted her face, fingers aiming for her mouth.

Tom kept his gaze locked with Leslie's. "You went into it planning to end it as soon as you'd won your case, didn't you?"

"To be honest, I haven't thought beyond the case."

He nodded. He didn't know what he wanted her to say, exactly. As she'd pointed out, they both knew why they'd married. And for now, the motive still applied. "I suppose as long as Pendleton's monitoring us, we'll have to present the appearance of an average married couple."

"I suppose so."

He massaged the back of his neck. "And it will probably be best if we don't tell anyone else the real reason for the hasty wedding. It's enough that you and Mom and I know the truth. Everyone else can simply believe that this was something we planned in private."

Leslie frowned. "Even Zach?"

Tom shrugged, bothered again by the guilt that had flashed through him in the restaurant earlier, when Zach had looked at him with hurt in his eyes. But something in him rebelled against telling Zach that Leslie had married him only because she'd felt she had no other choice. "For now, I think it's best that we keep our reasons to ourselves."

Looking troubled, Leslie chewed her lower lip and rocked the baby.

Tom felt himself going on the defensive. "What's the problem?"

"I guess I didn't think of how many lies we'd have to tell. How much deception would be involved."

"Yeah, well, that's what happens when you run a scam. Takes a lot of work to keep the ruse going."

It was obvious that she didn't care for his choice of words. "We're not—mmph." Kenny's playful hand had landed squarely in her mouth, muffling her words.

Tom smiled a little. "Looks like he wants to play."

Kenny crowed, as if in agreement.

On an impulse, Tom reached out and plucked the baby from Leslie's arms. "You've been wearing that suit all day," he said to Leslie, shifting Kenny comfortably into the curve of his arm. "I'll watch the kid while you change."

Leslie was tempted. "I am ready to get out of these heels," she admitted with a slight smile.

"Take your time. Kenny and I will do some male bonding. I'll show him pictures of power tools and teach him the Tim Allen grunt."

He was gratified when his weak joke drew a small laugh

from her. "Well, as long as you're contributing to his education..."

Tom watched her walk out of the room. The white skirt clung sleekly to her hips and emphasized her long, shapely legs. He'd always thought Leslie had a real talent for making a tailored business suit look incredibly sexy. He didn't try to delude himself that she would reappear in something short and slinky suited to a typical wedding night. Not that it would matter. Regardless of how many layers of clothing she wrapped around her, Tom would still want her.

He had never stopped.

Her wedding night. Sometime around three in the morning, Leslie lay alone on the bed in the guest room. Kenny slept soundly in the portable crib set up in one corner of the room, occasionally sucking on his pacifier.

It certainly wasn't like any wedding night Leslie would have envisioned, had she ever imagined herself getting married.

After the way Tom had kissed her in his exercise room, she might have expected at least a good-night kiss before they'd turned in. Or more—they had, after all, been lovers at one time. And that part had been very good between them.

Tom had played with the baby for a while and then handed him over to Leslie when it was time for a bottle. He had then changed into a T-shirt and sweatpants, disappeared into the exercise room and, judging from the noises she'd heard from there, proceeded to use every piece of equipment he kept in there. It had been almost an hour before he'd reappeared, sweating and tired looking, his limp pronounced. She'd already put Kenny to bed by then.

Tom had given her a quick smile. "I'm going to hit the shower and turn in," he'd said lightly. "I leave for the office at 7:45 in the morning. If you aren't awake by then, I'll leave the number for you in case you need to reach me."

She'd been sitting on the couch, pretending to read while she'd waited for him, wondering how the day would end. She hadn't thought it would be quite so abrupt. "Um, good night," she'd said.

He'd nodded and disappeared. Just like that. She'd heard the shower running, then the sound of his bedroom door closing. She could only assume he'd been asleep ever since.

Leslie hadn't slept a wink.

Arriving home from work late the next day, Tom found Leslie sitting on his couch, reading a magazine. She looked fresh and comfortable in a dark-green chenille sweater with faded jeans and green socks on her shoeless feet. Little Kenny lay on a baby blanket on the floor, kicking his feet and batting at colorful toys that dangled from a molded plastic contraption that arched over him.

The simple domesticity of the scene hit Tom hard. He'd never realized how dull it was to come home to an empty house until he'd compared it with this.

Leslie looked up with a distracted expression. "I didn't know that careless smoking is the leading cause of residential fires."

Obviously, she was reading one of his professional publications. "Read that again," he advised her.

She looked back down at the page. "Oh. It's the leading cause of residential fire deaths."

"Right. Cooking, arson and alternative heaters are the more usual causes of residential fires. Fires caused by smoking cause so many deaths because the smoker has often fallen asleep, or passes out when the fire begins."

Leslie flipped pages in the magazine, paused, then read a few more words. "Have you studied the 'Standard Test Method for Ignitable Liquid Residues in Extracts from Fire Debris Samples by Gas Chromatography'?"

He smiled. "ASTM Standard E 1397-95. And yes, I've studied it. I've done a lot of reading about fire investigation during the past year."

She closed the magazine and set it aside. "So you're the fire marshal now."

"Assistant fire marshal," he corrected her. "One of two."

He put his radio on a table, along with his car keys. He was wearing the standard fire department uniform of blue shirt and pants with black shoes, the clothes rumpled now after a full day at work. The walkie-talkie would stay on and close at hand while he was away from the office this week, since it was his turn to be on call. He would be summoned by the firefighters to every fire for which a cause was not immediately obvious, he explained to Leslie, preparing her in case he was called away that evening.

"Fire investigation sounds fascinating," she said tentatively, her eyes searching his face.

He shrugged. "It's interesting. That's only a small part of my job, of course. Mostly I do routine fire code inspections of local businesses. Every existing business has to be inspected at least once a year, and every new business before opening. There's a lot of paperwork involved."

She rose from the couch, still watching him. "Do you like it?"

Again, a shrug seemed appropriate. "It's a living."

Abruptly, he changed the subject, "Man, something smells good. Don't tell me you cooked dinner."

"I cooked dinner," she replied lightly. "It gave me something to do while Kenny took his afternoon nap. I hope baked chicken and wild rice are okay."

"Sounds great. I'll go wash up."

"Take your time. It won't be ready for another half hour."

Tom meant to go straight to his bedroom to change, but he found himself suddenly kneeling on the floor by the baby. Kenny met his eyes, looked humorously surprised for a moment, then broke into a slobbery grin.

Tom ran a finger across the baby's chubby, dimpled cheek. "Hey, pardner, how's it goin'? What's this you've got here, hmm?" he asked, thumping a dangling plastic yellow bird and making it sway from the bar to which it was attached with a nylon strap.

"It's called a baby gym," Leslie said. "See the little round hand grips? I think they're intended to build upper-body strength. He hasn't learned to pull on them yet, though. He just likes to watch the toys swing.''

"A gym, huh?'' Tom shook his head. "Forget it, kid. You'll never build real muscles with this sissy contraption. We'll spend some time in my exercise room and really work on those abs and pecs.''

Kenny chortled. Tom laughed in response to the funny sounds the baby made. This was a seriously cute kid, he decided. It was no wonder that Leslie had been willing to do just about anything to keep him.

Thinking there might be time for a fast shower before dinner, he started to rise. A curse pushed itself out of his throat when the entire lower half of his body seemed to clench. He stumbled, tried to steady himself, and stumbled again.

Leslie was instantly at his side, her full weight against him as she supported him until he regained his balance. "Are you all right?''

The pain was there, as it so often was, angry and quick. A thin film of perspiration had broken out on his face and beneath his clothing. He shouldn't have tried to rise so hastily from his kneeling position. Even after over a year, he still sometimes forgot that there were things he could no longer do as easily as before.

Sharply reminded of all those things, he felt the laughter drain out of him. It both embarrassed and annoyed him that Leslie had witnessed his weakness. "I'm fine,'' he growled, pushing away from her. "No problem.''

"Tom—''

"I said I'm fine.'' He was already moving toward his bedroom, cursing his limp, cursing his temper, cursing himself.

He figured that Leslie should be well aware by now that the man she'd left behind so many months ago was not the man she had married.

Nina put the last cut-flower arrangement in the big refrigerator unit that lined one side of her florist shop and closed the door. And then she sighed and pressed a hand to the middle of her back. It had been a trying day. Not as exhausting as last Friday, of course, with its hectic Valentine's Day rush, but still busy.

It was closing time. She'd already sent her employees home, telling them that she would lock up today. After all the extra effort they'd given her last week, she'd figured they deserved an extra half hour off today. They'd accepted her offer with alacrity.

She caught a glimpse of her reflection in the chrome trim on the cooler. She looked tired, she thought critically, tucking a strand of salon-perfected ash-blond hair behind her ear. Everyone was always telling her that she looked younger than her age, but today she felt all of her forty-seven years. Maybe it was because she'd left her childhood so early, had been forced by poor choices and circumstances to take on almost overwhelming responsibilities at such a young age. Or maybe it had to do with her awareness all day that her thirty-year-old son was now married, and himself at least partly responsible for a child.

She was practically a grandmother, she'd realized with a start. And while there was a certain pleasure in that acknowledgment, it was also a bit daunting.

Maybe she should try a new hair color, she mused, gazing into that somewhat distorted reflection.

"Finished for the day?"

The question, asked in a deep male voice from behind her, made her gasp and jump. She'd been so lost in her thoughts that she hadn't even heard the bell chime when the front door had opened, she realized. Not a particularly secure feeling, since she was alone in a small business in nearly deserted downtown Fayetteville.

She turned to gaze at the tall, dark-haired, brown-eyed man leaning against her counter, dashing and handsome in a leather pilot's jacket, a soft-looking sweater and jeans.

"Hello, Steve," she said, making no effort to hide her surprise. "I thought you'd gone back to Little Rock today."

"I've taken a few days off. I haven't spent much time in Fayetteville, so I played tourist today, mostly at the university."

"You're a Razorback fan?"

His smile was rueful. "Isn't nearly everyone in this state?"

"Is there something I can do for you?" she asked, wondering why he'd shown up at her business this way. She'd told him a bit about her shop last night when they'd chatted over lemon pie, but she certainly hadn't expected to see him here today.

"Have dinner with me?" Though he spoke lightly, he was looking at her closely.

Taken aback, she blinked, then suddenly understood. "You want to talk about Tom and Leslie," she said.

He shook his head. "I think we've covered that subject well enough already. To be honest, I'd just as soon *not* talk about them tonight."

"Then why…oh, of course. You don't really know anyone else here in town, do you?" Obviously, he wasn't a man who enjoyed eating alone.

Steve shrugged. "I know a few people I could have called. Business associates, mostly. But I'd rather be with you."

His sudden grin made her heartbeat skip. She told herself sternly that she was much too old to react that way to a beautiful male smile.

She smoothed her palms nervously over her neatly tailored black pantsuit. "Well, I—"

"If you have other plans, I'd certainly understand. You needn't feel that you should entertain me or anything. I'm perfectly capable of dining alone."

The look he gave her was so pitiful that she had to smile. "I have no other plans," she heard herself saying. "I'd be happy to have dinner with you."

An innocent dinner between friendly acquaintances. That was all it would be, she assured herself.

Steve's smile was a bit smug. "Great. I'll wait until you lock up and we'll leave from here, okay?"

"Yes, that will be fine."

Just dinner. And there was no reason at all that she shouldn't enjoy herself, she thought with a touch of defiance at the little voice inside her that kept asking what in the world she thought she was doing.

"This is great," Tom said, his plate nearly empty. "You're a great cook, Les."

He'd been trying to be pleasant while eating the dinner she'd cooked for them. He regretted snapping at her earlier. She hadn't deserved it.

Leslie shrugged and toyed with her own food. "Thanks. I've always liked cooking, when I had the time."

Tom glanced at Kenny, who sat in his seat, gumming a plastic teether and watching them eat. "He's bright eyed tonight, isn't he? Looks like he'd love to join in the conversation."

"Mmm." She glanced at the baby, then sipped her iced tea without further comment.

Leslie hadn't been responding very well to Tom's friendly overtures. Polite, but distant best described the way she'd acted during the meal. He suspected that he'd hurt her feelings earlier. And, he realized without relish, it was apparently going to take an apology to mend them.

He drew a deep breath. "Leslie, I'm sorry. I shouldn't have snarled at you."

He didn't figure he needed to be more specific, and apparently he was right. She gave him a look that told him she knew exactly what he was talking about.

"Forget it," she said, but it was obvious that she hadn't.

He frowned. "It embarrassed me to lose my balance in front of you," he explained reluctantly. "I don't like being reminded of my...limitations." He said the word with distaste.

Her expression revealed nothing. "When did you say you had your accident?"

"Almost fifteen months ago. Barely four months after you left."

"And you've been sulking and feeling sorry for yourself ever since?"

Her question knocked the breath out of him. He stared at her, stung by the unfairness of her accusation. Apparently, she hadn't yet realized exactly how serious his injuries had been.

"I almost died," he snapped. "I came within an inch of spending the rest of my life in a wheelchair, paralyzed from the waist down."

Her left eyebrow quirked. "But you *aren't* in a wheelchair. It looks to me as if you get around pretty well, with the exception of a slight limp. And maybe you lose your balance occasionally. On the whole, you were actually pretty lucky."

He was genuinely stunned. "I lost my job. I loved being a firefighter, being on the search-and-rescue team. I can't do that now."

"Maybe." She didn't look entirely convinced. "But you're still working in the field you like, and there are probably talents you could contribute to the search teams other than climbing mountains and rappelling down cliffs."

"You don't understand." He felt betrayed by her attitude. Damn it, everyone else seemed to realize how much he'd suffered, how much he'd lost. Why didn't Leslie?

"I'm sorry." Her tone was too polite. "Did you want me to feel sorry for you, too?"

He cursed and pushed himself away from the table. He didn't have to sit here and take this. This time he was able to stand without stumbling, to his relief. "I've got some paperwork to do and then I'm going to work out. Leave the dishes. I'll get them later."

"I'll get them myself. I have nothing else to do. I'm the one who lost everything, *including* my career, remember?"

The bitterness in her voice took him aback. "Damn it, Leslie—"

She stood, holding her plate, and turned her back on him. "Go play with your exercise toys. I have work to do in here."

With a scowl, he left the room. He heard Kenny babbling behind him, but he didn't hesitate. All of a sudden, he didn't feel as if he belonged in his own kitchen.

Chapter Eight

"I love spicy food." Nina reached for her glass of water as she spoke.

Smiling, Steve watched her swallow a fourth of the glass of cold liquid. "I can tell you have no problem with spicy food at all."

She smiled sheepishly and blotted her lips with a red-checked napkin. "I really do enjoy it. Even when it burns the lining of my mouth."

They had chosen a trendy new Southwestern restaurant in the old downtown square, within walking distance of Nina's shop. The room was rather dark, and the candles flickering in the center of each table provided most of the illumination. The tables were small, and arranged to provide a comfortable feeling of intimacy, encouraging low-voiced conversation. Nina and Steve had been taking advantage of the opportunity to chat about a wide variety of subjects, from sports to politics, from art to literature, from music to movies.

Nina hadn't enjoyed a meal this much in years.

"Tommy always makes fun of me when we eat Mexican food," she commented. "I always drink gallons of water to counteract the peppers. No food is too hot for him. He eats jalapeños as easily as if they were sweet pickles."

"You talk about your son a lot," Steve observed, pushing his empty plate away and leaning comfortably back in his chair.

Nina frowned. Was he criticizing her? If so, he might as well know that her son was the most important part of her life. She couldn't help talking about him.

Steve seemed to read her thoughts from her expression.

"That wasn't a criticism. Just a comment. You're obviously very proud of him."

She relaxed a little. "Yes, very. He's a wonderful son."

"You deserve a great deal of credit for raising him alone the way you did."

Pleasantly embarrassed, she shrugged lightly. "I did my best. It helped that he was always such a good boy."

"He never met his father?"

Shifting in her seat, Nina shook her head. "No. Ron never wanted to see Tom. He gave up all claim to fatherhood the day I told him I was pregnant, and he said he never wanted to see me again. He moved out of the state not long after Tom was born. I don't know where he is now—if he's even still alive, though I assume that he is. When Tom turned eighteen, I told him his father's name and gave him some personal information I thought would interest him. I told him I didn't mind if he felt he needed to track Ron down someday, for his own curiosity."

"And what did Tom say to that?"

"He said he had no interest in meeting the man who'd contributed nothing to his development except a Y chromosome. He said that as far as he was concerned, he had only one parent and he needed no other." Nina couldn't keep the pride out of her voice that time, though she tried to speak matter-of-factly.

"Good for Tom."

"I told you he's a wonderful son. And a fine man. You'll like him, I think, once you get to know him better."

"I certainly intend to try."

"For Kenny's sake," Nina murmured with an approving smile.

"Partly," Steve agreed, gazing at her over his wineglass.

Something in his expression made her clear her throat and look hastily away.

"How about some dessert?" a bronze-skinned young server asked as he approached the table with a smile. "Sherbet? Key lime pie? Fried ice cream?"

"Sherbet sounds good," Nina agreed, seizing the change of subject. "What about you, Steve?"

"Yes, I'll have that, too."

Nina told herself that she was being silly again. Imagining undercurrents that simply weren't there. *You're having a lovely evening, Nina Lowery. Don't blow it.*

After lingering for a time over dessert and coffee, Steve paid for dinner, then walked Nina to her car, which she'd left parked in its usual space behind her shop. She was very conscious of him beside her as she huddled into her coat against the February night air. He loomed so tall over her, appearing so strong and virile in his leather jacket and denim jeans. And yet the smile he slanted down at her was so kind and gentle that she couldn't help feeling safe with him.

In some ways, she mused, he reminded her of her son. But Steve Pendleton evoked no maternal feelings in her at all.

She slid her key into the lock of her car and looked upward. "Will you be going back to Little Rock tomorrow?"

He leaned a forearm against the top of her small car. "No, I don't think so. I'd like to hang around here a few more days. I haven't had any time off in a while."

"You'll want to see Kenny, of course. I'm sure Leslie will welcome you, though you can't blame her for being a bit wary at first. I'll talk to her for you, if you like. Explain to her that you want to get on a more friendly footing with her."

"Thank you, but that won't be necessary. I'll talk to Leslie myself."

"That would probably be best." Her hand on her door handle, she cleared her throat. "Dinner was lovely, Steve. Thank you."

"I thank you for giving me the pleasure of your company this evening."

His old-fashioned courtliness appealed to her...as did so much about this man. "Well...good night."

"I was able to nab two tickets for the basketball game tomorrow night. Will you go with me?"

Her fingers clenched spasmodically on the car handle. "Um..."

The vapor lights overhead illuminated Steve's enticing smile. "I hope you have no other plans. I'll be terribly disappointed if you do."

"Steve, I—"

He reached out to touch her cheek with a disarmingly gentle fingertip. "Nina," he said, imitating her tone. "Why do you look so nervous? I'm only asking you for a date."

A date. She moaned. *Now* she was nervous. Surely he didn't mean...

"A second date, I should have said," he corrected himself. "Counting tonight."

"Oh, but tonight wasn't a date," she protested automatically.

His eyebrow quirked. "No? What do you call it when a man and a woman who like each other and are attracted to each other spend time together to get to know each other better? We call it a date where I'm from, but maybe you have another term for it here."

He was teasing her—but beneath the humor he was quite serious, she realized. He considered the dinner they'd just shared a date. And...oh, heavens, had he just said he was attracted to her?

"Steve, I—"

He leaned over to feather his lips over hers. "Say yes," he murmured.

"Yes," she repeated blankly, and since she suddenly couldn't remember the question, she hoped she hadn't just agreed to anything illegal or immoral.

"It's a date, then."

Again, there was that touch of smugness she found both annoying and somehow intriguing.

"Would you like for me to follow you home? Just to make sure you get there safely?"

"Thank you, but that won't be necessary."

"All right. I'll see you tomorrow, then. I'll call the shop in the morning to arrange a time, okay?"

"Yes, that will be fine." Her response was mechanical.

He saw her into her car, and waited until she'd buckled in and started the engine, before turning to lope toward his vehicle.

Nina sat for several long moments, making no effort to drive away, her fingertips brushing her still-tingling lips. And then she realized that Steve was also sitting in his car, watching her, apparently waiting for her to leave before he himself pulled out.

Abruptly, she shoved the gearshift into Drive and pressed the accelerator. She suddenly had a great need to be alone in her apartment, where she could spend some quiet, private time trying to decide exactly what had happened this evening.

Leslie hated feeling guilty. Her parents had always conveyed to her that guilt and regrets were a waste of time, apologies a waste of breath. "What's done is done," her father had often said. "Get over it."

It was how he'd lived his entire adult life. And he'd hurt a lot of people along the way, she thought morosely. Without ever even acknowledging the pain he'd caused.

Whatever her father's philosophy, she knew she owed Tom an apology. The things she'd said to him had been cruel...even if there was truth in them.

Of course, he had owed her an apology, as well, she thought with a momentary return of the irritation that had spurred her to utter those unkind words. He shouldn't have snapped at her earlier just because she'd seen him at a moment of weakness. She'd offered assistance, not pity. If he didn't know the difference, then he didn't understand her at all.

And then her annoyance faded again as guilt crept back in. She really shouldn't have said what she had. Tom *had* suffered. It had been obvious to her ever since she'd first arrived back in town. He had loved his job, and he'd lost it. Of course, she'd lost her job, too—but it had been her choice to take that chance by placing Kenny's interests first, she reminded herself. Tom's choices had been taken away from him.

He'd said very plainly that he didn't want pity. And then he'd gotten mad at her because she hadn't shown him enough. Just what *did* he want from her, anyway?

Her emotions ping-ponging between self-censure and indignation with him, she sighed deeply and went in search of Tom after putting Kenny to bed. Tom had been very careful to avoid her since dinner, spending time first in his bedroom, then his workout room, and then lingering a long time in the shower. She'd known that he was looking for excuses to stay away from her.

She'd heard the phone ring a few times, but each time Tom had answered in another part of the house. Since he never summoned her to the phone, she assumed all the calls were for him. She couldn't help wondering if any of the calls were from women, though she chided herself for thinking like a jealous wife again.

Leslie had spent the evening cleaning the kitchen, playing with the baby, doing a couple of loads of laundry and berating herself for her behavior. Now it was time to confront Tom and get back on somewhat more comfortable footing with him. They certainly couldn't go on living in the same house without speaking to each other.

She tapped on his bedroom door. "Tom?"

His voice was muffled by the wood between them. "What?"

"Could I talk to you for a minute?"

She thought she heard a sigh. And then footsteps. A moment later, the door opened.

He was wearing a white cotton T-shirt and gray fleece pants. His feet were bare, his dark-blond hair still damp from the shower. There was no expression in his shuttered green eyes.

Fighting down her automatic rush of attraction to him, she managed to keep her voice steady. "I want to apologize for the things I said earlier," she told him. "I was out of line."

Partially, she wanted to add, but didn't because she knew that was no way to settle a quarrel.

"Apology accepted," he said flatly. "Good night."

He started to close the door. She caught it with one hand, her temper kicking in again.

"Just what is with you, anyway?" she demanded. "Do you want me to leave? Is that it? Do you want to forget I ever came back to Fayetteville?"

"No."

"You're obviously sorry you married me. It was another of your impulsive gestures, wasn't it? And now you regret it."

"No," he repeated more firmly. "I knew what I was doing."

"What? Sacrificing yourself to help poor little me?" She couldn't keep the bitterness out of her voice, didn't even try. "Well, thanks, but no, thanks. I don't want pity any more than you claim to want it."

Tom lifted a weary hand to massage his temple. "Let's not fight any more tonight. This is getting us nowhere."

"I don't want to fight," she admitted. "I just need to know that you don't dislike having me here. That I haven't ruined your life. If that's the way you feel, I need to know so I can make other arrangements for Kenny and me."

"I don't want you to go," he repeated.

Taking her by surprise, he wrapped a hand around the back of her neck and pulled her to him. His lips covered hers in a kiss that almost made her forget they'd ever quarreled. By the time he lifted his head, she was trembling.

"It's getting late," he murmured. "And I have an early breakfast meeting tomorrow. Maybe we'd better go to bed."

She was certainly willing, if a bit nervous. Maybe she'd feel more like a married woman after she and Tom made love again. She glanced at his bed, then up at him. He smiled down at her, his eyes still unreadable to her.

"Good night, Leslie," he said.

And politely closed his bedroom door in her face.

She stood in the hallway, staring at that closed door. And then she shook her head as though to clear it.

Just what was going on here? she asked herself as she walked reluctantly back to the guest room. There'd been a time when Tom couldn't keep his hands off her. When they'd taken advantage of every spare minute to dive into bed and into each other. Physically, they'd been a perfect match.

What was holding him back now? And how could she let him know that if he was holding back for her sake, he needn't bother?

He was her husband, darn it, she thought glumly. How long would they go on sleeping in separate beds?

Since Tom's office wasn't far from Nina's shop, they had lunch together fairly often. He called her Tuesday morning and arranged to meet her at a deli within walking distance for both of them, about halfway between them.

It was a beautiful day, a bit windy, but still pleasantly warm for February. A nice day for a walk. As he maneuvered the lunchtime busy downtown sidewalks, Tom nodded to several acquaintances, who'd apparently felt the same way.

He and Nina arrived at the deli almost simultaneously. He bent to kiss his mother's breeze-blushed cheek. She looked stunning in her swingy black coat over a black-and-white-patterned pantsuit, and he told her so.

"Thank you, dear," she murmured, patting her ash-blond bob into place. "I like your outfit today, too."

Since he was wearing his uniform, he chuckled, as his mother had intended. "We'd better get in there and grab a table before they're all gone," he said, taking her arm.

They found one of the last empty tables for two, commandeered it and ordered sandwiches and salads from a harried young server. Only then did Nina open a conversation. "How are Leslie and the baby?" she wanted to know.

"They're fine."

"Does Kenny sleep through the night?"

"Yeah." Or at least Tom assumed he did. He figured he would have heard Leslie get up with the baby during the night. Since he'd slept very little, he'd been attuned to every sound.

"So how does it feel being a new dad?" she asked, only half teasing.

The question caught Tom off guard. He hadn't really thought of himself as Kenny's dad. Leslie had made it clear enough that she considered the baby hers. She hadn't hesitated to ask Tom's help to keep him, but marriage had been the extent of her expectations. He wasn't even sure she wanted him to start taking an active interest in raising Kenny.

"I guess it's too soon to tell," he said.

Nina toyed with her salad. "Steve's expecting you and Leslie to start adoption proceedings soon. Have you discussed it yet?"

"No," Tom admitted. "We were just married the day before yesterday, Mom. There hasn't been a lot of time for making plans."

"No," she conceded. "I'm sorry. I don't mean to push you."

"You aren't pushing me. I know you're curious about what's going on. It's just that I don't have much to tell you yet."

Nina nodded, then asked, "How are your friends reacting to the news? What did Zach say?"

"I had at least a half-dozen calls last night demanding to know if the rumors were true. I thought Chris Patton was going to have to storm into my house and see Leslie for herself before she'd believe it. I managed to convince her to wait a few days until Leslie and I were ready to get out and socialize. Zach and Kim were dining at the same restaurant Leslie and I chose Sunday evening, so we broke the news to them then. I haven't had a chance to talk to him since.''

A fleeting frown crossed Nina's face. "Well? How did he react?''

"He congratulated me," Tom answered lightly. "Said we'd have to get together with the wives soon. He was surprised, of course, but he managed not to put a foot in his mouth.''

"You told him the details, of course.''

Tom shook his head, avoiding his mother's eyes. "I thought it best not to. For Leslie's sake, I don't want everyone to know that she came here to propose to me. That we married for convenience, rather than the usual reasons.''

"Everyone? Tom, we're talking about Zach.''

Suppressing a wince, Tom sipped his iced tea before answering. "Zach doesn't need all the details. I have to consider my wife's feelings before my friend's curiosity.''

"Your wife," Nina repeated with a misty smile. "You said that so naturally.''

Tom blinked. "Yeah. I guess I did.''

Nina reached across the table and covered his hand with her own. "Is it really only a marriage of convenience, Tom? You were so fond of Leslie before. I don't think you ever really got over her. Weren't you actually pleased that she came to you for help now?''

Tom set his glass down with a thump. "To be honest, Mom, I don't know what I feel anymore.''

It felt pretty good to admit that. To let someone know that he was confused and uncertain, that he didn't quite know what to do next. He'd been hiding his feelings for so long that it had become habit. And there were times when he needed to open up to someone. His mother had always been the only one he'd occasionally allowed inside his emotional walls. There'd been a time when he'd considered making a new opening for Leslie. That was before she'd left him, of course.

"And what does Leslie feel?"

"I don't know that, either."

"Then maybe it's time you talked to her."

He sighed. "When we talk, we quarrel. It's probably better if we don't talk."

"You don't really believe that," she chided gently.

"No. I guess not."

She pulled her hand away and returned to her lunch. "It's understandable, of course, that Leslie would be a little wary about marriage. Especially with her parents' histories. Steve said that her father made little effort to be a real husband or parent, and that Leslie's mother always seemed more interested in her own problems than in Leslie's. She's probably seen few examples of happy marriages. It will be good for her to spend time with your friends. Especially Zach and Kim, and Sherm and Sami, who are all blissfully happy in their marriages."

She sighed. "Of course, you didn't have that example, either, since you've never known what it was like to be a part of a conventional, two-parent family."

"And never missed it," he assured her, truthfully for the most part. "You made a good home for me, Mom. You didn't need anyone else to help raise me."

"Thank you, sweetheart. But it would have been nice for you to have a father in your life when you were growing up. You're very sweet to want to reassure me, but I know there were times when you were aware of what you had missed. You adored Zach's father, and I heard you say once that you wished he were your father, too."

Disconcerted, he shifted in his seat. "Everyone loves Zach's dad. And George treated me like another son, for the most part. If I ever needed a man's guidance, I always knew he was there for me."

"You and Zach really are like brothers in many ways. As much as he loves his sisters, you always understood him best, ever since you were in first grade together."

A ripple of regret went through him as Tom remembered a

time when he and Zach had shared everything. When they'd known each other's thoughts. Prior to the accident, the only thing Tom had ever kept from Zach was the way he'd felt after Leslie had left. He'd made a point of shrugging off the breakup as a lost cause, a mistake best put behind him. Afraid that Zach would feel sorry for him—or, worse, tease him mercilessly—Tom hadn't let on how much Leslie had meant to him then. He'd never even hinted that the thought of marriage and permanence had entered his mind on a few occasions before Leslie had received the job offer from Chicago.

Zach had behaved much the same way when he'd fallen for Kim, Tom remembered. Zach hadn't told Tom about the first date he'd had with Kim, letting Tom find out by unexpectedly catching them together. And then, when Zach and Kim had broken up for a few weeks, Zach had pretended it didn't matter. Had shrugged it off—just as Tom had under the same circumstances.

As for the months since the accident—well, Tom no longer understood Zach at all. He only knew that he missed their closeness. Their easy camaraderie. He hated it when Zach acted too solicitous to him now. He wished he understood what, exactly, had come between them.

He was tempted to blame it all on Kim. His and Zach's friendship wouldn't be the first that was strained by the arrival of a new bride. But somehow he knew that Kim had nothing to do with it. In fact, she seemed to have done everything she knew how to keep the friendship alive.

It wasn't her fault that her efforts didn't seem to be working.

Because it made him uncomfortable to talk about Zach, Tom abruptly changed the subject. "You've mentioned Steve Pendleton's name a couple of times," he said. "Have you been talking to him again? Was it you who convinced him to drop the custody battle?"

He was surprised when she blushed and looked quickly away.

"He made that decision on his own," she replied. "I merely

stated my opinion to him and he gave me the courtesy of considering what I said.''

"I'm not sure Leslie would thank you for pleading her case with him. You know how prickly she can be.''

"I, er, just happened to bring it up during a conversation. Steve's really quite reasonable, Tommy. He simply wanted to make sure his nephew was being cared for. And he's grieving for his sister, and the relationship they never had. You can't blame him for that, can you?''

"I can blame him for being so brutal to Leslie. She was grieving, too, for the relationship she *did* have with Crystal. Instead of thanking her for being his sister's loyal friend, he blamed her for everything that had gone wrong between Crystal and him. That was unfair and unkind.''

"He knows that now, I think,'' Nina said soothingly. "He was hurt, Tommy. And angry with fate. He shouldn't have taken that anger out on Leslie, but I'm sure he'll be more sympathetic now that he's had time to reflect. And once he has a chance to really observe her with Kenny, he'll understand what a wonderful mother she'll be to that baby.''

Tom set his fork down and leaned back in his chair, looking closely at his mother. He knew her too well to miss the nuances in her tone, her manner. "Just when did you have all this meaningful dialogue with Pendleton, anyway?''

"We, er, had dinner together last night. To talk about things,'' she added quickly, still looking flushed, her gaze focusing anywhere but on Tom.

Tom's eyebrows rose. "I didn't realize he was still in town yesterday.''

"He's taking a few days off. He did some sight-seeing yesterday and has tickets for the basketball game tonight.''

"How did he cop those? That game's being shown on ESPN. Been sold out for months.''

"He said he pulled a few strings.''

"I didn't realize he had any strings to pull in these parts.''

"Apparently, he has some prominent business associates in Fayetteville.''

Tom wondered just how much those influential business associates could have helped Pendleton if the custody battle had gone to court. It was possible, he thought, that he'd underestimated the guy. "I suppose he's going to the game with one of those associates?"

Nina cleared her throat. "No…"

Tom frowned. "Mom?"

She lifted her chin. "I'm going to the game with Steve tonight."

His frown deepening, Tom asked, "You're spending a lot of time with this guy, aren't you? Are you doing this just for Leslie's sake? If so—"

"It isn't for Leslie's sake. It's for my own. I like him."

"So you're…what? Dating him?" He asked the question a bit facetiously.

His mother was quite serious when she finally met his eyes and said, "Yes, I suppose I am. At least for tonight."

"This is a *date?*" Tom repeated the word as if he'd never heard it before. "I mean, a real date?"

"Steve defined it as a social outing between a man and a woman who are attracted to each other and enjoy being together. A date, to be quite specific."

He almost asked her if she'd lost her mind. There had to be a dozen reasons his mother should not even consider going on a date with Steve Pendleton. The guy had to be ten years younger, for one thing. And Tom had seen him at his arrogant and domineering worst. Not to mention that it had been because of Pendleton's threats that Tom had ended up married to Leslie.

A little voice at the back of his mind asked Tom if it bothered him that his mother was going out with Steve Pendleton—or if the truth was that he wasn't comfortable having her go out with *anyone.* She was his mother, for Pete's sake. And he was still squirming at her mention of "a man and a woman who are attracted to each other." He didn't even want to follow that statement to its logical conclusion.

It was with a great effort that he said none of those things, only "Be careful, Mom, okay?"

"I'm an adult, Tommy. I'm quite capable of taking care of myself," she reminded him with a touch of wry amusement at his emotional reaction.

He believed her. But he still didn't like it.

Nina glanced at her watch. "I have to get back to the shop. Lisa has an appointment with her obstetrician and I promised her I wouldn't be gone long."

"Yeah, I have to get back, too. I have several inspections to do this afternoon. I'll, er, call you tomorrow, okay?"

"Of course."

His mother was dating. And dating a man who was less than ten years older than Tom. As Tom walked slowly back to his office, he tried to come to terms with that staggering fact.

During the past eighteen months, Tom's life had changed almost faster than he could keep up. First Leslie had left, then he'd been in the accident that had changed his health and his career. Zach and Kim had married. Then Leslie had returned—baby in tow—and Tom had married her. And now his mother had announced in a slightly defiant tone that she was dating, and that, basically, Tom had nothing to say about it.

He wasn't at all ready for whatever surprise was awaiting him next.

Nina sat at the dressing table in her apartment, her face in her hands.

She should have called Steve and canceled this date. She shouldn't have agreed to go out with him in the first place.

Tom didn't approve. It had been obvious that he thought she was making a mistake—which she probably was. That Steve was too young for her—which he was. Nina was in danger of making a fool of herself over a man—which she had been so determined not to do again.

Her doorbell rang, and she looked up in panic at the woman in the mirror. She'd taken great care with her makeup, but it hadn't completely masked the fine lines at the corners of her eyes. Lines carved by laughter and tears, smiles and frowns, worry and joy. She wasn't ashamed of them, had never considered doing anything to remove them—but she was definitely aware of them tonight.

She sighed and pushed away from the dressing table, casting one last glance at her outfit of gray slacks with an apricot turtleneck and matching wool blazer. She knew that red was the traditional color to wear to a Razorbacks game, but she had never looked very good in red. Vanity had won out over team spirit this evening.

It was only a date, she reminded herself. She'd been on them before, though rarely in the past few years.

It was only a basketball game. She'd been to many of those, often cheering her son as he'd loped down the court to the shouts of his admiring classmates.

It was only one evening. It certainly wouldn't change her life.

The doorbell rang again, and she fancied she heard mocking laughter in its strident tone.

Chapter Nine

Leslie made dinner again Tuesday. Pasta primavera. Crusty garlic bread. Cheesecake for dessert. She cheated on that part by using a boxed mix.

She'd spent the day thinking about how she would act when Tom came home. They couldn't go on growling at each other, avoiding each other or kissing and then snapping again. For one thing the tension couldn't possibly be good for Kenny. Not to mention that it wasn't at all good for her.

The point was, they were married. And for now they would stay married. Steve had made it clear enough that he had given in—provisionally—on the custody battle primarily because Leslie had married Tom. And while she still resented the implication that she wasn't capable of raising Kenny alone, that she needed a man at her side to guide her, that she was somehow incomplete on her own—her rash plan had worked. Steve had dropped the suit, if not his intention to monitor her care of his nephew.

Once the adoption was final, when Steve no longer had as

much leverage over her, she and Tom could make plans for the future. She found herself reluctant to think of the end of the marriage, but told herself that was only because she didn't know when, exactly, it would be.

In the meantime, she decided, there was no reason that she and Tom couldn't deal amicably with each other. The house was large enough that they wouldn't be in each other's way. He apparently had little interest in returning to their former, intimate relationship, and that was fine with her, she thought firmly. They could be friends, roommates, partners in the matter of providing for Kenny's future with her.

She would cook Tom's meals, clean his house—the least she could do in return for all he'd done for her—and she would find a job so he would not be financially responsible for her and Kenny. She would be pleasant, but distant. Polite, but reserved. Patient, but decisive. Cooperative—to a point.

And when it was time for her to go, she would do so with dignity, expressing her undying gratitude to him and making it clear that she would never ask another favor of him.

Vaguely depressed by the path her thoughts had taken, she had to make an effort to smile when Tom came into the house.

"You've cooked again," he observed unnecessarily, sniffing appreciatively at the air.

"I thought you'd be hungry since you had to work late today," she replied. He'd called her earlier in the afternoon to tell her he would be detained. He'd asked about Kenny, offered to pick up something on the way home and urged her again to make herself comfortable in his house. The entire call had lasted less than five minutes.

"You know me. I'm always hungry."

Actually, she didn't know him. She'd once thought she did, but that had been another time, almost another man. Even then, there'd been parts of him she'd never known at all.

"Dinner's ready, but I can keep it warm if you want to shower or change first," she said.

He shook his head. "I'll just wash my hands. Be right in."

She turned back to the stove as he left the room. Maybe it

GET FREE BOOKS AND A WONDERFUL FREE GIFT!

*TRY YOUR
LUCK AT*

Welcome to the casino!
Try your luck at the roulette wheel ...
Play a hand of Twenty-One!

HOW TO PLAY:

1. Play the Roulette and Twenty-One scratch-off games, as instructed on the opposite page, to see if you are eligible for FREE BOOKS and a FREE GIFT!

2. Send back the card and you'll receive T

It's fun, and we're giving away FREE GIFTS to all players!

PLAY Roulette!

Scratch the silver to see where the ball has landed—7 RED or 11 BLACK makes you eligible for TWO FREE romance novels!

PLAY TWENTY-ONE!

Scratch the silver to reveal a winning hand! Congratulations, you have Twenty-One. Return this card promptly and you'll receive a fabulous free mystery gift, along with your free books!

YES!

Please send me all the free Silhouette Special Edition® books and the gift for which I qualify! I understand that I am under no obligation to purchase any books, as explained on the back of this card.

Name (please print clearly)

Address   Apt.#

City   State   Zip

Offer limited to one per household and not valid to current Silhouette Special Edition® subscribers. All orders subject to approval.   PRINTED IN U.S.A.

(U-SIL-SE-02/98)   **235 SDL CE6Q**

The Silhouette Reader Service™ — Here's how it works:

Accepting free books places you under no obligation to buy anything. You may keep the books and gift and return the shipping statement marked "cancel." If you do not cancel, about a month later we'll send you 6 additional novels and bill you just $3.57 each plus 25¢ delivery per book and applicable sales tax, if any.* That's the complete price — and compared to cover prices of $4.25 each — quite a bargain indeed! You may cancel at any time, but if you choose to continue, every month we'll send you 6 more books, which you may either purchase at the discount price...or return to us and cancel your subscription.

*Terms and prices subject to change without notice. Sales tax applicable in N.Y.

If offer card is missing write to: Silhouette Reader Service, 3010 Walden Ave., P.O. Box 1867, Buffalo, NY 14240-9952

BUSINESS REPLY MAIL

FIRST-CLASS MAIL   PERMIT NO 717   BUFFALO NY

POSTAGE WILL BE PAID BY ADDRESSEE

SILHOUETTE READER SERVICE
3010 WALDEN AVE
PO BOX 1867
BUFFALO NY 14240-9952

NO POSTAGE
NECESSARY
IF MAILED
IN THE
UNITED STATES

wasn't going to be as easy as she'd hoped to remain politely detached from Tom. All he had to do was walk into the room, windblown and rumpled from a day's work, and her pulse lurched into a frantic rhythm. Sexual attraction she could handle, she assured herself. But the feelings she harbored for Tom that went beyond desire—well, those would take a bit more effort.

She heard him come back into the room and she turned, a covered dish in her hands. She was surprised to see that Tom was now carrying Kenny, who bounced happily against Tom's chest.

"Look who's awake."

The smile Tom gave the baby almost made Leslie jealous because he hadn't smiled for her.

"He was babbling in his playpen, and I'm pretty sure he ordered me to pick him up and bring him in here. I think he smells the pasta and wants his share."

"I'll make another batch for him—in about a year or so," Leslie replied, quickly setting the bowl down before she dropped it. The sight of Tom holding little Kenny was entirely too enticing—much too hazardous to the practical plans she'd spent all day making.

"I'll get his seat," she said, moving toward the kitchen doorway. "He can watch us eat."

"Oh, man, that's cruel." Tom chuckled and tickled the baby's tummy, eliciting a gurgle of delight. "Don't worry, kid, I'll slip you a bite when she's not looking."

Leslie told herself she should be pleased that Tom was being so kind to the baby—and she was, of course. She assured herself that she wasn't jealous of a four-month-old baby. That would have been ridiculous. She was glad that Tom seemed to enjoy playing with Kenny. Tom needed to laugh again.

She just wished he hadn't apparently forgotten how to laugh with her.

"Leslie, that was fantastic," Tom said after cleaning his plate and putting away a good-sized slice of cheesecake. "I insist that you let me clean the kitchen this time."

"You've worked all day," she reminded him. "And I clean as I go, so all that's left to do is stack the dishes in the dishwasher."

"You've worked all day, too. The house is spotless. You didn't have to do that. I have someone who comes in every couple of weeks to handle the heavy stuff."

"I have to do something during the day," she said lightly. "Daytime television doesn't interest me, and Kenny still takes a couple of long naps a day, so that leaves me with several free hours on my hands. I might as well be cleaning."

He started to say something, then apparently changed his mind. After a moment, he spoke again. "Want to get out of the house for a while? We could take in a movie or something."

"I'm not sure Kenny would stay quiet through a movie, and I've always hated it when other people allowed a crying baby to disturb an audience."

"I could ask Brandi to baby-sit," he offered. "She's the teenager who lives next door. Nice girl. Does a lot of baby-sitting in this neighborhood."

Leslie shook her head. "Not tonight. But thank you for offering."

He nodded. "Some other night, then."

"Sure. The basketball game's on TV tonight, isn't it? We could watch that."

A frown crossed Tom's face. "Yeah," he muttered. "We could do that."

She tilted her head curiously. "What's wrong? Have you lost interest in Razorback sports? I find that awfully hard to believe, considering what a fan you were."

"No."

But he was still frowning, apparently bothered by something.

"Tom, what is it?"

"My mom's going to that game."

"And that's a problem?" She still didn't understand.

"She's on a date."

The way he said it, the word sounded almost obscene. Trying not to smile, Leslie inquired, "Someone you dislike?"

"Someone I don't trust," he corrected her. "It's Steve Pendleton."

Leslie felt her jaw drop. "Your mother is on a date with *Steve?*"

Tom nodded grimly. "That's what she told me."

"Wow." Not certain how she felt about the news, Leslie sank back into her seat and tried to decide if there was any reason to worry.

"You don't suppose Steve is using her somehow to get to us, do you?" She felt more than a little paranoid asking the question, but she could tell by the look on Tom's face that he'd wondered the same thing.

"I don't know," he admitted. "It's not as if my mom's unattractive or anything, of course...."

"Your mom's beautiful," Leslie corrected him. "And a lot of fun to be with. I can certainly understand how any man would be attracted to her. It's just..."

"It's Steve Pendleton," Tom said for her. "He paid someone to follow you here, then arrived himself with the sole purpose of causing trouble for you. He threw around a lot of thinly veiled threats, tried to intimidate you, said some unpleasant things about your family. And now he's going out with my mother."

"There's certainly reason to be a bit concerned," Leslie conceded.

Tom's face hardened. "If he does anything to upset her, I'll rearrange his face."

"Your mother's a grown woman," Leslie felt compelled to state. "I'm sure she can take care of herself."

"Why would she want to go out with him, anyway?" Tom was bewildered. "She hardly ever dates, but when she does it's always men she knows well. Men her own age or older, dependable, respectable, well-known in the area. Not total strangers.''

The way he described his mother's occasional escorts made them sound dull, Leslie found herself thinking. She wondered if perhaps Nina had felt the same way about them.

"Steve is a very good-looking man,'' she admitted grudgingly. "Girls were always drawn to him when he was a teenager.''

"My mother isn't interested in a man's appearance,'' Tom countered a bit scornfully.

Leslie couldn't help laughing. "Your mother isn't blind, Goose. And she's certainly still young enough to appreciate a pair of dark eyes and a great male body.''

The look of utter revulsion that crossed his face made her laugh again.

"Cut it out, Les. This is my *mother* you're talking about.''

"Who is perfectly capable of deciding whom she wants to go out with. Try not to worry about it so much. Maybe she just felt sorry for Steve because he doesn't know many people in town. She has such a kind heart, and she enjoys entertaining. Once he goes back to Little Rock, she'll probably not give him another thought.''

Tom seemed to take some reassurance from her words. "You're probably right. Maybe I'm reading too much into it.''

"I'm pretty sure your mom had something to do with Steve's giving up the custody suit. Maybe she's still working on him, convincing him to leave me alone.''

"Maybe. That doesn't bother you?''

Leslie shrugged. "I'm not particularly thrilled with the idea of being discussed that way, but if it lets me keep Kenny without any further trouble from Steve, then no, it doesn't really bother me. Surely you've realized by now that I won't let pride or anything else interfere with my fight to keep Kenny.''

He nodded and looked at the baby, who grinned back at him. Tom's face softened. "Yeah, I understand that. Maybe

Mom can help. That's probably exactly what she wants to do."

"I'm sure it is. I've always loved your mother."

For a moment, Tom's eyes met Leslie's, and the warmth in them brought a lump to his throat. "I'm glad," he murmured.

And then he suddenly looked away. Cleared his throat. Reached precipitously for his dessert plate. "I'll help you load these into the dishwasher," he said brusquely. "Then we'll watch the game."

Leslie swallowed and gathered her own implements. Desire, she reminded herself, had no business coming between platonic roommates. She'd better keep reminding herself of that as long as she was living with infinitely desirable Tom Lowery.

The telephone rang during halftime. Leslie was feeding the baby, so Tom snagged the receiver off the end table close to him and lifted it to his ear. "H'lo? Oh, hi, Sami."

A few moments later, he pressed the phone to his shoulder and looked at Leslie. "It's Sami," he said. "She, er, wants to throw us a party. Kenny's invited, too. Are we free Friday night?"

"I'm free every night," Leslie answered matter-of-factly, steeling herself to face an evening with Tom's understandably curious friends.

Tom nodded and returned to the call. "Leslie's delighted," he assured his friend's wife. "We'll be there."

Leslie made a face at him and shifted Kenny into a more comfortable position in the crook of her arm.

She could do this, she assured herself. Compared with facing Tom every evening, dealing with a couple dozen of his friends would be a snap.

So why was she suddenly dreading Friday night?

Pleasantly tired from the basketball game, at which she'd had a wonderful time despite the disappointing final scores, Nina smiled at Steve as he pulled into a parking space at her apartment complex. "I had a lovely evening. Thank you for asking me."

"I'll walk you to your door," he said, reaching for his door handle.

Nina waited for him to come around and open her car door. She knew that wasn't the way things were done anymore, but she'd been raised with old-fashioned manners and she liked such niceties. Steve himself seemed to enjoy them. He'd made a point each time he was with her of opening doors, walking near the street, standing when she stood. Yet he still treated her as an intellectual equal, showing interest in her words, respecting her opinions. A true gentleman, she thought with pleasure.

"Do you mind if I ask you a personal question, Steve?" she inquired impulsively as they strolled down the sidewalk toward her brightly lit apartment entrance.

"Of course not. Ask me anything you like."

"Have you ever been married?"

"No."

Tentatively, she asked, "Did your parents' bad experience sour you on marriage permanently?"

He placed a hand at the small of her back to guide her around a slender branch that had fallen onto the sidewalk from a huge oak nearby. "Actually, I was engaged for almost two years. Three weeks before the wedding, my fiancée died in a car accident."

Though he spoke without emotion, Nina was appalled. "Oh, Steve, I'm so sorry. I shouldn't have asked."

"Of course you should ask. How else will we get to know each other?"

"How long has it been?"

"Eight years. I had just turned thirty."

Tom's age now, Nina thought automatically. So young to face such a tragedy. She wondered if he still grieved for his lost dreams. "You must have loved her very much," she murmured, thinking that must be the reason he'd never found anyone else to marry.

"Yes. She was very special. I was devastated at first. I was hardly functional for several weeks after the accident, and then I overcompensated by throwing myself into my business. As time passed, it became easier to smile when I remembered Jessie. She would have wanted me to remember her that way."

He spoke easily, obviously comfortable with sharing that part of his life with her. With every new facet Nina discovered in this man, she grew more intrigued.

They had almost reached the entrance of her building.

"What about you, Nina? Why did you never marry?" Steve asked.

A bit embarrassed by the question, but knowing it was only fair after she'd asked the same of him, she shrugged lightly. "It just never happened for me," she admitted. "I'm afraid I haven't shown very good judgment where men are concerned."

"Just because you made a mistake when you were a teenager? Nonsense."

"It wasn't only that," she said with a frown and a shake of her head as a bitter memory stabbed her. But she had no intention of sharing that humiliating story with Steve tonight. "Let's just say that with my Tommy to raise and my business to start, I've stayed quite busy."

"Your Tommy is thirty years old," Steve noted mildly. "He's been raised for quite some time."

"That's true, of course. But we've remained very close. And after the accident that caused his limp just over a year ago, he needed me very badly. There were long months of physiotherapy, weeks when he wasn't able to get around on his own. I moved in with him for a while, until he was literally back on his feet. And then I came back to my apartment so that he could rebuild on his own."

"You'll have to tell me more about that accident sometime."

Was he implying that there would be another date, or acknowledging that they would probably see each other because of his connection with Kenny? Nina cleared her throat. "Yes, sometime."

They were within a couple of feet of the door, when something large, dark and hairy jumped out of the bushes lining the side of the brick building. The dog spotted them, barked and dashed toward them, feathery tail pumping the air.

Nina shrieked and instinctively tried to climb Steve as though he were a six-foot tree.

He caught her close. "Hey, it's okay," he said as the dog circled them, sniffing and whining. "He looks friendly. His tail is wagging."

Nina jerked and shuddered when the dog poked his nose against her leg. "Please get me inside," she gasped, hardly able to breathe through the panic that tightened her throat.

As though suddenly aware of the extent of her fear, Steve tightened his arms around her. "Go on, get out of here," he snapped at the dog.

The shaggy beast whined and wriggled closer to them, blocking the sidewalk between them and the door. Nina buried her face in Steve's comfortably broad shoulder. The top of her head came barely to his chin.

"You heard me. Get." Steve spoke more harshly this time, his meaning unmistakable, even to this dopey-looking animal.

Appearing dejected, the dog turned and ran back into the bushes, clearing the way for Nina and Steve to proceed.

"He's gone, Nina," Steve murmured comfortingly, without loosening his hold on her. "Come on, let's go in."

She was trembling so hard she could barely walk straight. She was both grateful for Steve's support and humiliated at the way she was acting. But she couldn't help it. She'd been terrified of dogs ever since she could remember. To have such a large, boisterous one jump out at her from nowhere like that was a scene straight from one of her childhood nightmares.

Steve stayed with her in the elevator and down the short hallway to her apartment. He took the key from her shaking hand and opened the door himself. And then he escorted her in and closed the door behind him.

She might have stepped away from him then, but he turned her into his arms and gathered her against his broad, firm chest.

"Are you all right?" he asked, his cheek resting against the top of her head.

She was still quivering like a leaf, her breath hitching, pulse racing. Only now she no longer knew how much of that reaction had to do with the dog and how much of it came from being held so tightly in Steve Pendleton's arms.

"I'll be fine," she said in a voice that was nearly an octave higher than her usual tone. "I feel like such an idiot."

He stroked her back soothingly. "You have a fear of dogs."

She nodded against his shoulder. "A phobia, really. It's so foolish. I've tried to overcome it. But when he jumped out like that…"

"He was a big dog. Anyone would have been frightened by his sudden appearance. For all you knew, he could have been dangerous."

She shuddered again. "Thank you for trying to make me feel better, but I know my reaction was totally out of proportion. You wouldn't believe how many times poor Tommy had to chase away dogs when he was growing up. Sometimes the dogs were bigger than he was, but he was never afraid of them. Never afraid of anything, really."

She was babbling now, a combination of reaction to her fright and nervousness about her current position. She felt Steve press a kiss against the top of her head. His voice was a rumble against her cheek.

"I'll share a little secret with you," he murmured. "I'm terrified of heights. No way you'll ever catch me on a ladder or an observation tower or one of those stupid swinging bridges other people seem to like so much. I like my feet planted firmly on solid ground."

Nina couldn't imagine Steve's ever being "terrified." He seemed much too calm and controlled for such an endearingly human weakness. As for having one's feet planted on the ground—she was afraid that didn't apply to her at all at the moment. She couldn't have sworn her feet were touching the floor beneath them, so heady were the feelings Steve's wandering hand was arousing in her. Firmly, deliberately, he stroked from her nape to her waist, tracing the curve of her back, stopping just before he reached the swell of her hips.

She trembled again, and she knew exactly what caused it that time.

"I, um, I'm surprised. I wouldn't have guessed you were afraid of heights," she managed to say with some semblance of coherence.

"Comparing me with your paragon of a son?" he asked, just a touch of censure in his voice. "Don't do that, Nina. I prefer to be judged on my own merits—or lack of them."

That brought her head off his chest. She craned her neck to look up at him. "I wouldn't presume to judge you, Steve. And I'm not comparing you with my son."

His mouth quirked. "Good. He sounds just a bit too perfect for my peace of mind."

"Tommy isn't perfect. Though he's close," Nina couldn't resist adding, meaning every word of it.

"I can see where a man could become a little jealous of your devotion to him," Steve mused, bringing his hand around to trace her still-unsteady lower lip. "I admire your maternal loyalty, of course, but I can't help wondering if you've left any room in your heart for anyone else."

She didn't know how to answer that. Didn't understand quite how to interpret his words. Was he simply making an observation, or could he possibly be speaking from a more personal position?

He smiled. "You look thunderstruck. Why?"

"Er, I—" She stumbled helplessly to a halt.

"Maybe it has something to do with this," he muttered, and bent his head to cover her mouth with his.

A frantic little moan lodged in her chest. And then dissolved into a sigh as she went up on tiptoes to wrap her arms around his neck.

It was the most spectacular kiss of her life. It lasted for a very long time. Until Nina suddenly came to her senses.

She tore herself out of Steve's arms with a gasp. What on *earth* was she doing?

"This is not right," she said shakily.

His eyes had darkened to near black, and his face had gone taut with his reaction to the kiss. "It felt damned right to me," he groaned.

She lifted her hands to her cheeks, her fingers feeling ice-cold against her flaming face. "No. It's not...we can't..."

"We can't what?"

"Get involved—that way." Lord, she felt like a fool.

Hands on his lean hips, he cocked his head and frowned at her. "You're telling me you aren't attracted to me?"

She could hardly make him believe that, considering the way she'd just plastered herself against him. She drew a deep breath and tried for logic, instead. "Be reasonable, Steve. I'm much too old for you."

"You're forty-seven," he replied evenly. "I'm thirty-eight. They're only numbers, Nina."

"Well, yes, but it's more than that. You're Kenny's uncle, and you'll be seeing him and my son when you visit. I don't want any awkwardness between us if we should happen to run into each other in the future."

His left eyebrow shot upward. "If we should happen to run into each other in the future?" he repeated. "You make it sound as though I'm interested in a one-night stand. I can assure you that's not at all what I have in mind."

She eyed him warily. "Then what *do* you have in mind?"

"I want you," he said, holding her gaze with his.

Her heart skipped a beat.

"But," he added before she could speak, "I'm not interested in a one-time fling. I've been attracted to you since you walked into your son's apartment carrying a chocolate pie and looking at me as though you weren't sure whether to throw me out or invite me to dinner. When you chose the latter, even understanding why I was there, I realized you were someone

I wanted to get to know better. The time we've spent together since has only convinced me that we can have something very special with each other.''

''Oh, Steve.'' She sank bonelessly onto a dainty chair, trying to clear her mind.

''I haven't felt like this about any other woman since Jessie died,'' he went on relentlessly. ''It isn't just lust, Nina, though there's definitely some of that involved.''

The corner of his mouth twitched with a suppressed smile. ''You're beautiful. And you're kind and loyal and generous and funny. Is it any wonder that I've fallen for you?''

She groaned and hid her face in her hands. ''Don't talk like that,'' she pleaded. ''I don't know what to say.''

''It's too soon for you.'' Regret colored his deep voice. ''That's okay. We'll take it slowly.''

Her hands fell to her lap. ''Steve, I don't think this is a very good idea.''

He stood his ground. ''Tell me you don't feel the same way I do, and I'll leave you alone. I would never try to force my attention on any woman who isn't interested.''

Not interested? She might have laughed had this not been so very serious.

She was most definitely interested. She just wasn't sure she was willing to take the gamble of doing anything about it. She'd settled into a comfortable, safe, relatively risk-free routine and she'd been content, for the most part, with the life she'd made for herself. Was she really ready to open herself up to heartbreak again, just when she'd put the mistakes of her past firmly behind her?

Steve seemed to find encouragement in her silence.

''Give me a chance, Nina. Let me show you how good we can be together.''

His voice was pure seduction, playing on her nerve endings in a way that started her shivering again.

''I won't rush you. I won't expect more than you're willing to give. But please don't say you don't want to see me again.''

"This is insane," Nina murmured, shaking her head. "I can't imagine what Tom will say."

Steve scowled. "This has nothing to do with your son. This is strictly between us."

Her chin lifted then. "I didn't say I have to ask Tom's permission, but you must understand that I will always consider his feelings, no matter what choices I make."

He held up both hands, palms outward in a sign of surrender. "I'm not trying to come between you and your son."

"No one could."

"Do you think I don't know that? I'm only asking you to make a little room in your life for me. Won't you try to do that?"

"What do you want from me, Steve?"

"Say you'll go out with me again. I have to go back to Little Rock tomorrow, but I can be back in Fayetteville this weekend. I'd like to see Kenny, but most of all, I'd like to spend time with you. Say you will."

She stepped to the edge of a very steep, very hazardous cliff. And without looking back, she jumped. "All right."

He narrowed his eyes. "You will?"

"Yes. Just—don't rush me."

"I promised I wouldn't."

"I know. And I'll hold you to that promise. It's...been a while since I've dated anyone regularly. Give me a little time to get used to the idea again."

His smile was devastatingly beautiful.

"All the time you need. As long as I know you'll be spending part of that time with me, I can be very patient."

It wasn't his patience that worried her. It was her own. She'd always had a little problem with impulsiveness, and being around Steve Pendleton definitely brought out her impetuous side. But she was a mature adult, she reminded herself. She was perfectly capable of taking things slowly, making careful decisions, calling a halt if she could see she was headed for a mistake.

His smile deepened, carving deep creases into his tanned cheeks.

"You are most definitely worth waiting for, Nina Lowery."

Oh, Lord. So much for being mature and levelheaded. That smile was almost enough to make her pounce on him right there in her living room. "Behave yourself," she ordered him.

He laughed. "I'll try."

He leaned over to kiss her again, firmly, boldly, just a tad possessively. "Good night, Nina. I'll call you."

Trying not to gulp, she nodded. She didn't quite trust her voice that time.

Steve let himself out.

Nina sat perched on the edge of that chair for a very long time, her mind whirling with nagging doubts and breathtaking possibilities.

Chapter Ten

Though she'd spent all week dreading it, Leslie was almost relieved when it was time to depart for the party at the Gilberts' house Friday evening. The novelty of keeping house and cooking Tom's dinner had worn off fairly quickly, leaving her bored and restless during the days while he worked. She enjoyed being with Kenny, but he was such a good baby that his care was hardly a full-time job. He liked spending time on his tummy on the play blanket, kicking his feet, gumming his bright plastic toys, generally entertaining himself.

Leslie wished that she were so easily amused.

She wasn't accustomed to having nothing to do.

The weather had turned cold again, so she chose a plush black sweater and charcoal wool slacks, which she paired with short black boots. She brushed her auburn hair until it gleamed, letting it fall free and wavy to her shoulders. Her jewelry consisted of a large, open-heart silver pendant on a glittering silver chain, cascades of silver hearts dangling from her ears, and several silver bracelets. And, of course, the plain gold band that she still wasn't quite used to wearing after five days.

She emerged from the bedroom to discover that Tom had also chosen to wear black. A black shirt, open at the collar and black denims smoothed over black Western boots. His black belt was studded with silver. With his dark-blond hair brushed back and gleaming in the lamplight, his green eyes glittering and his mouth curved into a smile as he played with Kenny, he looked good enough to cause any woman's heart to flutter.

Leslie's heart was fluttering like crazy.

She cleared her throat. "Looks like we coordinated our outfits tonight."

He glanced up, lifted an eyebrow and chuckled. "Yeah, it does. Want me to take mine off?"

She nearly melted into the carpet as her mind suddenly filled with images of his doing just that. In which case, they would never make it to the party if she had her way.

"I don't think that will be necessary," she managed to say.

Tom was sitting cross-legged on the carpet, with Kenny sitting precariously in front of him, supported by Tom's strong hands. The baby pumped his arms and cooed, nearly toppling over before Tom steadied him.

"He's getting this sitting-up thing almost knocked," Tom said, looking back at Kenny proudly. "As soon as we conquer this, we're going to start working on his passing game."

To say that Tom had bonded with the baby during the past week was a slight understatement. Every day when he had come home, he'd headed straight for Kenny, who now greeted him with grins and squeals of delight. Leslie had been forced to remind herself on several occasions that it was incredibly petty to be jealous of an infant.

But just once, she would have liked for Tom to greet her with the same fond smile he seemed to reserve for her ward, instead of the polite formality he displayed with her.

He hadn't even touched her in days.

Tom glanced away from the baby for a moment. "Ready to go?"

"Yes, I suppose."

"Try to restrain your enthusiasm."

Leslie wrinkled her nose. "It's not that I don't want to see your friends again. It's just…well, it could get awkward."

"Being feted as happy newlyweds?" He shrugged. "So we'll pretend."

"It really doesn't bother you to deceive your friends that way?"

"Leslie, we *are* newlyweds. And I'm not particularly unhappy, are you?"

"Well, no, but…"

"It's not such a great deception. Any further details are no one's business but our own."

"Zach will be there, won't he? I'm pretty sure his wife said he wasn't on duty tonight."

"Yeah, he'll be there. I ran into him earlier today and he told me he'd see me tonight."

"He's off tomorrow, too. If the two of you want to hang out or something, don't feel that you have to change your plans for my sake."

Tom shook his head. "Zach and I don't have any plans for the weekend. I thought maybe you and I could do something with Kenny tomorrow. Maybe go for a drive in the hills or something."

He and Leslie had once loved taking long leisurely country drives. Often, she remembered, in the tiny classic MGB that had been his pride and his hobby. She'd asked about the car a couple of days ago. Tom had told her without expression that he had sold it after his accident.

She missed that little car almost as much as she missed the way Tom had been before.

She almost cringed as she remembered the cutting things she'd said when she'd left him. How she'd accused him of being reckless and foolhardy, frivolous and irresponsible.

What she wouldn't give to have him back that way again,

instead of this quiet, prickly, physically and emotionally wounded man he'd become.

He got carefully to his feet, making certain he kept his balance on the way up. And then he reached down to hoist Kenny into his arms, wincing only a little with the motion. Watching him, Leslie thought that Tom wasn't nearly as hindered by his injuries as he'd convinced himself. There were still many things he could do, and do well. It was his confidence that was still in need of healing.

She wished there were something she could do to help him with that.

They bundled the baby into a warm fleece coverall over the red-striped shirt and cute denim overalls he already had on, then wrapped him in a blanket. Tom carried him out to Leslie's car, which they'd chosen because the baby's safety seat was still fastened into it. Leslie carried the ever-present diaper bag. Growing increasingly proficient at the task, Tom strapped Kenny into the car seat.

Leslie tossed him the keys. "You drive. You know the way."

It was the first time he'd driven her expensive sports car. Within a few miles, he was hooked.

"Drives great, doesn't it?" He leaned back into the deep leather seat, hands comfortably around the leather-wrapped steering wheel.

"Yes. Of course, I bought it because I wanted to impress the partners at the law firm," she admitted wryly. "That was back when I was still playing the-one-who-dies-with-the-most-expensive-toys-wins. Before I discovered what really mattered."

"Takes some folks a lifetime to learn that status symbols don't equal success as a human being," Tom said with a shrug. "Or to figure out how wrong it is to make possessions more important than people. I've seen families lose everything they owned in fires and yet still consider themselves truly blessed because they hadn't lost one another."

"I still plan to sell this car. Though it's paid for, I really can't afford it now. I'd be better off with a lower-maintenance economy car.''

"If you're really attached to it, we'll find a way for you to keep it.''

"It's just a car,'' she said with a faint smile. "It won't hurt me to sell it any more than it probably bothered you to get rid of the MG.''

He grimaced. "That smarted a bit,'' he admitted.

"Then why did you sell it?''

He shrugged and focused grimly on the road ahead. "I was off my feet so long after the accident that I wasn't sure when I would be able to work on it again. You probably remember how much time it took keeping it tuned and running smoothly, especially in the winter. Someone made me a generous offer for it, and I accepted.''

"And now you regret it.''

He cleared his throat, looked quickly at her and then away. "No, not really. It was a practical decision at the time.''

Arriving at a modest, relatively new housing development on the east side of town, he made two right turns, then pulled onto a street lined with several cars and trucks at the curb. "That's Sherm's place,'' he said, nodding toward a yellow-sided, ranch-style house with a nice-sized fenced yard in which two big dogs waited to greet arriving guests.

"I see he still has Killer and Bruiser,'' Leslie commented, recognizing the mutts. "They've gotten bigger.''

"They were little more than oversized pups last time you saw them. They're full grown now.''

"Still friendly, I hope.''

"Ridiculously so, considering the names Sherm saddled them with,'' he assured her. "They love everybody. Kim even sort of likes them, and she's usually afraid of dogs.''

"She shares your mother's phobia?''

Tom shook his head. "Not that bad. Kim's just not a 'dog person,' in her words. But nobody can help liking these two clowns—with the exception of my mom, of course.''

"Looks like quite a few people are here," Leslie observed, and twisted her fingers nervously in her lap.

"I think Chris Patton and Mike Henry are on duty tonight—oh, and Jeff Samples and Leroy Kuykendall and Billy Joe Brownlee. The rest of the gang is probably here. Everyone shows up when Sherm and Sami have parties. In fact, it was just a week ago tonight that they threw their last one, a small dinner party in honor of Valentine's Day."

"Which is where you'd been the night I came back to town," Leslie remarked.

"Right. It's Sami's cooking that draws everyone. She's still the best cook in Washington County—with the exception of *my* wife, of course," he added hastily.

Leslie giggled. "You'd better say that if you want me to keep making your dinners."

Tom turned off the car and reached out to run a finger down the side of her cheek. "I like hearing you laugh that way," he murmured. "I've missed the laughter between us."

"So have I," she whispered, reaching up without thought to capture his hand against her face.

He leaned over the console to kiss her. She didn't know if he was trying to boost her confidence for the ordeal ahead, or if there was more to it than that, but at the moment she didn't really care. It seemed so long since he'd last kissed her. And she silently acknowledged now that she'd been wanting him to ever since.

She closed her eyes and savored, storing the memory of his caress for the long, lonely night that lay ahead.

Tom seemed in no hurry to end the kiss. And then Kenny piped up from the back seat, making a high, questioning sound that seemed to ask what in the world was taking them so long to get out of the car.

Tom's mouth curved into a smile against Leslie's lips. Without drawing away, he said, "Just a minute, kid. I'm kissing your mom."

Leslie was so surprised and touched at hearing Tom call her Kenny's mom that she practically melted against him when he pressed his lips to hers again. It was so dangerously easy to fantasize about the three of them being together like this—

A thump on the roof of the low car broke them apart.

"Hey, Lowery," Zach McCain called through the window glass. "Cut that out. You've got an innocent kid in the back seat, for crying out loud."

Tom sighed and pulled back from Leslie with a gratifying show of reluctance. "Looks like the party has already begun," he said. "You ready?"

She took a deep breath and nodded. "As ready as I'm going to be."

"You get the diaper bag. I'll get the kid."

She only nodded again, thinking that Tom seemed almost eager to be the one to carry Kenny into the house.

He opened his door. "McCain, you pervert," he complained loudly as he climbed out from behind the wheel. "What are you doing sneaking around peering into windows?"

Zach retorted with something equally insulting, and Leslie was lost for a moment in nostalgia for the way it used to be. And then she glanced at the ring on her left hand, took another deep breath and told herself she'd better keep her thoughts in the present if she was going to handle this evening with any semblance of dignity.

Tom and Leslie were surrounded the moment they walked into the Gilbert house. Even if they hadn't been making their first appearance as newlyweds—a dramatic enough moment on its own—the baby would have drawn a crowd.

Tom was almost amused at his own surge of pride at having his friends see him with Leslie at his side and Kenny in his arms. He felt very much the new husband and new father, and even knowing that this was only an illusion in many ways, he allowed himself to enjoy the sensation.

It sure beat the "Poor Tom" image he'd been fighting among his friends for the past fifteen months.

Leslie remembered many of Tom's friends, though several

new faces had joined the circle while she'd been gone. Tom allowed Sami, ever the gracious hostess, to make most of the introductions, while he fended off questions and teasing comments. Kenny didn't seem to mind the attention; just the opposite, in fact. He grinned and gurgled in response to the inevitable funny faces and baby talk, his chubby little hand clutching Tom's shirt collar for balance, his feet kicking happily.

Sherm Gilbert made his way through the crowd, carrying his tiny, five-week-old daughter in the crook of his arm much as he'd once carried footballs. His ebony face creased with a smile at the sight of Tom holding Kenny. "What you got there, Lowery?"

"This," Tom said with a grin, "is Kenny."

"Hey, there, Kenny." Sherm chucked the baby's chin with a sausage-sized finger. "This is my daughter, Katie. You can be her friend, but keep your hands to yourself."

"Practicing for when she's a teenager?" Tom leaned over to admire the tiny cherub in her frilly white dress. A white hair bow was clipped among her thick black curls, and her huge brown eyes dominated her smooth face with its perfect rosebud mouth. "You just might have cause for concern."

"Gives me cold chills just thinking that far ahead," Sherm admitted.

Tom wondered suddenly what the odds were that he would see little Kenny as a teenager. But thoughts about the future left him feeling empty and unsettled, so he pushed them aside.

"By the way, Tom, congratulations on your marriage," Sherm said warmly. "I always thought you and Leslie made a nice couple, though I have to admit I was floored when I heard that you'd up and married out of the blue like this."

Tom would have liked to know what rumors were circulating about that hastily arranged ceremony, whether anyone believed the official explanation that he and Leslie had remained in contact after she'd left town, and had decided to marry when she'd become responsible for her stepsister's orphaned son, both for the baby's sake and because they wanted to be together. It made a nice little story. Did any of his friends buy it?

Tom saw that Leslie was chatting easily enough with Sherm's exotically pretty wife, Sami—probably swapping baby stories, he guessed. Kim approached the group and joined in the conversation just as Zach strolled to the relatively quiet corner where Tom and Sherm stood with the babies. Zach's hands were full of samples of the delicious finger foods Sami had prepared and displayed in enticing groupings on every available surface. Former social worker Sami Gilbert was a whiz at throwing a party, somehow making it look easy. More than a few had suggested that she go into business helping others plan and host social events, but Sami seemed content to be a stay-at-home wife and mom for now.

Tom couldn't help wondering how long Leslie would be satisfied in that role. Already he was seeing signs of restlessness in her. Remembering how driven and ambitious she'd been in her law career, he found it hard to imagine that she would be able to stay away from it for long.

"Man, look at you two," Zach jeered after swallowing a stuffed mushroom in two big bites. "What are you talking about—which disposable diaper keeps baby's butt drier?"

Unperturbed, Sherm rocked his drowsy daughter and grinned. "You just wait until you and Kim have kids of your own. You'll probably be the proudest pop around."

"You could be right," Zach acknowledged, glancing across the room toward his wife, his expression softening.

The men were suddenly descended upon by Leslie, Sami, Kim and several other determined-looking women.

"You guys have hogged the babies long enough," Sami announced, reaching for her daughter. "It's our turn to play with them."

Leslie held out her hands to Kenny, who grinned and reached for her. "You should check out the food tables," she advised Tom. "I've already sampled and everything is scrumptious."

"'S good," Zach agreed, his mouth full of something.

Everyone laughed. Kim sighed, rolled her eyes and punched her husband's arm. "Try not to embarrass me in front of your friends, will you?" she begged him, though she sounded resigned to the inevitable.

Zach swallowed with a gulp. "Are you going to hold the babies?" he asked her. "Sherm seems to think we should be practicing."

Kim blushed, but looked with renewed interest at the infants. "I don't know if I should hold them. They're both so little, and I haven't had much experience with babies...."

"You'll never get over your fear of holding one until you give it a try," Zach told her cheerfully.

For as long as Zach and Kim had been together, Tom had watched Zach challenge Kim to overcome the many fears she'd once suffered from, and he'd watched Kim slowly gain confidence as a result of Zach's unwavering belief in her. It was a partnership that worked well: a man who feared nothing and a woman who'd once been afraid of everything. They balanced each other nicely, in Tom's opinion.

As though he fully understood the conversation, Kenny lunged toward Kim, arms outstretched. Perhaps he was drawn by her brightly colored sweater and shiny, dangling earrings, but he made it clear in his baby-arrogant manner that he wanted to visit her. Laughing, Leslie handed him over to Kim, who held the baby awkwardly at first and then increasingly comfortably as he babbled and snatched eagerly at her earrings.

The women carried the babies off, leaving the guys empty-handed.

"I don't know about you two," Sherm said, already moving, "but I'm heading for the food."

"Right behind you," Tom assured him.

"Me, too." Zach obviously didn't want to be left behind. "I'm ready for a second helping."

Nina had spent the past three days convincing herself that she'd overreacted to Steve after the basketball game Tuesday evening. Maybe she'd been thrown off balance by her fright after the large dog's sudden appearance. Maybe she'd simply been awkward and uncertain because it had been so long since she'd been on a date with an attractive man.

The point was, she'd acted like a flustered schoolgirl, which was ridiculous for a woman her age. Just because Steve had kissed her senseless, had indicated that he was attracted to her on both a mental and a physical level, had more than implied that he had an intimate relationship in mind for them, she shouldn't have dithered around like an idiot. She was a mature, experienced woman. She was perfectly capable of deciding who she would or would not see. When or if she would go to bed with a man. And it was up to her to determine how that decision would affect the rest of her life.

She could enjoy Steve's company without allowing herself to get carried away with unrealistic fantasies, she assured herself firmly. She knew from experience how to say goodbye when the time came, how to carry on when a relationship ended. How to find comfort and contentment in the life she'd built for herself long before Steve Pendleton had entered it.

It wouldn't last long, she warned herself. There were too many counts against them—from geography to age, from mixed loyalties to past histories. But darn it, everyone deserved a little fun, and she had so much fun with Steve. She should savor it, not fear it.

And that was exactly what she would do, she decided with a determined nod as she opened her door in response to the doorbell Friday evening.

Steve leaned with his right arm against the doorjamb, his leather coat dangling by one finger over his left shoulder, his dark hair falling onto his forehead, his firm body clad in a soft maroon sweater and slim-fitting jeans. It was a sexy, male-model pose that might have been deliberately assumed, except that it looked so perfectly natural for this man. And, predictably, Nina nearly dissolved into incoherence again.

So maybe this thing wasn't going to be quite so breezy and

amusing as she'd hoped. But she could still handle it, she vowed, even as he reached for her and she tumbled into his arms.

The party had hardly gotten under way before Leslie saw exactly what Tom had meant when he said his friends no longer treated him the way they had before. It wasn't that they treated him badly—just the opposite. They were so eager and solicitous that as the evening went on, Leslie could almost see him reinforcing the walls he'd built around his emotions.

He would hate being treated differently, she realized. He must have cringed inwardly every time someone kindly asked how he was doing. Or when people suddenly changed the subject each time one of their more adventurous physical exploits of the past year was mentioned—a skydiving outing, a rock-climbing expedition, a full-contact football game in the park, none of which Tom had been invited to participate in. When Tom offered to help Sami carry a heavy tray of appetizers from the kitchen, several others jumped to take his place, all making it clear they thought he shouldn't be straining himself that much.

Leslie saw the shuttered resentment in his eyes, and she ached for him. Only now was she beginning to understand how much he had really lost in that accident, and that it had nothing to do with his back or his leg.

She suspected that it wouldn't give him much comfort if she were to point out that his friends were behaving this way because they loved him.

He was talking to Zach and a couple of other guys from the fire department when she approached him as the evening was drawing to an end.

"Will you hold Kenny?" she asked Tom with a smile. "He's getting a little fussy and wants to be held, and my arms are tired."

"I'll take him awhile, Leslie," Zach immediately offered, even as Tom reached for the baby.

"I've got him," Tom answered, easily handling the hand-off, as though from long experience.

Kenny snuggled comfortably against Tom's chest and stuck his finger in his mouth, appearing content.

"You've been standing for a long time, Tom. Want to sit down with him?" Sherm suggested, motioning toward a comfortable-looking armchair.

Tom shook his head, his head bent toward the baby. "I'm fine," he said, just a bit curtly.

"Tom's getting used to this," Leslie explained with a chuckle. "Kenny had a tummy ache night before last and threw a fit every time we tried to lay him down. Tom walked him around the house for over an hour until Kenny finally fell asleep. My arms would have worn out long before Tom's did. I guess all that bodybuilding he's been doing has paid off in more than attractive muscles," she added, giving her husband a teasingly flirtatious look.

Those who were standing closely enough to overhear her glanced automatically at Tom's broad shoulders and strong arms. Leslie wondered if they'd really looked beyond his limp during the past few months to see what excellent shape he was in otherwise. She had certainly noticed right away, but perhaps that was because she hadn't seen him immediately after the accident, when he'd probably looked pretty bad.

A pang went through her at the thought of how much he must have suffered. If she had known—if anyone had called her—she would have come to him, she realized abruptly. The accident had happened just as Leslie was getting well established at the law firm in Chicago, but she would not have hesitated to leave her job behind if she'd thought Tom needed her.

It was, after all, what she had done for Crystal. What she would do for anyone she...

Loved.

The word echoed in her mind, terrifying her. She immediately retreated from it by turning to their hostess and saying quickly, "You really must give me the recipe for those mint brownies, Sami. They're fabulous."

* * *

An hour later, most of the party guests had departed. Since both the babies had made it clear that they wanted to be fed at about the same time, Sami and Leslie had carried them to the nursery, inviting Kim to join them while the men examined a new fly rod and reel Sherm had recently purchased.

"That man does love to fish," Sami said fondly, sitting in a huge rocker, tiny Katie nursing hungrily at her breast.

"So does Zach," Kim agreed, cross-legged on the floor nearby. "Not that he ever catches anything."

Leslie was sitting on a cushioned window seat, Kenny in her lap with his bottle. "Does Tom still fish with them?" she asked.

"I think Tom and Sherm went out in Sherm's boat last fall," Sami replied with a slight frown as she tried to remember. "Sherm is a warm-weather fisherman. He hasn't been out since the weather turned cold, though he's looking forward to spring so he can get out on the lake again."

Kim appeared troubled.

Leslie studied her expression. "Kim? Do Tom and Zach still fish together? I remember they used to sit in a boat for hours, just talking and wasting worms."

"Actually, I can't remember the last time Zach and Tom went fishing," Kim admitted.

"Do they spend *any* time together anymore?" Leslie inquired, sensing that this was somehow important to her understanding of just how much had changed for Tom since she'd left.

Kim bit her lip, then sighed. "Not much. At least, not without including me or others. Maybe it's my fault, though I've always encouraged Zach to take time to be with his friends. I'm not one to need him around all the time to entertain me."

"I don't think it's your fault," Leslie said, hazarding a guess. "I think it has something to do with the accident."

She watched as both Kim and Sami stiffened in reference to that terrible event.

"How much has Tom told you about the accident?" Kim asked curiously.

"Enough for me to know that he could have died or been left paralyzed. That he was extremely fortunate to have recovered to the extent that he has."

Kim shuddered. "I'll never forget the way he looked the first time I saw him afterward. It was a couple of weeks later, and I drove to Little Rock to see him in the hospital there. He was so pale and thin and frail looking. There were all those tubes stuck into him, and it was still uncertain how much mobility he would regain."

"I saw him like that, too," Sami agreed somberly. "It was heart-wrenching."

"I wasn't here then," Leslie admitted. "Tom and I had broken up for a while and I suppose no one thought to call me. Maybe people thought he wouldn't want them to contact me. But when I look at him now, I see a strong, healthy man who limps a little and has some occasional back pain. I wonder if the rest of you don't still see that broken man in the hospital."

There was a moment of shocked silence in the bright, pretty nursery. Sami stopped rocking, her eyes widening as she stared at Leslie.

"What an odd thing to say," she said after a moment. "What do you mean, Leslie?"

"Tom thinks everyone is treating him differently since the accident. That everyone feels sorry for him because he has some lingering disabilities and because he can no longer work as an active-duty firefighter. Tom's a very proud and capable man. He can handle everything that has happened to him except the pity."

Leslie knew Tom wouldn't thank her for speaking for him this way. In fact, he was more likely to be furious with her. But someone had to do something about the situation she'd witnessed between Tom and his friends this evening, and since no one else seemed to be taking that first step, Leslie figured it was up to her. She owed Tom this much, she told herself.

"Tom thinks we pity him?" Kim was stunned. "Oh, Leslie,

I had no idea. You're right, that would be unbearable for him."

"And completely unjustified," Sami agreed thoughtfully. "The guy's still more handsome than any man has a right to be. He's got a good job. Friends. The respect of the community. And now he has a beautiful wife and an adorable little boy."

"That's exactly what I've been telling him," Leslie said approvingly. Then blushed at the way that must have sounded. "Except for the 'beautiful wife' part, of course."

"It's all true, though," Sami said with a smile.

Her eyes held a new understanding, and Leslie guessed that Sami would be talking to her husband later about the preservation of a man's pride.

Kim had drawn her legs up and wrapped her arms around them, unhampered by the loosely constructed knit pantsuit she wore. Her expression was grave. "I've known for a long time that something was wrong between Zach and Tom," she admitted unhappily. "I haven't known how to explain it, but—"

Kim took a deep breath. "Zach and I had dated only for a few months before he and Tom were in that accident," she explained for Leslie's sake. "Actually, we'd broken up just a few weeks earlier—a stupid argument that we blew all out of proportion. But during those earlier months, I spent time with Zach and Tom on several occasions, and I could see the relationship they had. They were so close. Closer than brothers. They finished each other's sentences, laughed at jokes no one else heard, said more in a glance than other people say in entire conversations."

"That's the way I remember their friendship, too," Leslie murmured with a pang of regret.

"It isn't like that between them anymore."

Leslie sighed. "I know."

"You know," Sami interrupted, "it's no one's fault, but relationships between friends, even longtime friends, change when one of them marries. It happened to me and my best friend, for example. I didn't have as much time to spend with her after I married Sherm, and now that Katie's here, I have even less. She's still dating and going to parties, and I'm spending my weekends doing laundry and scrubbing the house with disinfectant. I know Kim never asked Zach to spend less time with Tom, but it was only natural that Zach would want to be with his new wife. Everyone knows he adores her.''

Kim blushed and looked both pleased and troubled at the same time.

"Not to mention the different jobs,'' Sami went on. "Before, Zach and Tom were a team. Partners. Same schedules, same work experiences. Now Zach puts out the fires and Tom comes in afterward to investigate the causes. It gives them common ground, but it's still different from the way it used to be.''

"Everything you've said makes sense,'' Leslie agreed, "but somehow I think there's more to it.''

"So do I,'' Kim said.

"Did Zach and Tom have a fight?''

Kim shook her head. "Not that I know of. And I think Zach would have told me.''

"Has he talked to you about Tom?''

Again, Kim bit her lip before answering. "Not much. When I bring Tom up, Zach usually ends up changing the subject.''

"Tom does the same about Zach.'' Leslie sighed. "I wish I knew what was wrong.''

"Looks like it's going to be up to you two to set things right,'' Sami said matter-of-factly.

Leslie and Kim exchanged searching glances.

"Sami,'' Leslie said, "you could be right.''

Chapter Eleven

Leslie and Tom left the Gilberts' home less than half an hour later. Zach and Kim departed at the same time.

"Here, Tom, you take the baby," Leslie said, handing a well-fed and warmly bundled Kenny to Tom. "I'll get the diaper bag."

"Want me to carry him for you, Tom?" Zach reached out as Tom juggled the soundly sleeping, utterly limp infant into a secure position.

"Looks to me like he's doing just fine," Kim said briskly to her husband. "Here, you carry these extra brownies Sami gave us."

"The baby weighs all of twelve pounds," Sami agreed dryly. "I don't think he'll be too much of a burden for a guy with Tom's muscles."

Zach and Sherm seemed surprised by their wives' comments. Tom shot a suspicious look at Leslie, who gazed back at him with bland innocence.

"What did you say to them?" Tom demanded the minute he and Leslie were alone in the car, he behind the wheel again.

"I don't know what you're talking about," she bluffed, glancing over her shoulder to make sure Kenny had settled comfortably into his car seat.

"Leslie." Her name was a growl.

She sighed. "Okay, I might have said something when we were feeding the babies."

"And just what might you have said?"

She'd known he would be mad, but his accusatory tone was beginning to annoy her. "All I said was that you weren't an invalid and no one should treat you like one. That any man would resent being treated that way by friends."

"Damn it, Leslie!"

The words exploded from him, startling the baby into a squawk of protest from the back seat. Leslie and Tom both stiffened until Kenny settled down, and then Tom spoke again, his voice considerably lower this time.

"No man wants his wife fighting his battles for him, either. You think that's any easier than being treated like an invalid?"

"I wasn't trying to fight your battles for you," she snapped. "I simply made a comment. How they choose to act on it is their decision. And for the record, Sami and Kim think you have every reason to be annoyed with the way you've been treated and you won't have to deal with it from them anymore."

"I'm supposed to thank you for that?"

"God, the male ego." She exhaled gustily. "It must get tiresome carrying that burden around all the time."

They were still sniping at each other when they reached Tom's house. He carried the baby inside, then handed him over to Leslie, who swiftly exchanged Kenny's overalls and striped shirt for a soft sleeper snapped over a clean diaper. She tucked him into the portable crib, then braced herself to go into the living room to rejoin Tom.

He was sitting on the couch, staring at his hands, lost in thought. He looked up when Leslie entered the room, and opened his mouth to speak. He fell silent when a siren suddenly made itself heard inside the quiet room. The wail grew louder as the vehicle sped past the house, then faded into the distance.

Leslie watched Tom as he went tense, his head turning to follow the sound. "Fire truck?" she asked.

"Sounded like one."

"And you wish you were hanging on to the back of it." It wasn't a question.

He didn't try to equivocate. "Yeah. Knee-jerk reaction, I guess."

"Will you be called if it's a fire?"

"Depends on what they find when they get there. If it's a small kitchen fire or whatever, I won't be needed. I'll be called only if it's a fire of suspicious origin, or if the cause isn't immediately apparent."

"Do you really hate your new job so much?"

He looked a bit surprised, then thoughtful. "No, I don't hate it. The inspections get kind of boring at times, and I'll never like paperwork—but I enjoy the investigation part. I've been doing a lot of studying in that area, and I'd like to get even more deeply into it."

"So it's not all bad."

"No." His smile was wry. "It's not all bad."

She smiled in return.

"What about you? How badly do you miss *your* career?" he asked, turning the tables on her.

She made a face. "I don't miss the firm in Chicago. It didn't take me long to know I'd be miserable there. But the job— well, I miss that. It was what I trained for, what I wanted to do."

He nodded in total understanding.

Leslie pushed a hand through her hair and sighed lightly. "I still hope to find a new job, using my training and my experience. But given another choice between work and Kenny, I will always choose Kenny. No career could ever make me feel the way that he does."

"So it isn't all bad." Tom threw her words back at her with gentle mockery.

She wrinkled her nose. "No. It's not all bad."

He held out his hand to her. She placed hers into it without hesitation. She didn't resist when he drew her toward him and pulled her down to sit beside him on the couch.

"We're quite a couple, aren't we?" he mused without releasing her. His thumb stroked the back of her hand, his fingers entwining with hers.

Odd how such a light touch could cause such a dramatic reaction inside her. She cleared her throat. "I suppose you could say that."

He lifted his gaze to hers. "Leslie..."

She held her breath.

The telephone rang just as Tom leaned close to Leslie, his mouth hovering only inches above hers. She felt his breath on her anticipation-parted lips when he hissed a frustrated curse.

"Hold that thought," he said, pushing away from her. "I'll be right back."

But to her mingled relief and disappointment, he wasn't able to take up where he left off. It turned out that his input was needed at the nearby fire scene after all.

"I don't know how long I'll be," he said. "You don't need to wait up for me."

She searched his face and saw his regret at the interruption...as well as a flicker of interest in whatever he'd been told over the telephone. His job was calling to him, she could see. She was glad, for his sake, that he was still able to find challenge and incentive in his work, even if he'd been forced onto a new career path against his will.

"Be careful," she said.

"I'm always careful these days," he replied.

If there was any bitterness in his words, it wasn't apparent. So Leslie only smiled and said, "Good."

He leaned over to brush a kiss across her lips. And then he left, locking the front door behind him.

Bemused, Leslie leaned against the back of the couch and

exhaled slowly. What a strange evening it had been. It seemed to her as if she and Tom had been either fighting or kissing since they'd left the house earlier.

Raising her fingertips to her still-tingling lips, she told herself that, on the whole, she much preferred kissing.

Trying to be as quiet as he could, Tom scrubbed the familiar smell of smoke out of his hair, then ducked his head under the shower head to rinse. The house had been quiet and dark when he'd gotten home, the door to the guest bedroom closed. Though he hadn't really expected Leslie to wait up for him, since it was quite late when he'd returned, he'd been a bit disappointed nevertheless.

Walking into that quiet, dark house had made him think of all the other nights he'd come home alone, to be greeted only by silence and shadows. In less than a week of marriage, he was becoming spoiled about having Leslie and Kenny welcome him home. That realization unnerved him, reminding him how badly he could be hurt if he wasn't very careful. How empty the house would be again when they were gone.

He stepped out of the shower, swiped at his wet skin with a towel and wrapped another around his hips. Combing his wet hair back from his face with his fingers, he walked out of the bathroom and into his bedroom. And then he froze.

Leslie was sitting on the side of the bed. Her auburn hair tumbled around her shoulders, and she'd removed her makeup, leaving her face looking fresh scrubbed and somehow more vulnerable. She wore a thin black satin robe over a matching black satin nightshirt. Her feet were bare.

She looked so beautiful it took his breath away.

"Is, er, something wrong?" he asked automatically, trying without success to read her expression.

Her fingers twisted in her lap—the only outward sign of nerves. "No. It was just…lonely in there."

In uncharacteristic shyness, her gaze lowered, then widened. He saw the shock that crossed her face before she could mask it.

Though he'd been expecting this moment, he hadn't looked forward to it. "The scars aren't exactly pretty, are they?"

She bit her lip, as though to steady it, then said with commendable composure, "They took me by surprise. But they're not so bad."

He knew exactly how he looked with the dark-red lines streaking his visibly damaged right leg and hip. If he was to turn around, she would see more scars on his back, mute evidence of two operations. He wasn't ready to turn around just yet.

He clung to his towel. "I just got out of the shower," he explained, then felt stupid for making such an obvious statement.

Leslie nodded. "Do you want me to leave?"

With every molecule of his battered body, he wanted her to stay. Yet the jolt of nerves inside him startled him. He and Leslie had made love before, of course, so he shouldn't be so apprehensive about it. They had been spectacular together before, and he suspected that they would be again. Even though it had been a long period of abstinence for him, he was still reasonably confident that he could perform satisfactorily.

What worried him most was the thought that if he made love to her now, he would never be able to let her go again. And he wasn't at all certain that she would feel the same way.

"No," he muttered. "I don't want you to leave." *Not tonight—not ever.*

Her fingers twisted more tightly, knuckles bleached white with strain. "I just thought..." She stopped to moisten her lips. "We *are* married, after all."

"That's true." His voice was more husky than he would have liked. Silently, he cleared his throat.

She made a muffled sound of frustration. "This is so awkward," she murmured. "It was so easy between us once."

He took a step closer to her. "A lot has changed since then. For both of us."

Leslie nodded, her hair swinging down to hide her face. "It

has crossed my mind that maybe you aren't still attracted to me in the way you were before.''

Another step brought him beside the bed; less than a yard separated them. "That's one thing that has *not* changed. I can't imagine ever not wanting you," he said frankly.

Her gaze shot up to his face. Her cheeks darkened as her hands went quiet in her lap, still clenched. "Tom?" she asked, her voice uncertain.

He sat beside her on the bed and reached for her, releasing his grip on the towel. Probably he would pay for this, he thought fleetingly. But there was no way he had enough will-power to resist her tonight.

He covered her lips with his, drank in the taste and feel and warmth of her. *So long.* The words played over and over in his head. He had been so long without her.

Her arms went around him, her palms flattening against the bare, damp skin of his back. He shivered in reaction. So long since she had touched him like this.

Her robe fell away from her shoulders and he ran his hands lingeringly over the bare skin of her arms and her back, brought one hand between them to cup her right breast through the thin barrier of black satin. Her back arched in reaction, and he heard her murmur something against his lips.

"So damned long," he muttered in response.

She trailed her right hand down his back, fingers lingering to stroke and tease, and then she slipped that inciting hand beneath the towel lying loosely across his lap. A jolt of electricity shot through him, forcing a moan from his throat.

Her fingertips lingered on a knot of scar tissue. She seemed more distressed than repelled. "I wish I had been with you when this happened," she whispered. "If I had known—if anyone had told me—I would have come."

He had no doubt that she would indeed have come to visit him had she heard. He grimaced at the thought of her seeing him as he'd been after the accident, hooked up to tubes and wires, still in doubt that he would even walk again.

"Don't worry about it," he said more gruffly than he'd intended. "Obviously, I survived."

At least I won't be around to watch you kill yourself. He wondered if he was the only one who heard the echo of the bitter prediction she'd made the day she'd left him, a prophecy that had come all too close to proving true.

But he wouldn't think now of the words they'd exchanged on that painful day. They were together again tonight, and he would be a fool not to savor every moment. Just as it would be foolish for him to worry about how long it would last this time.

His hands tightened spasmodically on her, then moved swiftly to strip away the thin fabric that concealed her from him. She cooperated eagerly.

Together they tumbled to the bed. Tom winced when his awkwardly twisted back twinged in protest of the movement, but he ignored the momentary discomfort. Leslie, however, did not.

"Your back," she said, stiffening against him in alarm.

"Forget it. I'm fine."

"Would you admit it if you weren't?" she asked with a touch of wry humor.

He leaned over her and brushed a strand of hair away from her flushed cheek. "I'm fine," he repeated firmly. "I'm still perfectly capable of making love with you."

She reached up to touch his cheek. "I suppose you would know."

He spoke with a confidence he sincerely hoped was justified. "That's right. You know how I feel about being coddled, Les. Don't start it—especially now, for God's sake."

She smiled and moved sinuously beneath him, making him catch his breath in immediate reaction. "I just want to make you feel good."

He pressed her more firmly into the mattress. "Be still," he ordered her hoarsely. "I don't want to feel *too* good...not yet, anyway."

Leslie laughed softly, but Tom hadn't exactly been joking.

"You should probably know," he said, his voice gruff, "I haven't been with anyone since you left."

Her smile faded. "You haven't?"

"After my accident," he explained, embarrassed, "I was in pretty bad shape. Lovemaking was the last thing on my mind."

She trailed a finger across his chest, through the dusting of sandy hair. "And before the accident?"

"I was missing you."

Her eyes were luminous in the lamplight when she looked up at him then. "I missed you, too," she murmured. "And, Tom—there hasn't been anyone else for me since the day I met you."

Somehow he had known. Despite all the changes that had taken place in their lives since she'd moved away, the bond between them had remained unchanged. Still tentative, still undefined, still fragile—but still inarguably there.

It was as if they'd both been aware that they'd separated without closure. That they were not truly free to go on with their lives until they'd resolved whatever they'd begun two years ago.

Memories of the time they'd spent together flashed through his mind as he kissed her again, deeply, slowly.

The day they'd met. Leslie had been standing in front of him in a long, slow-moving line at a bank. They'd started talking. By the time Leslie made her deposit, Tom had inveigled a first date.

Their first kiss. The first time they'd made love…six weeks after that first meeting. As clichéd as it sounded, Tom had known afterward that nothing would ever be quite the same for him. And nothing had been.

A day at the lake, when Leslie had stood poised on a rock just prior to diving in, sleek and pretty in her bright-red bathing suit, her wet auburn hair glinting in the sunlight. Tom had gazed at her and felt his chest ache in a way it never had. And he'd wondered if that was how it felt to be in love.

The day she'd left. The way she'd looked when she'd turned

on her way out the door to look at him one last time, a word-less plea in her eyes, messages he didn't quite understand passing between them. And all he'd said was, "See you." And both of them had known he hadn't believed it.

He tore his mouth from hers, remembering that painful day, the way he'd felt after she'd left. Losing his physical agility, his position in the fire department—those disappointments had been painful. But what he'd never wanted to admit—even to himself—was that losing Leslie had been even harder.

Could he go through it again without losing an important part of himself?

"Leslie—"

He didn't know what he might have said. Whatever it was fled his mind when she slipped a hand around the back of his neck and lifted her face to his.

"Make love to me, Goose," she whispered, her breath caressing his lips.

He groaned. Locking the warnings of his common sense into a mental closet, he tightened his arms around Leslie and dove mindlessly into her warmth and softness.

The baby woke them sometime during the night. Leslie had left both bedroom doors open so that she would be sure to hear Kenny if he cried out. She and Tom both jerked upright in response to the baby's first demanding wail.

"I'll get him," Tom offered, sliding from the bed. "You think he wants a bottle?"

Leslie blinked and tried to clear her fuzzy mind. "Probably just a diaper change, but—"

"No problem. Go back to sleep."

Clutching the sheets to her throat, she sank back into the pillows. She heard Tom moving around in the other room, talking softly to Kenny. She heard him laugh quietly at something Kenny did, and then the creak of the rocker-recliner in the den. She pictured Tom sitting there in the shadows with the baby in his lap, rocking the baby back to sleep, his strong hands warm and gentle.

His very talented hands, she added silently with a shiver of memory at the feelings those hands had recently evoked in her. Whatever lingering physical problems remained from Tom's accident, none of them had affected his skill as a lover.

She closed her eyes and allowed herself to drift in satiated contentment, the sound of Tom's murmurs and the rhythmic creak of the rocker lulling her back into sleep.

Nina Lowery awoke slowly Saturday morning. Her eyes fluttered and opened, squinting against the full sunlight streaming through the lacy curtains. She didn't usually have the luxury of sleeping so late.

Hers was the bedroom of a woman who'd been living very comfortably alone. Lace at the windows and on the bed. Soft colors and dreamy paintings on the walls. A chintz-covered chaise lounge where she'd spent many hours with her books and cups of tea, enjoying the music from the high-quality compact stereo Tom had given her one Christmas and then installed in an entertainment cabinet in one corner of her bedroom, along with a small TV and VCR combination. A collection of porcelain figurines, most of them gifts from Tom during the years, were displayed on a corner curio unit.

The pair of men's jeans thrown over the back of the lounge were a jarring contrast to the blatant femininity surrounding them.

Memory jarred her fully awake. The sound of running water from her bathroom made her wince and run a hand through her tumbled hair.

She quickly pushed thoughts of her son to the back of her mind. This was definitely not the time to think about Tom, she told herself.

"Stop worrying about him, Nina."

Steve Pendleton stood in the doorway to her bathroom, frowning and wearing nothing but a pair of navy boxers and a thin gold chain on which hung a small gold cross. The chain and cross had been a gift from his late mother, he'd explained when Nina discovered it the night before. He always wore it.

She swallowed hard at the sight of him, and then frowned at his words. "Stop reading my mind."

His mouth quirked into a faint smile. "It wasn't your mind I was reading. It was that maternal-guilt expression on your face. I've learned to recognize it."

Her face warming, Nina looked away from him.

"You've done nothing wrong, honey."

"I know that," she assured him hastily. "It's just... well..."

"It's just been much too long since you've given any thought to your own needs," he cut in gently, his tone warm with understanding.

She shrugged. "Perhaps."

"Definitely. As a matter of fact—"

He headed toward her, hips rolling in a sexy, sauntering gait that made her heart stop and then start again with an all-new tempo.

"Thinking of my needs, are you?" she asked, the light words belied by her husky tone.

"Actually, I was thinking of my own needs this time."

She tossed aside the bedclothes and held out her arms. "Once again, you read my mind," she purred as he came down to her.

Having gotten distracted and missed breakfast, Tom and Leslie were having an early lunch, when the telephone rang. Since Tom was holding Kenny in his lap as he ate, Leslie answered. She looked troubled when she returned to the table.

"Is anything wrong?" Tom asked, immediately concerned.

She shook her head. "Not exactly. That was your mother."

He frowned, growing even more concerned. "What did she say?"

"She and Steve will be here in an hour."

Tom frowned. "Oh."

"She said Steve wants to visit Kenny."

"And he thought my mother should be the one to set it up? He couldn't just call us himself?"

Leslie looked at him uncertainly. "I, er, think he was there with her when she called. At her apartment."

Tom glanced at his watch. "Pretty early for him to be visiting her, isn't—" He stopped speaking suddenly. He almost felt the color leave his face. "Hell."

"You don't think—"

He drew a sharp breath and shrugged. "None of my business how long he's been there, I guess."

He said the words as much to convince himself as Leslie. He hoped she accepted them more easily than he did.

Looking thoughtful, Leslie bit her lip.

Kenny tugged at Tom's shirt and babbled in a bid to reclaim his attention. Grateful for the distraction, Tom willingly complied.

It was just over an hour later when Nina and Steve arrived. Tom tensed when the doorbell rang, and it was the first time in his adult life he'd ever done so at the thought of seeing his mother. He hated that.

Leslie hovered behind him when he opened the door. Her hands were twisted in front of her in that nervous gesture he knew so well.

Nina looked as nervous as Tom felt, though she made an effort to mask it with a bright smile that didn't fool him for a minute.

"Hi, sweetheart," she said, going up on tiptoes to kiss his cheek. "I brought you something."

She pressed a covered dish into his hands.

"Chocolate pie?" he asked hopefully, his own grin feeling somewhat strained.

"Black forest cake," she corrected him. "Still chocolaty enough to satisfy you, I think."

"Come on in. I'll put this in the kitchen. Er, hey, Steve," he added a bit awkwardly, uncertain what to say to the man who stood way too close to his mother.

"Hello, Tom." Steve smiled easily enough as he spoke, but his eyes were guarded.

Nina swept past Tom to hug Leslie. "Leslie, dear, you look wonderful. I love that dark-green sweater on you."

"Thank you. And you look beautiful, as always," Leslie replied fondly. She, too, stiffened a bit when she turned to Steve. "Hello, Steve."

"Leslie." He didn't seem to know whether to shake her hand or kiss her cheek. He settled for a smile and a nod, before he pulled a hand from behind his back to reveal a small, silver-wrapped gift box. "I brought you a wedding gift. I haven't had an opportunity yet to congratulate you both on your marriage. I hope you'll be very happy."

Leslie's gaze flew to Tom before returning to Steve. "That's very nice of you. Thank you."

"I'll just set this in the kitchen," Tom said, motioning with the cake dish. "Anyone want any coffee or anything?"

"I'll help you," Nina offered quickly, slipping her hand beneath his arm. "Leslie, you and Steve sit down and get comfortable. Tommy and I will serve the cake and coffee."

"Is the baby sleeping?" Steve asked as he and Leslie moved toward the sitting area.

"Yes, he always takes a nap after lunch. He should be awake soon."

Reassured that Leslie and Steve would probably spend the next few minutes discussing Kenny—amicably, he hoped— Tom braced himself for a talk with his mother in the kitchen.

He set the cake on the kitchen counter and opened a cabinet to pull out dessert plates. Leslie had already made a pot of coffee, so Nina assembled cups and saucers, sugar and creamer on a serving tray.

"You and Leslie seem to be getting along well," she commented, glancing sideways at Tom.

He went warm as he thought of the preceding night. And this morning, for that matter. He and Leslie had certainly gotten along very well then. Surely his mother didn't read him *that* well. "How can you tell that? You've been here only a couple of minutes."

"I can tell," she said.

And she probably could. No one knew him the way Nina did.

Of course, the reverse was also true. He eyed her glowing eyes and rosy cheeks, and frowned. "You and Pendleton are still an item, I see."

"We're still seeing each other," she said, busying herself with pouring coffee.

Tom didn't at all like her tone. He turned to face her, narrowing his eyes on her suspiciously flushed face. "Mom—"

"Should we carry the desserts into the living room or would you rather sit at the table?"

Her fluttery manner confirmed his worse suspicions. He opened his mouth to speak, then closed it when he realized he had nothing to say. For once in his life, he'd found something he couldn't talk about with his mother. Her love life. It wasn't anything that had ever come up between them before. He'd stupidly supposed that it never would.

"Maybe we'd better eat at the table," he said without enthusiasm. "It's easier that way."

Nina cast him a somewhat pleading glance, then nodded. "All right. Why don't you ask the others to join us while I set these things out?"

Tom could almost feel her gaze on him as he turned to leave the room. She wanted something from him—approval, understanding, encouragement, perhaps. He found himself incapable of offering any of those at the moment. He needed time to accept this, he thought grimly. For now, it was all he could do to handle his own tangled relationship.

Chapter Twelve

Conversation during the dessert was stilted, to say the least. Leslie was unusually quiet, throwing occasional surreptitious, suspicious looks at Steve, gazing curiously at Nina at times, darting questioning glances at Tom. She did show Tom the gift Steve had brought them—a heavy silver picture frame—but even that she handled a bit cautiously, as if uncertain what the gift implied.

Steve talked, but his conversation was superficial, limited mostly to the weather, Nina's good cooking, questions about the baby, comments about the area. Tom answered when spoken to, and tried not to stare at his mother or glare at Steve.

Nina was the one who worked hardest at keeping the conversation flowing; she chattered brightly, asked dozens of questions, made comments that practically dragged responses out of the other three. Tom felt somewhat guilty about not helping her out much, but his head seemed to be stuffed with oatmeal. He wasn't thinking clearly—about anything.

They all appeared relieved when Kenny cried out from his crib.

Tom and Leslie both moved at the same time to respond, but Leslie was faster. "I'll get him," she said. "I'll be right back."

"Why don't we move into the living room," Nina suggested cheerily. "We'll be much more comfortable there. Unless anyone wants more cake?"

Both men shook their heads. Tom glanced down at his plate and noted that it was empty, though he hardly remembered taking a bite. He was going to have to stop eating his mom's desserts while under stress, he thought idly. It was such a waste of good chocolate.

Steve stood when Leslie carried Kenny into the living room. His eyes were focused on his nephew. "He looks like Crystal," he murmured.

Tom watched as Leslie's eyes went misty. "Yes, he does."

"Actually," Nina said, "he looks a little like you, Steve. Did you and your sister favor each other?"

"Yes," Leslie answered for him. "There was a strong family resemblance."

Steve drew a breath and reached out to touch Kenny's cheek. "Those eyes are Crystal's. She and I both had brown eyes, but hers were lighter than mine—amber, like Kenny's."

He lifted his eyes to Leslie's. "I loved my sister, Leslie. I didn't like the way she lived, and I couldn't help telling her—but I loved Crystal. Always."

"I know," Leslie said, her voice shaken. "And she loved you, too, in her own way."

"Then why wouldn't she let you call me when she was—when she was dying?" It was obvious from his tone that the question had been haunting him.

"She didn't want you to see her the way she looked at the end," Leslie answered simply. "She didn't want you to attempt to interfere with her pregnancy, even for her best interests. And she didn't want to have to admit that she'd been wrong to keep you at a distance before, wasting the time you could have spent getting to know and understand each other better. But most of all, she didn't want you to try to keep her from me at the end. She needed me, and I needed to take care of her. We were sisters, Steve, in spirit, as much as she was your sister by blood. I loved her, too.''

He sighed and pulled his hand away from the baby to run it wearily through his hair. "I know. And—well, I realize I haven't shown it, but I'm…I'm grateful that you were there for her. At the end." His slight, uncharacteristic stammer underlined his sincerity.

Tom frowned. "You have an odd way of showing it. Trying to take Kenny away from Leslie after she'd nurtured him from the day he was born was cruel and vicious. She sacrificed everything for your sister and your nephew. You owe her a hell of a lot more than an offhanded thanks."

"Steve owes me nothing, Tom," Leslie replied before Steve could speak. "I didn't do anything for him. Only for Crystal and the baby. For myself. But if he wants to make amends, for Kenny's sake, I'll do my part to cooperate."

She turned to Steve then with a smile that apparently disarmed Steve as much as it surprised Tom. "Would you like to hold your nephew?"

Steve backed off instinctively. "I, er, I've never held a baby that small."

"You were going to fight for custody of him. You didn't intend to even hold him if you won?" Tom asked pointedly.

"Tom." Nina placed a hand on his arm.

He fought an urge to shake her off. Damn it, he wasn't quite as forgiving as everyone else seemed to be. Steve Pendleton had put Leslie through pure hell, frightening her so much that she'd been willing to enter into a marriage she didn't want just to keep the baby.

Leslie threw Tom one quick, warning look, then turned back to Steve. "You won't break him," she said. "Tom hauls him around like a sack of flour, and Kenny seems to thrive on it."

Steve rose immediately to the bait. If Tom could do it, he could, too, his expression seemed to say as he reached for the child. Kenny, friendly and sweet natured as usual, went happily into his uncle's arms and snatched eagerly at the glint of gold chain just visible inside Steve's open-collared, long-sleeved, rugby-styled shirt. Steve carried the baby to the couch, where he sat carefully next to Nina, who couldn't resist cooing at the baby and touching his soft, chubby little hands.

Frowning at the tableau, Tom felt Leslie slip her hand beneath his arm. "It's okay," she murmured to Tom. "I want Kenny to know his uncle."

He relaxed a little, but there was no way to explain to her that it wasn't just the sight of Steve with Kenny that bothered him. It was this new vision of his mother as a woman with a life and interests that didn't include him. The pang he felt when his mom smiled fondly at a man who wasn't Tom. And his fear that she would be hurt if something went wrong in this impetuous and—in Tom's opinion—ill-advised affair.

Tom and Leslie settled into the matching recliners that faced the couch and watched the other couple play with the baby. Pleased with the attention he was receiving, Kenny performed for them, pumping his arms, crowing, grinning and blowing bubbles. Even Tom was chuckling before long; it was impossible to watch this baby without smiling.

"He really is cute," Steve mused, smoothing the baby's wispy, dark hair with one big, awkward hand. And then he lifted his gaze to Leslie and Tom. "I suppose you two will start adoption proceedings soon?"

"Yes," Tom said immediately, overriding whatever Leslie would have said. She shot him a startled glance, making him wonder just what she'd had in mind as far as Kenny's adoption was concerned. Had she planned to leave Tom out of that transaction entirely? If so, they needed to have a very long talk.

"You'll call him 'Kenny Lowery'?"

Tom liked the sound of it. "Of course."

Leslie cleared her throat. "'Kenneth Pendleton Lowery.'"

Steve's eyebrows lifted, but he nodded approval. "It's a good name. Better than—" He stopped abruptly.

GINA WILKINS   179

"Better than 'Harden'?" Leslie asked coolly.

He grimaced. "I didn't say that."

"But you were going to."

"It crossed my mind," he admitted. "I haven't changed my feelings about your father, Leslie. I'll never forgive him for what he did to my family. But I shouldn't have blamed you for any of it. You were only a kid yourself at the time. It couldn't have been any easier for you to be in the middle of the mess than it was for Crystal and me."

"It doesn't really matter what name he uses, as long as he is raised with love," Nina said firmly. "'Kenneth Pendleton Lowery' is a good name, and Kenny can be proud of it. I know that I will be very proud to call him my grandson."

Tom was watching Leslie's face, and he saw the flicker of her eyelashes. What was she thinking? he wondered. Was she asking herself again if she'd made a mistake bringing Tom and his mother into her life and Kenny's? Wondering if she'd given away more responsibility for the baby than she'd originally intended? Had she really thought Tom would be content for long to be her husband in name only, standing quietly in the background while she raised the child without his interference, for as long as she chose to stay?

If that was the case, he couldn't help wondering why she had come to him last night, knowing exactly what would happen when she did.

Nina and Steve didn't stay much longer. Leslie was feeding the baby when they left, so Tom saw them out. Nina turned to him at the door.

"I'll call you later," she promised.

She looked at him with that same half-pleading look that had shaken him before. He tried to reassure her with a smile. "Of course." He leaned over to kiss her cheek. "See you later, Mom."

Just as Tom closed the door behind them, he saw Steve Pendleton slip an arm around Nina's shoulders as they walked to his car.

* * *

Back at her apartment, Nina paced the living-room floor, her arms crossed tightly in front of her, her movements agitated. "This isn't going to work," she lamented. "I've made a terrible mistake."

"Nina." Steve sounded as though his patience was getting strained when he stepped in front of her to physically halt her pacing. "Would you please stop this?"

"Oh, Steve, I'm sorry, but surely you understand. We have to put an end to this."

"No, I do *not* understand. I'm not going to let you throw away what we've found together just because your son is too selfish to share you."

Her chin rose. "Tommy is not selfish."

"Tom is most definitely selfish if he doesn't want you to have your own life or find happiness with someone other than him," Steve retorted firmly. "He's not a saint, Nina. I'm sure he's a fine man because you've raised him to be, but face it. You've spoiled him."

She wanted to argue. She even opened her mouth to do so. But she shut it when she realized that it would do no good. Steve was right, of course. She had spoiled Tom a bit. Understandable, of course, considering that he'd been her whole life for the past thirty years. Her career, her friends, her few, very brief relationships—none of them had come even close to meaning as much to her as her son.

She shivered, thinking of the invisible wall that had been between her and Tom earlier. She'd seen him use it to keep others at a distance, but he'd never kept her outside before. Not even after his accident, when he'd been wounded and dispirited, angry and withdrawn. He'd always let her in.

He hadn't let her in today. And it had broken her heart.

"I can't allow anything to come between Tom and me," she whispered, willing Steve to understand. "Not even you."

A look that might have been hurt flashed across his handsome face, but it was quickly replaced by an expression of stubborn determination. "I won't come between you and Tom, Nina," he assured her. "But I'm not walking away, either.

You mean too much to me for me to give up that easily. If I have to win Tom over as well as you—well, I'll do my best. But I'm not just going to disappear. Not unless you can convince me that it's you who wants me out of your life, and not Tom.''

He tugged her into his arms and bent to kiss her. And she moaned softly into his mouth, knowing that she would never be able to convince him that she wanted him to disappear. God help her.

As Tom drove home from work Wednesday, he found himself singing along with the country song blaring from his radio. It was a chilly, rainy evening, already dark, but Tom didn't even notice the weather.

The sound of his own voice startled him. He hardly remembered when he'd last felt like singing. He'd never been very good—in fact, certain friends had been known to beg him not to join in sing-alongs—but there'd been a period when he'd sung all the time, particularly when he was alone. Lately, he'd spent most of his days alone thinking about how things used to be, rather than simply enjoying the moment.

He was enjoying the moment now. He'd had a pretty good day at work, and he knew that Leslie and Kenny would be waiting for him at home. Despite the problems that were never far from his mind—his physical shortcomings, his precarious future with Leslie, his inexplicable awkwardness with Zach, his mother's worrisome relationship with Steve Pendleton—Tom was surprisingly more content than he'd been in a very long while.

It wasn't hard to pinpoint the cause of that.

He thought of the passion he and Leslie had shared last night. She'd slept in his bed every night since she'd come to him Saturday evening. They'd made love; they'd slept tangled in each other's arms; they'd awoken with smiles and kisses and sometimes more lovemaking if Kenny wasn't yet up. They hadn't talked about it—they didn't talk about their relationship or the future at all—but Leslie seemed increasingly content with the way things were progressing between them. She'd certainly made no complaints.

Tom was almost afraid to say anything for fear of rocking the boat. Every time he allowed himself to think of how happy he was—now, for example—he started to worry that it wouldn't last. He'd experienced too many losses in the past year or so to take happiness for granted now.

He was smiling when he walked through his front door, shaking raindrops out of his hair, to be greeted by the tantalizing aroma of home-cooked food and the enchanting sound of Leslie's laughter.

Damn, it was good to have the music and the laughter back in his life, he thought, trying to ignore the nip of apprehension that accompanied the thought.

Leslie was sitting on the floor beside Kenny's play quilt, supporting Kenny as he sat in front of her, his arms beating the air as if he were attempting to fly. Leslie looked up when Tom came into the living room. Her smile of greeting made him go warm all over.

"Is the kid performing for you?" he asked, tossing his coat over the back of a chair and trying to mask his unusually happy emotional state.

"He's in a great mood."

Tom bent to kiss Leslie's smiling mouth and then scoop the baby into his arms. Careful to use his knees for lifting, he picked Kenny up and held him high in the air. "Hey, pardner. What's up with you?"

In answer, Kenny gave him a loud, wet raspberry.

Tom burst into laughter, as did Leslie. Kenny crowed with apparent self-satisfaction.

"He's been doing that all day," Leslie explained, still giggling. "He thinks he's discovered a delightful new talent."

"*Pb-b-b-bt.*" Kenny was even noisier that time. And then he laughed, a clear, happy baby chortle that would have melted even the hardest of adult hearts.

As far as this baby was concerned, Tom's heart had melted long ago. As soon as he'd stopped trying to be cautious and detached—which hadn't lasted very long, he admitted now—he'd tumbled head over heels. And now he was hopelessly in love with both his wife and their tiny charge, though he didn't know how long he would be able to hold on to either of them.

He hugged the baby, inhaling the fresh scents of soap and powder, and brushed a kiss against impossibly soft skin. "You're a genius, kid," he murmured, struggling to keep his voice light. "Not just any four-month-old can blow a good raspberry."

And then he turned to loop an arm around Leslie and pull her into the group hug. He covered her mouth with his, dimly aware that Kenny was still laughing and making bizarre noises. Could it get any better than this? Tom wondered.

Leslie's eyes were warm and soft when she drew back to take a breath and smile up at him. "I made a pot of seafood gumbo for dinner. Corn bread and salad on the side."

"I love seafood gumbo," he assured her. "I love—"

You.

He smoothly substituted, "I love anything you cook."

She frowned a bit, as if sensing that he'd started to say something else, but he continued briskly, "I need to wash up first, but I'll hurry. I had a light lunch, and I'm starved."

"You're always starving," Leslie accused indulgently, taking the baby from him. "You and Kenny are just alike when it comes to that. Like father, like son, I sup—"

Apparently, she'd spoken without thinking. The instant the words left her mouth, she stammered to a stop, her eyes going wide.

"Er—"

Tom pretended he hadn't noticed a thing. He patted Kenny's head and quipped, "We growing boys have to eat, right, pardner? Be back in a sec."

He headed for the bathroom with a haste that was just short of running. His pulse was still racing as a result of Leslie's carelessly spoken and obviously unintentional words. *Like father, like son.*

He'd never known his own father. Had spent a lifetime pretending he didn't miss what he'd never had. But he knew that he wanted to be Kenny's father with an intensity that bordered on physical pain.

The gumbo was perfect. Thick with small, tender okra, shrimp, scallops, tomatoes, onions and peppers. Spicy enough to wake up all Tom's taste buds. He slathered butter on a cornbread muffin and sighed. "Man, this is good."

Leslie seemed pleased by the sincere compliment. "I'm glad you like it. I got this recipe from a college friend who grew up in Baton Rouge. Kenny and I made a grocery run this afternoon, and since it was such a damp, cool day, hot soup sounded good for tonight."

"Great idea." Then Tom frowned. "You bought groceries today?"

She nodded and helped Kenny, who was lying in his infant seat at one end of the table, retrieve his fallen pacifier. "We were getting low on quite a few things."

"How did you pay for them?"

Her left eyebrow rose. "I wrote a check."

"From your own checking account?"

"The store clerks tend to frown when I write a check on anyone else's account. Forget it, Tom. I had enough to cover a few groceries."

He shook his head. "We'll have to go to the bank this week and get your name put on my accounts. I hadn't even thought about it before now."

Her cheeks were red, and she looked very uncomfortable. Leslie was a woman who was accustomed to paying her own way, being dependent on no one. Tom knew she didn't like the idea of being supported by him, and he wished he could convince her that he didn't mind at all. In fact, there was an old-fashioned, probably chauvinistic side of him that rather liked the idea.

"We'll talk about finances later," she muttered around a

bite of corn bread. She swallowed, took another sip of her tea, then said, "I got a call from Leo Weiss today."

Tom looked up from his meal in surprise. Leo Weiss was a longtime attorney in the area who had been Leslie's boss before she'd accepted the position in Chicago. "How did Leo find out you were here?"

She shrugged. "You know Leo. He seems to find out everything that goes on in this part of the state. Someone apparently told him that I was back in town and that you and I were married. He said he wanted to offer his congratulations—and to ask if I'd be interested in working for him again."

The taste of gumbo went suddenly flat on Tom's tongue. He set down his spoon. "He offered you a job?"

She nodded. "He said I was the best legal researcher he'd ever worked with. He told me I could work as many or as few hours as I wanted. At home or at the office or the university law library, as needed. Whoever told him about us also told him about the baby, I guess."

"He's being very accommodating." Tom knew he should probably sound a bit more enthusiastic. Leo *had* made a very generous offer, and Tom should be pleased for Leslie's sake. Not so selfishly worried on his own behalf.

"Yes."

Tom crumbled the last quarter of his muffin onto his bread plate. "So, what did you say?"

"First I asked him if he'd heard that I was fired from the firm in Chicago."

Tom wasn't surprised. Leslie was nothing if not honest. "Did he know?"

"He knew. He said he didn't care. He wants me on his team, and he's willing to work around my responsibilities to have me there." A slight crack in her voice illustrated how much her blunt-spoken, no-nonsense former employer's confidence meant to her.

Tom knew the answer even before he asked, "Are you going to do it?"

"Of course," she answered simply. "I worked too hard to get my education not to put it to use. As long as Leo is willing to be flexible so that I can be available whenever Kenny needs me, there's no reason for me not to work and pay my own way here. I told Leo I would start interviewing nannies and day-care centers and I'd get back to him as soon as I made arrangements for Kenny. I said it shouldn't take longer than a couple of weeks."

"Well." Tom used his thumb to shift his empty bowl away from him. "This is good news, Les. I knew you'd want to get back to work soon, and you always seemed happy with Leo and his associates."

"I was happy," she admitted. "I was such an idiot to walk away from...from everything I had here."

"You thought it was the right move at the time."

"I was wrong."

He didn't want to argue anymore about that. Probably because he secretly agreed with her. "I'll help you ask around about child care," he offered. "We'll want a lot of recommendations, of course."

She nodded. "I want the best for Kenny. I'll try to minimize the time I spend away from him, but when it's necessary for me to leave him in someone else's care, I want to be certain it's someone who loves children and is very experienced at taking care of them."

"Maybe Mom will know someone. I'll ask her next time I talk to her."

"She called this afternoon, by the way."

"She called you?" As far as Tom knew, Nina hadn't tried to phone him at the office.

"Yes. She said she just wanted to see how things were going, and to ask about Kenny. She said she wanted to have us over for dinner again soon."

Tom nodded and, knowing he was being petty, hoped that Steve Pendleton wouldn't be included.

"She asked if we'd started adoption proceedings yet," Leslie added. "She said she wanted to start bragging about her grandchild soon. And she said she wanted photographs to bore her friends with.''

Tom forced a smile. ''Mom's always loved babies. We'll have to watch her or she'll spoil Kenny rotten. But, then, that's what grandmothers are for, right?''

''Tom, were you really serious about wanting to adopt Kenny?'' Leslie asked the question tentatively, concealing her own feelings. It was the first time they'd mentioned adoption since Steve had brought the subject up on Saturday.

''I was very serious. I definitely think I should be included on the adoption papers. For one thing, everyone—especially Pendleton—would wonder why if I wasn't. And I want to do it. It's for Kenny's own protection. If anything happens to me, he'll be legally included in my insurance and estate and whatever. Or—God forbid—if anything happens to you, I would still have a right to keep him. I wouldn't want his future left unsettled again. You, er, *would* trust me to raise him, wouldn't you?''

''I wouldn't have come to you for help with him if I hadn't thought you'd make a wonderful father,'' Leslie answered simply, and to Tom's relief. ''If anything should happen to me, there's no one else I would rather entrust Kenny to. It's just—well, adoption is a lifelong commitment, Tom. No different from having a child of your own. Even if you and I...if something changes between us—''

''I would still consider myself Kenny's father,'' he interrupted flatly. While he understood why she needed to bring it up, he hated Leslie's implication that their marriage might not last. The thought of being without her again created a painful hole in his chest. ''I know exactly what I'm taking on, Leslie. And I want it.''

He glanced at the baby. Kenny was working his pacifier and staring back at Tom as if paying close attention to this important conversation. Tom reached out to touch the baby's cheek, and Kenny smiled around the pacifier.

''I want this, Leslie,'' Tom repeated. ''I'm not trying to take him away from you. I'll never threaten you the way Steve did. I only want you to include me in Kenny's life. I never had a dad, and I don't want Kenny to grow up as aware of that lack as I was.''

She drew a deep breath. "You've never really told me how you felt about not having had a father."

He shrugged, self-conscious as always at revealing his most private feelings. "It wasn't all that bad," he assured her. "My mom and I were always so close that I hardly felt abandoned or anything. And Zach's dad was a part of my life from the time I was just a little kid. He took us fishing, taught us both how to throw and catch, gave us those stern talks men have with their teenage boys, just as if I were Zach's brother. It was just…I would have liked a father of my own. And I want Kenny to have someone like that in his life. I want it to be me.''

"We'll talk to Leo," Leslie said, seeming to reach a decision. "I'm sure he'll start the proceedings for us."

Tom nodded, unable to find the words to express his emotions. He was deeply gratified, of course, that Leslie trusted him to become such a vital part of this child's life. He knew it wasn't easy for her to share the baby she had raised as her own from the day he was born. But he also knew that Leslie would never want to deny Kenny anything, including a devoted, willingly responsible father.

He wanted to tell her how much her faith in him meant to him. How much *she* meant to him. He wanted to ask her to promise she would never leave him again. He wanted to know that his wasn't the only heart at risk in their relationship. That their marriage was as real and as important to her as it was to him.

He wanted to tell her that he loved her. That he always had.

But that emotional wall he'd constructed kept him imprisoned as surely as it locked others out. The words remained trapped inside him.

And then Leslie spoke, and the moment was gone. "I have raspberry sorbet for dessert. It seemed appropriate today, for some reason," she added wryly, with a smiling glance at Kenny.

Tom managed to chuckle in response to her quip. "Let me help you clear these dishes away first, and we'll have our sorbet afterward."

Leslie didn't argue with that plan.

Zach telephoned later that evening. "The weatherman's calling for a nice weekend, highs in the low sixties," he said. "Want to go fishing Saturday morning?"

Tom was surprised. "Fishing?" he repeated blankly.

"Sure. It's been forever since we got out on the lake. Still remember how to cast?"

"I think I could handle it if I put my mind to it," Tom drawled.

"So, how about it? Or do you need to ask the little woman's permission first?"

Tom could hear the grin in Zach's voice. "Maybe you'd like to repeat that question—in just those words—to my wife," he suggested.

Zach laughed. "No, thanks. Lawyer Leslie would have me for a snack and go lookin' for lunch. She always did scare me, you know."

"She scares the hell out of me, too." Tom hoped Zach took the words as a joke. Tom wasn't so sure they were.

"So are we on? Saturday morning?"

"What time?"

"I'll pick you up at six. We'll catch the fish while they're still too sleepy to be smarter than we are."

Tom chuckled. "I don't know. Combined, we might have the IQ of the average fish. But we'll try to outsmart a couple of them, anyway. See you Saturday."

Sounding pleased, Zach completed the call quickly.

Sitting on the couch playing pat-a-cake with Kenny, Leslie looked up. "Was that Zach?"

"Yeah. He called you 'the little woman.' But he told me not to tell you because he was afraid you'd hurt him."

"And so he should be," Leslie said with a ferocious scowl.

"He, um, asked me if I wanted to go fishing early Saturday morning."

"Did he?" Leslie made a face at the baby, though she directed her words at Tom. "You'd better dress in layers. The mornings are still very cool."

Tom frowned at how easily she accepted his words. "Did you have something to do with this?"

She looked up at him then. "What do you mean?"

"Did you say something to Zach? Maybe suggest that he ask me to go fishing?"

"Of course not. I haven't spoken to Zach privately since the party."

"What did you say to Kim and Sami the other night?"

"Back to that again?" She sighed. "Tom, I had nothing to do with Zach's calling you. What's the big deal? You two used to go fishing all the time."

"We haven't fished together since the accident." Tom's words hung starkly in the air, expressing much more than he'd actually said.

"Then it's past time for you to go again, isn't it?"

He spoke through clenched teeth. "I don't want Zach taking me on some sort of pity outing."

"Quit being an idiot, Goose."

He blinked in response to her blunt comment.

She held his gaze firmly with her own. "Zach loves you. You were raised as brothers, and he still sees you as one. Just as you still feel the same way about him. Whatever it is that has come between you, you have to talk about it. And sitting in a fishing boat on a quiet, peaceful lake seems like a good time to start."

Tom frowned. "We're going fishing, not having a touchy-feely therapy session." Zach, he knew, was no more likely to have that kind of encounter in mind than Tom was. Even when their relationship was closest, they hadn't needed to use words to understand what the other was feeling.

She shook her head. "No one's asking you to bare your soul, Tom. We know better than to expect that from you."

He was taken aback by the touch of bitterness in her voice and by her use of the word "we," but she went on before he could speak.

"Just go fishing with him," she said a bit wearily. "If you want to talk, talk. If you don't, fish. But don't give up on a relationship that has lasted twenty-five years just because you've hit a little rocky spell."

"*Pb-b-b-bt.*"

"I think Kenny's telling me he's hungry again," she said, standing with the baby on her hip. "We really should start thinking about solid food soon, I guess. He seems to be hungry all the time now."

"Speaking of which," Tom said, deliberately pushing thoughts of Zach and the fishing trip to the back of his mind, "were there any of those cookies left that you made last night?"

Leslie rolled her eyes, then smiled at Kenny. "Like father, like son," she murmured.

And this time Tom knew her choice of words was deliberate.

It was with decidedly mixed emotions that he followed her to the kitchen in search of chocolate.

Chapter Thirteen

Ignoring the usual noisy bustle of the popular deli, Nina smiled at her son, who sat on the other side of the tiny corner table. "I'm so glad you were free to have lunch with me today," she said. "It seems like a long time since we were alone together."

"It's been a busy couple of weeks," Tom replied, looking up from the daily menu.

Two weeks, Nina mused. It had been only two weeks today since Leslie Harden had come back into Tom's life. And look how much had changed—for all of them—in such a short time. "It certainly has been busy," she murmured.

Tom set his menu aside. "How's business?"

She shrugged. "A bit slow this week. It usually is for a couple of weeks after Valentine's Day, but it will pick up again soon for Easter and proms and spring weddings."

"How's your very pregnant assistant? She looked ready to pop last time I saw her."

"Due any day. And still at the shop every morning at the

usual time. Lisa says she couldn't bear to sit at home and wait for a labor pain, so she would just as soon be working. Her doctor says it's okay, as long as she doesn't overtire herself, but I can't help fussing over her. I have this continuing nightmare that the baby's going to be born right there behind the sales counter.''

"Not the type of delivery your shop usually advertises, right?"

"Hardly." She was pleased that Tom had made a joke, however lame. He'd looked a bit somber when he'd arrived, making her worry that their lunch would be awkward. "And how are things in your household?"

"Pretty good," he answered, reaching for the iced water the server had brought with the menus. "Different, of course. After living alone for so long, it feels strange—but nice—to be sharing the house with two other people."

Nina smiled. "That sounds very promising."

He looked into his water glass. "We're making arrangements to have Leslie's things from Chicago delivered. She's been busily organizing the house so there will be room for everything she wants to keep. She says she didn't keep all that much, but she has a lot of legal books in storage there. As well as a computer and a fax machine and some other equipment. We'll have to find room for it all."

"That shouldn't be so hard."

"Yeah, I know. I told Leslie to do whatever she wants to the house. She can paint it orange, if she wants to. As far as I'm concerned, it's as much her home as it is mine now. It annoys me when she acts like a guest there."

"Give her time. It's an adjustment for both of you."

"Yeah, I know."

But Tom still looked troubled, she noticed. Since he had always talked to her about his problems, she asked carefully, "Is something wrong, dear? You are happy that you married Leslie, aren't you?"

His answer was succinct, and apparently sincere.

"I have no regrets about marrying Leslie."

"No regrets about taking on responsibility for the baby she brought with her into your marriage?" Nina suspected she already knew that answer.

Tom's eyes warmed and his expression softened, giving her his response before he said the words. "No regrets about that, either. Kenny's a great kid."

It was obvious that Tom had fallen head over heels in love with little Kenny, and Nina couldn't be happier about that. She suspected that his feelings for Leslie were more complicated, but no less intense.

"What about Leslie?" she asked, still choosing her words with care. "Do you think *she* has regrets?"

Tom was given a temporary reprieve from answering when the server approached to take their orders. After they'd made their selections and were alone again, he said, "I think Leslie's still convinced she made the right decision under the circumstances."

Nina frowned. "That sounds a bit bland. As if she'd had no other choice."

"She didn't think there was another easy choice. When she arrived, Steve seemed determined to take Kenny away from her. After we announced our marriage, he backed off. She accomplished what she wanted."

"And what about you, Tommy? Why did you marry her?"

"Because she needed me," he answered simply.

That had always been such a powerful motivation for Tom. Taking care of his mother, looking out for his friends, choosing a career helping and rescuing people—Tom was a man who desperately needed to be needed. But in this case, she didn't think he was telling her the entire story. Leslie wasn't the only one who needed something from this marriage.

She decided not to push that point just yet. "Leslie told me that Leo Weiss has invited her to rejoin his firm," she said, instead.

She watched the expression that crossed her son's face, and silently analyzed it.

"Yeah," Tom muttered. "She was really pleased by the

call. It meant a lot to her that he had so much faith in her, even after she'd left him to take that job in Chicago. And even after she was fired by that firm.''

"Leo is a good man. I've known him for years. He realizes Leslie is a committed and competent woman and that the circumstances in Chicago were beyond her control.''

Tom suddenly looked at his mother with narrowed eyes. ''You called him, didn't you?''

She cleared her throat and busied herself with checking her utensils for spots. ''I might have run into him a time or two lately.''

"And you just happened to mention that Leslie was back in town?''

"Of course I told him that you and Leslie were married now. That's big news in our family.''

"And maybe you just happened to tell him the details of why she lost her job in Chicago?''

"Maybe I did,'' she admitted.

"Damn it, Mom—''

"Why would you mind that?'' she asked, going on the offensive. ''It was obvious that Leslie's confidence had been shaken by her experiences, and I knew Leo would understand how difficult it must have been for her to have to choose between her family and her career. Leo is a man who has always valued family over everything else, and he has nothing but respect for others who do the same. I certainly didn't ask him to call Leslie and offer her a job. That was a choice he made on his own, and I'm sure he considers himself very fortunate to have her back on his team.''

"I'm sure he does.'' Tom's tone was unexpectedly grim.

Nina eyed him. ''You don't like it that Leslie's going back to work.''

"Leslie is certainly free to work or not as she chooses,'' he answered stiffly. ''Although—''

"Although?''

"She'll have to make arrangements for Kenny, of course. I've heard some horror stories about child-care workers. It's certainly reasonable that I would have some concerns about whom she chooses.'' He sounded as though he was trying to convince himself as much as her.

"Of course. But Leslie's not going to leave that baby with anyone she hasn't checked out thoroughly. Knowing Leslie, she'll require a dozen references and an FBI background check.''

Tom didn't smile at the exaggeration. "I would hope so."

"Kenny will be fine, Tom. I had no choice but to use day care for you, since I was our only source of income, and you turned out very nicely.''

"That's because I had such a nice mother,'' he replied with a smile that looked genuine enough to satisfy her.

Their food arrived, and they concentrated on their meal for a few minutes. And then Tom spoke, sounding as if he were forcing the words out. "Have you, uh, heard from Steve lately?''

"He called last night," she admitted, annoyed because she felt her cheeks warm in response to Steve's name. "We talked for a while.''

Two hours, to be exact.

"Going to be seeing him again soon?''

"He'll be spending the weekend here in town again.'' She didn't add that he was driving to Fayetteville that very evening. She would be seeing him in only a matter of hours, she thought with a quiver of anticipation.

Tom broke a potato chip in half with a snap. "He must be running up quite a hotel bill.''

Nina nearly choked on a bite of turkey-and-avocado sandwich. She reached hastily for her water, took a couple of swallows and changed the subject. "You won't mind if Steve visits the baby sometime while he's here, will you?''

Tom frowned at her, but shook his head. "Just give us a call first.''

"Of course.''

She wanted to ask him how he really felt about her seeing Steve. She wanted to know that nothing between her and Tom had changed during these past two momentous weeks. She wanted to ask if he loved Leslie as much as Nina suspected that he did, if he was as afraid of his feelings for Leslie as Nina was about the rapidly intensifying feelings she had for Steve. She wanted to know if her son was as confused and worried and excited and terrified as she was.

She asked him nothing. She wasn't sure the words would penetrate that maddeningly frustrating invisible wall he'd slid between them at some point between the arrival of their food and his question about Steve.

It was going to take a major explosion to break through that wall that her son so often and so efficiently hid behind, she mused. She just wasn't sure she had the right ammunition to get through.

She wondered if Leslie held the only key. Or if Leslie even knew Tom well enough to be aware of the wall's existence.

Lunch with his mother had not left Tom feeling particularly good about himself. In fact, he felt like a first-class jerk, he decided as he drove home later that afternoon.

He was obviously a very selfish man. Instead of being pleased for Leslie's sake that she'd been offered a position in the career she loved, he worried that her job would come between them. Would change the pleasant routines they'd established during their two short weeks of marriage.

Instead of being happy that Nina had someone new in her life, he was being jealous and inconsiderate, much like a small boy who didn't like sharing his mommy's full attention. He could try to convince himself that he was only being concerned for his mother's well-being, that he worried that she would be hurt or disappointed, that Steve Pendleton was using her for some reason of his own—but the truth was, Tom just didn't like the possibility that someone else would take his place in his mother's heart. Even though he knew full well that Nina would always love him.

His friends would hardly treat him like "Saint Tom" if they

knew how petty and possessive he really was, he thought, squirming uncomfortably in the driver's seat.

He parked in his carport and swung his legs out of the vehicle. He winced when his back spasmed in protest of his abrupt, twisting movement.

Leslie had married herself a real winner, he thought morosely. He was aware that he was sinking into self-pity, but he wasn't able to shrug it off. He made an effort to mask his mood as he entered his house.

Leslie had been cleaning again. The place practically sparkled, and the smell of cleaners was just detectable beneath the sweeter fragrance of her favorite vanilla-scented air freshener. He found Leslie in the spotless kitchen. With Kenny in her arms, she greeted him with a smile and a light kiss.

"I haven't started dinner yet. I thought I'd throw some steaks on the grill and cut up a salad to go with them," she said.

"Why don't I make dinner tonight," he suggested impulsively. "You shouldn't have to do all the cooking. I'm perfectly capable of grilling steaks and making salad. You and Kenny go watch TV or something, and I'll let you know when dinner's ready."

She looked surprised, but agreeable. "I'd be happy to help," she offered.

He shook his head. "Not necessary. Go relax."

She reached up to kiss him again, lingering a bit longer this time. "Sounds like a good plan to me," she murmured. "And after dinner—when Kenny's asleep—maybe we should both relax, hmm?"

"I'll cook fast," he promised huskily.

Leslie laughed and carried the baby out of the kitchen. Feeling uncomfortably warm all of a sudden, Tom shed his jacket and rolled up his sleeves to wash up. He splashed some cold water on his face while he was at it.

Leslie woke before dawn Saturday to the sound of muted country music coming from the radio-alarm on the nightstand. Tom silenced it quickly with a slap of his hand.

"Sorry," he said, his voice morning husky. "Go back to sleep. I'll see you when I get back from the fishing trip."

The room was still pitch-dark, with Tom barely visible in the shadows. Leslie reached out to him, reluctant to give up the warm comfort of his body beside her in the bed. "Were you going to leave without saying goodbye?" she asked drowsily.

He leaned over her. She felt the brush of his hand against her cheek, the gesture tender and sweet. "I didn't want to disturb you," he said. "It's a ridiculous time to get up."

Leslie chuckled. "Why are you doing it, then?"

"Zach says we'll catch more fish if they're too sleepy to outsmart us."

"Sounds exactly like something Zach would say."

She slid her hand up his bare arm, guided by touch rather than vision, picturing the tanned skin and taut muscles in her mind. "Mmm," she murmured. "You feel so warm. Nice."

"Leslie."

His voice had taken on a deep undertone that she recognized.

"You're making it harder for me to get out of this bed."

She ran her hand across his chest, fingertips threading through the light pelt of hair. "I'm not trying to detain you," she assured him, and walked her fingers up his shoulder to tickle the hair at the back of his neck.

He groaned. "You certainly aren't pushing me out, either."

She lifted her head to brush a kiss across his chin. "No," she admitted.

His mouth sought hers, sliding over her cheek, settling onto her lips. The kiss was deep, slow, savoring. He didn't lift his head when he murmured, "I really should be getting ready. Zach will be here in an hour."

Knowing she should probably let him get up, she nuzzled against him anyway, enjoying the musky scent of sleep-warmed male, the rasp of morning beard, the accelerated beat of the pulse in his throat. There hadn't been one morning she'd spent away from him that she hadn't woken with thoughts of him at the back of her mind. The past week had brought back all the happy memories of the time they'd spent together before, as well as new insecurities about how long they would be together this time. But she couldn't imagine ever taking for granted the simple joy of waking in Tom's arms.

He shifted his weight against her, making no effort to hide the evidence of his response to her. He wanted her. She wasn't sure exactly what else he felt for her, but she had no doubt that he wanted her.

"An hour, hmm?" She pressed against him and nipped at his lower lip. "So how long does it take you to get ready for a fishing trip?"

"Fifteen minutes, if I have to hurry."

"I think you're going to have to hurry this morning," she whispered against his lips.

He rolled over to press her into the bedclothes with the weight of his body. "I think you're right," he muttered, and crushed her mouth beneath his.

"Running a little late this morning, aren't you? What did you do—oversleep?" Zach asked when he and Tom were under way, fifteen minutes later than they'd originally planned.

"Yeah, something like that."

From behind the wheel of his pickup, Zach slanted an amused look at Tom. "Uh-huh."

Tom cleared his throat.

"Hey, this is the first time we've had a chance to talk since you married Lawyer Leslie," Zach commented, as if the thought had just that moment occurred to him.

"Yeah, I guess it is."

"So, are you going to tell me how it all came about? I mean, you left Sami's dinner party a single guy, not even dating anyone as far as I knew, and the next time I saw you, a couple of days later, you were married. I gotta admit, it caught me off guard."

"I know." Tom knew, as well, that Zach had been hurt. Tom just didn't know how to express his regret of that in words.

He and Zach had never formally apologized to each other. Their rare and brief altercations had usually been settled by rueful grins and sheepish looks, a few halfhearted punches on the arm, a couple of beers. He didn't know if any of those would be appropriate in this case.

Maybe a fishing outing would serve a similar purpose.

But he supposed an apology wouldn't hurt, either. It was what Leslie probably would have advised him to do. "Er, sorry," he said.

"Sorry you didn't tell me, or sorry you got married," Zach quipped, proving he was no more comfortable than Tom with "touchy-feely" conversation between them.

"The, uh, former. Being married isn't so bad, actually." Tom couldn't help smiling as he remembered the way Leslie had seen him off that morning.

"It certainly has its benefits," Zach agreed, his own memories deepening his voice.

It was almost an hour's drive to the fishing spot they favored, so Tom shifted into a more comfortable position on the truck seat, adjusted his seat belt and reached for the large, insulated container of coffee he'd brought with him. "I need caffeine," he said. "Want me to pour you a cup?"

"Not yet, thanks. I drank half a pot before I left the house. Any more right now and I'll be bouncing out of the boat."

Tom chuckled and glanced automatically over his shoulder at the boat Zach towed on a trailer behind the pickup. It was still dark out, but he could dimly see the boat in the taillights of the truck. "The rig looks good. You've been working on it."

"Kim bought me new seats for Christmas. She thought it was a weird present, but I'd been wanting some. This will be my first chance to try them out."

Tom shifted in his seat again. His leg was aching a bit this morning. Probably from the damp, cold, early-morning air. Or maybe he'd been a bit too energetic with Leslie while still stiff from sleep. He recalled the over-the-counter painkillers he'd tossed into the pack he'd brought along with him, and thought he'd probably take one when he could do so without calling Zach's attention to his actions.

But he should have remembered that there wasn't much Zach missed.

"Your leg bothering you?" Zach asked a bit too casually.

"Just a little stiff," Tom replied, equally offhand. "It'll loosen up."

"So how have you been lately? Your back and all, I mean."

The gruff wording told Tom how carefully Zach was trying to question him without annoying him.

Maybe a couple of weeks earlier Tom would have shrugged off the well-intended questions, maybe even gotten chippy and defensive. But that was before Leslie had made him acknowledge to himself how badly he missed the closeness he and Zach had once shared. And to concede that he was at least halfway responsible for the awkwardness between them now. Which meant that he was going to have to make an equal effort to bridge the gap, no matter how badly he hated talking about his weaknesses.

"I'm okay, Zach," he said quietly. "I have a few bad days, but even more good ones. I went to Little Rock last month to see the orthopedic surgeon."

"What did he say?"

"That I've healed better than he expected when he first saw me fifteen months ago. That I probably won't heal any more than I have now, but with proper care, I won't get any worse, either. I guess that's a pretty good report."

"You, uh, never got all the movement or feeling back in your right foot?"

"No. The paralysis there is permanent. But it could have been worse," Tom said matter-of-factly. "I could have been left a paraplegic. Came pretty darn close, for that matter. Most days, I consider myself damned lucky."

"And on the other days?"

"I mope around and feel sorry for myself. Or at least I used to. Now when I start feeling like that, Leslie kicks my butt and reminds me of how good I've got it."

Zach chuckled. "She's a scary woman."

"Yeah. But good for me, I think."

"So do I. I was a little worried when you got married so quickly. Frankly, I wasn't sure if you knew what you were doing. I was aware you'd been pretty tight with Leslie before she moved away, but you'd convinced me that it had been an amicable parting and that you weren't carrying a torch or anything, so I wasn't sure why you suddenly married her. I thought it had something to do with her sister's kid..."

He let that sentence trail into a delicate question.

Tom shrugged and took a careful sip of hot coffee before answering. "Maybe to an extent," he said finally. "We both thought it was better for Kenny to have two parents. We're going to adopt him. His legal name will be 'Kenneth Pendleton Lowery,' and I fully intend to raise him as my son."

"He's a lucky kid. You'll be a good dad."

Tom was touched. "Thanks, Zach."

"And Leslie's obviously devoted to the boy."

"Completely. She's already his mother, in every way that matters. Crystal—the biological mother—knew what she was doing when she asked Leslie to raise her son."

"I never thought of Leslie as the maternal type. Thought she was all hard edges and career, you know? Looks like I was wrong."

Tom wanted to agree again. He wanted to believe that Leslie wouldn't be caught up again in her career when she went back to work. And he *did* believe it, in a way. He couldn't imagine her ever putting a job, any job, before Kenny. She loved that baby too much, had already sacrificed everything for him. She wouldn't hesitate to do so again.

As for where Tom stood in her priorities—well, that was the question that haunted him. She'd walked away from him for a career before. And while she'd made a few comments to the effect that she regretted doing so, he still worried that things would change between them when Leslie was back on her feet financially and emotionally.

When she no longer needed him.

Zach slowed for a steep, winding curve, negotiated it carefully, then picked up speed again, skillfully pulling the trailer along the twisting, mountainous roads toward Beaver Lake. This rural route wasn't heavily populated. A few old houses and mobile homes lined the road, only a few showing evidence that the residents were awake at this early hour on a Saturday morning.

The rosy sunrise was kind to the area, softening the peeling wood and patched roofs, the old cars sitting on blocks in dirt yards, the rusty dog pens and ramshackle storage buildings. Northwest Arkansas was a region of stark economic contrasts, containing both great wealth and staggering poverty. As a fireman, Tom had fought just as hard to save the old, decrepit homes as he had the expensive, country-club estates.

"Tom," Zach said after they'd driven a few minutes in silence. "I hope Leslie and Kenny will make you happy. God knows you deserve it."

"Zach, don't—"

"No, let me say this and then I'll drop it." Zach sounded as though he'd rehearsed a speech and was determined to deliver it, no matter what resistance he encountered.

"For the past year or so, I've felt so damned guilty around you. It wasn't anything you did," he added quickly, when Tom automatically started to protest. "It was my own guilt. I know you've never blamed me for that accident, and intellectually I realize it was more the fault of the guy who inadvertently slammed into us, if the blame falls on anyone—but I've never forgotten that I was driving. I've never forgotten the way you looked, all crumpled on the ground, bloody and absolutely motionless. At first, I—I thought you were dead."

The break in Zach's voice tightened Tom's chest. "Zach, this really isn't necessary."

"Damn it, Lowery, shut up and let me finish."

Scowling, Tom shut up.

"My point is," Zach said doggedly, "that I've felt lousy because, except for a bruised and sprained shoulder that healed in a couple of weeks, I wasn't even hurt in that accident. You went through hell, not knowing at first whether you'd ever even walk again, and then all those months of painful therapy, and being left with physical problems that kept you from returning to the only job you ever wanted to do. You were the one who talked me into being a firefighter, remember? It was your dream all those years, not mine, though I've loved every minute of it. But you were the one who had to leave it."

"I like my work now," Tom interrupted, feeling the need to make that point clear. "Not the mundane stuff, of course, but arson investigation is something that always interested me. Now I have a chance to get into it more fully. I'm signing up for classes all over the country starting this summer and I've been doing a lot of reading and studying. I might even teach a class or two sometime. I've also thought about teaching search-and-rescue classes. I've always liked sharing what I've learned."

"You'd be good at it," Zach said slowly. "You really want to be an instructor?"

"It's something I've been looking into. I have no intention of spending the rest of my life regretting a freak accident. I've still got things I want to do."

"I'm glad to hear that. For a while, you didn't even seem to want to talk about work or search-and-rescue or any of the things we used to do."

"For a while, I didn't want to talk about it," Tom admitted. "I had to go through my own adjustment period, I guess. Mom called it a period of mourning—which is an exaggeration, of course, but sort of true. It took me a while to form a new plan for my future, but I'm getting there."

Zach exhaled in relief. "Man, that's good to hear. I knew you'd come around, of course," he added quickly. "But I'm glad you're showing some enthusiasm for it."

"You knew I'd never be content to sit back and draw disability pay."

"I knew that never even crossed your mind," Zach agreed. "I thought you were going to take Art Sample's head off when he suggested it."

Tom snorted, remembering how furious he'd been when a former co-worker had advised him to draw total disability and spend the rest of his life fishing and taking it easy. Tom couldn't imagine a more boring and pointless existence. He was a giver, not a taker. As far as he was concerned, no one owed him anything he didn't earn with his own hands.

"Anyway," Zach went on, "it wasn't just work. It just seemed that I had everything I wanted. My health. My work. A wife I love more than anything. I hated the thought that you—the most deserving guy I've ever known—had been left without any of that. I felt...guilty."

"You should have felt stupid," Tom said bluntly, "because you were. I never begrudged you a damn thing, Zach McCain, and you know it. I never blamed you—or anyone else—for that accident, and I was nothing but pleased that you and Kim seemed so happy together. And I ought to punch your teeth in for letting some dumb guilt complex get between us."

"Hey, I wasn't the only one who let stuff get between us," Zach answered defensively, apparently more satisfied than offended by Tom's insults. "You've got to admit you've been acting weird lately. Finding excuses not to get together. Refusing to talk about the things we used to like. Keeping everything to yourself. Even getting married without telling anyone."

"Okay, so maybe I've been partly to blame," Tom conceded. "I had some issues to work out, and I needed to do that on my own. But mostly I couldn't stand the thought that any of you guys were feeling sorry for me. And sometimes you acted as though you did. You treated me like a noble martyr or something, and I hated that."

Zach's momentary silence told Tom that the words had struck home. Hard. "Damn," he said after a while. "Did I really act like that?"

"Yeah. Sometimes. You jerk."

"So how come you didn't beat some sense into me?"

"'Cause you probably would have apologized for hurting my fist with your face," Tom muttered. "And then I would have had to kill you. And that might have upset Kim, who didn't deserve it."

"Hell, Tom, I'm sorry. Trust me, I won't ever be nice to you again."

"You'd damned well better not."

"It's a promise. In fact, I might just make you bait my hooks today so I don't get those slimy old worm guts all over my nice, clean fingers."

"Up yours, McCain."

Zach laughed. It was the first time in months that his laughter sounded as easy and comfortable as it had before the accident. The first time since then that Tom felt he and Zach were really communicating. Not just verbally, but mentally, the way they always had before.

It felt good. Even if they had been forced to go through some "touchy-feely" stuff to get to this point.

Content, Tom leaned back against his seat and sipped coffee from the plastic lid of his thermos. The sky was growing much lighter in the east now. By the time he and Zach got to the lake, it would just be daylight. The closer they got, the worse the narrow roads would become, until finally they would be negotiating what was little more than a twisty, rutted, hair-raising trail. He and Zach had made the trip more times than Tom could count since the first time Zach's dad had taken them fishing together when they were still both missing their front teeth.

He entertained himself for a while listening to the country music from the radio and looking for signs of life in the few houses they passed. Tom had always liked getting out this early, watching the rest of the world come slowly awake. He liked being out on the lake on a cold, clear morning, listening to the water lap against the bottom of a fishing boat, watching his breath hover in the air in front of him, breathing in the pungent smells of outboard exhaust and fish.

He hadn't realized until now just how much he'd allowed himself to miss while recuperating.

He had opened his mouth to make some casual comment to Zach, when he suddenly sat bolt upright, the dregs of his coffee sloshing in the plastic cup. "Zach, look at that house!"

Zach looked inquiringly in the direction Tom indicated, swore beneath his breath and slammed on the brakes. Their experienced eyes had seen the same ominous signs—a red glow in the darkened back windows of an old wood-sided house, thin billows of smoke pouring from beneath the eaves.

The house was on fire. And if its residents were inside, they were probably still asleep, unaware of the danger surrounding them.

"Call it in!" Zach yelled, opening his door at the same time he cut the truck's engine. He was out of the vehicle and running toward the house almost before the words were out of his mouth.

Tom grabbed the cellular phone beneath Zach's dash. Moments later, assured that rescue crews were en route, he jumped from the truck and ran after Zach. Zach stood on a tiny, rickety front porch, hammering with his fist on the locked front door, yelling for someone to wake up and respond to him.

He glanced at Tom. "I just know someone's in there. I'm going in."

Already they could hear the mounting roar of flames, smell burning wood and insulation, taste the oily smoke billowing from beneath the eaves. "Go!" Tom shouted.

Zach raised his right foot and smashed at the flimsy wooden door. It took him only three solid kicks to splinter the jamb and gain admittance. Smoke poured out through the opening. Staying low, his jacket covering his mouth, Zach plunged inside.

Tom was right behind him.

Chapter Fourteen

Almost as soon as they were inside, Tom and Zach heard a woman suddenly start to scream from somewhere in the back of the house.

"Fire!" she shrieked. "Oh, God, Joey! Emily! Get out!"

Tom heard Zach crash into something heavy in the smoky shadows and swear, then yell in the direction of the hysterical voice, "Keep your head low and head for the nearest exit! Hurry!"

A heavyset woman in a flannel nightgown emerged suddenly from a hallway, screaming in panic. "The kids," she sobbed. "I can't find the kids. There's too much smoke back there."

Zach grabbed the woman's arms and swung her toward Tom. "Get her outside," he ordered. "I'll get the kids."

"Joey! Emily!" The woman sobbed and moved as if to run back down the hallway. Already flames were licking at the tops of the walls around them, sucking the air from the room.

Coughing, Tom managed to half drag the woman toward

the front door. She outweighed him, and panic made her movements awkward and unpredictable, so he didn't have an easy time of it. He wouldn't be able to carry her if she collapsed, he thought grimly.

"Zach will get your kids, ma'am," he kept saying, trying to calm her. "You have to get out of here now. You'll be waiting outside for them when he brings them out."

"Joey. Emily." She choked the names repeatedly, as if afraid to stop. "Please, help them."

Something cracked above their heads. Glowing sparks showered around them, stinging exposed skin. The house was old and would burn like tinder, Tom knew from experience. The air was thick and noxious. He shoved the woman out the front door, his thoughts remaining inside the burning building with Zach and the woman's children.

She was wailing now, no longer resisting him, but limp with despair. "My kids," she moaned. "My babies."

Tom had just managed to get her safely away from the house, when Zach stumbled out the front door, hacking and soot covered, a coughing boy about ten years old slung over his shoulder.

"Joey!" the woman screamed, and snatched at the boy, who was now crying and reaching for her. "Oh, God, where's Emily? Her room's the last one down the hall. *Emily!*"

Tom was already running, past Zach, who was bent double trying to catch his breath. The noise inside the house was deafening—the hungry shriek of fire, burning debris crashing down from the rafters, hot metals hissing, popping. And somewhere, in all that smoke and chaos, a little girl screamed, "Mommy!"

"Tom!" Zach shouted after him. "You can't—"

Ignoring the warning, ignoring his aches and discomfort, Tom covered his face as best he could with his jacket and threw himself into the inferno.

Nina woke with a start at just after 7 a.m. She didn't know what had disturbed her. Steve slept soundly in the bed beside her and the apartment complex was Saturday-morning quiet. There was no reason for her to have awakened with her heart pounding with dread, her pulse racing in anxiety.

She knew she wouldn't go back to sleep. She slipped silently from the bed and tiptoed to the window to peek outside, clutching her prim nightgown to her throat. She saw nothing unusual in the parking lot below her bedroom window; hardly anyone was stirring at this hour.

"Nina?" Steve yawned and rolled to sit on the edge of the bed. "What's wrong?"

"I don't know," she admitted, turning to face him.

"Bad dream?"

"I don't think so. Just…a bad feeling." She shivered.

Steve stood and crossed the room to wrap his arms around her. Though he wore nothing but close-fitting boxers, his body was warm against her. He kissed the top of her head. "I'll make some coffee and we'll talk about it."

She nodded, grateful that he hadn't brushed off her attack of nerves as foolish.

Already dressed in jeans and a sweater, Leslie was putting a load of baby clothes in the washer, when the telephone rang. It was still early, just after seven-thirty, but she hadn't been able to go back to sleep after Tom left, and then Kenny had woken up and demanded his morning bottle. She'd already fed him and put him in his playpen with some toys.

She understood now why parents of babies always laughed when other people talked of sleeping in on weekends.

It surprised her that anyone was calling this early. She wondered if it was Tom, telling her something he'd forgotten or changing the time he'd estimated that he would be home. She snatched up the receiver on the third ring. "Hello?"

"Leslie, it's Kim. I'm on my way over, okay?"

Leslie felt her knees lose their stiffening. She sagged against the counter. She had to force the words past the lump of fear in her throat. "What's happened to Tom?"

"I just got a call from Washington Regional. Zach and Tom

are there, but I've been assured that they're both going to be okay. I have to pass close to your house on the way, so I'll pick you and the baby up, all right?"

"Were they in an accident?"

"No. Apparently, they went into a burning house and saved a family." Kim's voice caught in a cross between a laugh and a sob. "Why was I not surprised to hear that?"

Leslie raised a hand to massage her suddenly aching forehead. "How soon can you be here?"

"Fifteen minutes. Will you be ready?"

"I'll be ready."

She hung up the phone and hurried to get the baby ready to go out. She felt as though she'd been transported back in time, to those months when she and Tom had been together before, when he'd worked as a firefighter and spent many of his days off on search-and-rescue missions. She'd always dreaded calls like this. Tom's reckless disregard of his own safety when it came to rescue work had been a constant source of fear for her. She'd been even more frustrated by his choice of recreational activities—rock climbing, white-water rafting, skydiving, bungee jumping—whatever took his fancy. Almost always something that involved a risk of life and limb.

Part of what she'd been running from when she'd left Fayetteville was her fear of something terrible happening to Tom. Even then, when she'd been afraid to let him know how strong her feelings for him really were, when the thought of a lifelong commitment had left her cold with fear born of painful childhood experiences, she hadn't been able to face the constant dread of a devastating telephone call.

She knew now that she'd lulled herself into a false sense of security since she'd returned to find Tom sidelined from the risk taking that had been so much a part of his life before. Obviously, it was time for them to talk—about their feelings and about their future. Knowing how Tom felt about showing his emotions, she was aware that it was going to be up to her to initiate that serious conversation.

If this marriage was going to work, one of them had to take

the first step. Her father had never bothered to stick around to work out the problems in his marriages; he'd always chosen to cut his losses and run when things weren't going just his way. Leslie's mother had never fought to save her first two failed marriages, but had whined and complained about how hard life was and had drifted into the next marriage with little hope for success.

Maybe Leslie had been following her father's poor example when she'd let her ambition and her frustration with Tom's emotional reserve spur her into leaving a job she'd loved to move to a city where she'd never really mattered to anyone until Crystal had found her there. Or maybe she'd been imitating her mother, giving up without a fight when a relationship started to fall apart.

Now it was time to find out if Ben and Martha Harden's daughter had what it took to make a marriage work—through both easy times and difficult ones. But first she had to make certain that Tom was all right.

She thought he must be safe—Kim surely wouldn't have been quite so calm if Zach or Tom had been seriously injured—but Leslie was consumed with a need to assure herself that her husband was unharmed. And it wasn't hard to figure out that it was love that prompted her fear for him.

"Feeling better?" Steve asked Nina later that morning. They'd breakfasted on coffee and orange juice and bagels with cream cheese. Nina had washed her face, combed her hair, brushed her teeth and dressed in comfortable, casual clothing. Steve had taken a quick shower and pulled on a sweatshirt and jeans. They planned to spend the day taking it easy, enjoying each other's company away from the curious eyes of Nina's neighbors and friends.

"Yes," she answered him. "I'm feeling much better. I don't know what came over me this morning."

"Must have been a bad dream you don't remember."

"Perhaps," she agreed, though she wasn't at all sure that explained it. She glanced at her watch. "I wonder if it's too early to call Tommy. Just to make sure everything's okay there."

Steve probably didn't intend for her to hear his faint sigh, but she did. And she bristled. "I just want to make sure," she said defensively.

"I didn't say anything."

"No, but you thought it. 'There goes Nina being the over-protective mother again.'"

He frowned reproachfully at her. "Don't put words in my head."

"I can't help it. It bothers me that you get all tense every time I mention my son."

"If that's true, it has nothing to do with whether I like your son or not. I do like him, as a matter of fact. I made that decision when I watched him with my nephew. My only concern is that you're letting him come between us. In fact, you seem to be deliberately putting him there."

Nina toyed with the bracelet on her right wrist—a thin, gold chain Tom had given her last Mother's Day. "I don't know what you're talking about."

Steve drew a deep breath. "I want to marry you, Nina Lowery. And I have a bad feeling that the first words out of your mouth when I propose are going to be something along the lines of 'what will Tom think?'"

She was stunned. Utterly, completely stunned. "You can't possibly be thinking about marriage."

"You're telling me what I'm thinking again," he grumbled. "And, again, you're wrong."

"Steve, we have known each other only two weeks."

"How long does it take to fall in love?" he asked quizzically. "Is there some sort of formula I haven't heard about?"

Love. Her knees folded. Fortunately, there was a couch behind her. She sat rather heavily, her hands falling limply in her lap.

Steve smiled without much humor. "I can see I've swept you right off your feet."

He sat beside her and took her cold hands in his warmer

ones. "I love you, Nina. I have from the beginning. I admire what you've accomplished. I respect your intelligence and your humor. I love your mind, your face, your body, your passions. I want you in my life every day, not just on convenient weekends."

"Do you always make up your mind this quickly about things?" she asked weakly, shaken by his ardent words.

"Always." His mouth twisted ruefully. "Unfortunately, that's one of the things about me that drove my sister crazy. When Ben Harden dumped my mother, four years after seducing her away from my father, he left her totally devastated. She was an insecure, dependent woman who wasn't accustomed to making decisions or facing responsibilities. My own father had remarried and moved away after the ugly divorce, and we saw him very rarely after that. Crystal was still just a kid, so someone had to step in and take charge of our family. I decided it might as well be me."

"How old were you?"

"Seventeen. A senior in high school. I got a job, helped mother find part-time work, and then I took over paying the bills and maintaining the household. I got in the habit of giving orders and having them followed without question. I'm afraid that I was never able to change that habit where Crystal was concerned. I always wanted what was best for her—and I guess I always thought I knew what that was. When she rebelled, I tried to coerce her into going along, until finally we weren't even speaking. I hated the way she lived, the choices she made, and she was equally determined to live on her terms, not mine. By the time I understood that she had the right to make her own decisions, it was too late to make amends with her. She wanted nothing more to do with me. I always thought that someday she'd forgive me enough to repair some of the damage between us…but then it was too late. Leslie called to tell me that Crystal was dead, and that her son was all I had left of my family."

Nina had heard most of this before, of course, but it still hurt her to hear the pain and self-recrimination in Steve's voice. "You can't keep blaming yourself, Steve. As you said, Crystal made her own choices."

"I know. And it's still difficult for me to accept them—which is the reason I instinctively resisted when I found out she'd asked Leslie, instead of me, to raise her son. That was probably the wisest decision Crystal ever made, actually. I see that now. I've been judging Leslie by her father's actions, and that was wrong."

"Yes. Leslie is a good woman. I'm very fond of her. I just hope..." Nina bit her lip.

"What?"

"She hurt my son very badly once. I pray that she doesn't do so again. But I'll admit Tommy was probably at fault in that himself. He can be a bit difficult at times. Still, no matter what happens between Tom and Leslie, they'll both make sure that Kenny doesn't suffer for it."

"I'm sure you're right. And so will I. He is my nephew—and once I persuade you to marry me, he'll be my...what? Stepgrandson?"

Nina shook her head and tried to pull her hands out of his grasp. "Don't talk that way. We can't—it's not—you aren't—"

"You're stammering," he interrupted gently, refusing to release her. "Slow down and tell me why you're so frightened at the thought of marrying me. I won't rush you. I'll give you all the time you need to make your decision. But I thought it only fair to warn you of my intentions."

"Steve, you aren't thinking clearly. We can't get married."

"Why not?"

"I'm too old for you." She rushed on when he opened his mouth to speak, a look of irritation on his face. "I know it doesn't mean much to you now, but think about it, Steve. I'm forty-seven. I have a thirty-year-old son who's making me a grandmother by adoption soon. I have a comfortable life and a thriving business here. I can't risk giving all that up only to have you decide later that you've made a terrible mistake."

"I'll never think that." His voice rang with sincerity as his fingers tightened forcefully around hers.

She refused to be silenced before she'd had her say. "You're a young man. Not even forty yet. You've never married, never had children of your own. You have plenty of time for all that now that your business is established and successful. I've raised my child. While I suppose I'm still biologically capable of having another baby, I simply don't want to start over at this point in my life. Even ten years ago, it might have been different, but now the thought of 2 a.m. feedings and diaper changes and colic and teething—well, I just don't want it. Do you really want to sacrifice your own chance at being a father?"

"If I had strong yearnings toward parenthood, don't you think I'd have done something about it before now?" he asked in return. "I was willing to raise Kenny, of course—ready to fight for him, obviously—but only because I felt obligated to make sure he would have a good home. At the time, I wasn't sure that Leslie was the best choice. Now that I know she is, I'm perfectly content to just be his uncle. I like children, but it's nice to be able to play with them and then send them home with their parents. I love the idea of having plenty of time with you—time for long walks and uninterrupted conversations, time to travel and explore new interests, time to enjoy the rest of our lives together."

She almost quivered with longing. Everything he said sounded heavenly to her—but could she really trust him not to change his mind later? When she turned fifty and he was only forty-one? Or ten years after that, when some men started looking for younger, "trophy" brides?

Was two weeks really long enough to fall in love, despite the intensity of what she felt for Steve now?

"I've made some serious mistakes in my past relationships," she admitted slowly. "I don't want to do so again."

"You were little more than a child yourself when Tom was born. You can't keep blaming yourself for that mistake."

"No. And I've long since stopped thinking of Tom as a

mistake. He's been nothing but a blessing to me. But I was a grown woman the next time I got involved in a disastrous affair. And it could have been devastating for me, and for Tommy, if I hadn't gotten myself out of it just in time.''

"What happened?"

She shrugged. "I had turned thirty. Tommy was thirteen, in school all day, and already involved in sports and outdoor activities. He spent a lot of time with Zach and Zach's father, and I encouraged that because I knew my son needed a good man's influence in his life. But I was lonely. And vulnerable. And when I met Al Campbell, I was an easy target for his romantic overtures.''

Steve winced. "This sounds very much like a married-man story.''

"That's exactly what it is,'' she said with a self-disgusted sigh. "I was such an idiot. Fell right into an old cliché. He was a traveling salesman, selling floral supplies to small shops like mine. He came to town twice a month, always during the middle of the week. We had long lunches together—first at restaurants and then at my apartment. He called me in the evenings, after Tommy was in bed, and we talked for hours, giggling like teenagers. He convinced me to keep our affair quiet at first, assuring me that it was much more romantic that way. He talked about the day we'd get married and he would become a father to my son, whom he'd never even met. And then I found out, quite by accident, that he already had a son. As well as a wife and two daughters. I was nothing more than the 'other woman.' A stupid, blind, pathetic dupe.''

"Nina, don't—"

She refused to look at him. This time, she was able to free her hands with a swift, firm tug. She wrapped her arms around herself, humiliated and depressed. "Thank God Tom never found out about that miserable episode. It was bad enough that I raised him as an illegitimate child, but to have him find out that I'd nearly destroyed another family was more than I could have borne.''

"Everyone makes mistakes, Nina. I've made plenty. My

sister died without telling me goodbye because I'd made so many mistakes with her. But should we spend the rest of our lives alone to atone for our misjudgments? Shouldn't we be given a chance to be happy, and to try to make wiser decisions in the future?''

"Don't you see?" she whispered. "That's exactly what I'm trying to do. For once, I'm trying to be cautious and sensible and not led by my emotions into making another mistake. I don't want to be hurt again. I don't want to hurt my son. And I don't want to let you rush us into a commitment that could easily prove to be all wrong for you.''

Steve was silent and still for several long moments. When he spoke, his voice was grim. "Now I know how much Crystal must have hated it when I tried to make decisions for her own good, when I didn't trust her to know her own mind.''

"It isn't that I don't trust you, Steve," Nina said anxiously.

His dark eyes were sad when he looked at her. "If you really trusted me, you would know that I would never make a promise I didn't absolutely intend to keep. If you trusted me, you would believe that I love you, and that I will never stop loving you. If you don't feel the same way about me— if I've misread your responses to me—I could accept that. I'd hate it, but I'd accept it. But I cannot agree to having you send me away out of some misguided sense that you're doing me a favor.''

Nina groaned softly and covered her face with her hands. She didn't know what to do. Should she follow her heart or her mind? Listen to the warnings of past mistakes, or heedlessly risk making new ones? Should she be strong and sensible, or let love overpower caution?

"What would Tommy say?" she murmured helplessly.

Beside her, Steve cursed beneath his breath. "I knew it," he said. "I knew that's what you would say. Damn it, Nina, do you love me or not?''

She dropped her hands and stared at him, a dozen different responses forming in her mind, only one of them true. And then the telephone rang, interrupting her before she could blurt out the answer.

It had been a very long time since Tom had felt like a hero. A long time since he'd thought of himself as one.

He'd grown accustomed to thinking of himself as damaged. Weakened. Slow. Someone confined to the sidelines while others did the rescuing. That image of himself had haunted him. Undermined his confidence. It had changed him in ways he hadn't quite realized until circumstances had forced him to take a new look at himself and his capabilities.

He'd almost let the accident take a lot more from him than his former physical agility.

Showered and changed, the smell of smoke at least partly eradicated, he sat at his dining-room table, Kenny in his lap. Zach sat across the table, also damp and fresh scrubbed, having borrowed Tom's shower and changed into clean clothing Kim had brought with her in response to his call from the hospital. Leslie had insisted on making lunch for everyone, and Kim had offered to help. Tom and Zach sat back and enjoyed the attention they were getting.

Tom balanced Kenny between his hands as the baby bounced on the balls of his tiny feet. "Look at him put his weight on his feet," Tom bragged, his voice still somewhat hoarse from smoke inhalation. "He'll be walking in no time."

"Running, you mean. Toddlers never walk when they can run," Zach, who had several nieces and nephews, remarked, his own voice gravelly. Both of them still coughed occasionally, their lungs irritated by the smoke and fumes and grit they'd inhaled.

Kenny plucked at the thick gauze bandage on Tom's left hand, then bounced again, babbling noisily.

"Your hand okay?" Zach asked casually, glancing at the bandage that had momentarily claimed the baby's attention.

"It's not the first time I've been burned. Won't be the last," Tom said matter-of-factly. There were other minor burns on his neck and his left shoulder, and one angry red streak down his left cheek, but none of them was serious. The muscle relaxers he'd been given at the hospital had dulled the spasms in his abused back. He was only dimly aware of the ache now, the medication making him float a bit.

"What about you?" Tom asked in return. "Doing okay?"

"Yeah. I'm fine." Zach, too, had a few burns and bruises from their impromptu rescue operation. He'd followed Tom back into the house in search of seven-year-old Emily, whom they'd found cowering almost unconscious in a corner in the very back of the burning building.

Tom had reached her first and had carried her out, with Zach supporting him and holding a bedspread over them to protect them as best he could from the rain of burning sparks and debris. By the time they'd gotten the little girl outside, all three of them coughing and gagging and dizzy from lack of breathable air, the first fire truck had arrived. Within minutes, they'd all been strapped into oxygen masks and hustled out of the way so that the crew could do what they could to contain the fire that had already destroyed most of the family's home.

Tom and Zach had broken all sorts of safety rules and procedures during that rescue, but neither of them regretted their actions. They were safe—though it had been a close call, as the house had almost collapsed around them. A family of three was alive, relatively unscathed, though little Emily would be kept in the hospital overnight for observation to make sure there was no lasting damage from her smoke inhalation.

Settling Kenny onto his knee, Tom reflected that he and Zach had been a team again that morning. They had always been stronger and more effective together than apart. How could he have forgotten that?

And how could he have allowed himself to believe that a few physical problems had made him less than he'd been before? He still had a lot to offer, he thought with a surge of satisfaction. Maybe he didn't have the strength or physical stamina he'd had in his twenties, but he still had training and experience and the intelligence to put them to use in new ways. He couldn't be a firefighter again, of course. Would never pass that physical again. But there were other things he could do.

He was a giver. A rescuer. And it was past time he got back into action.

Leslie and Kim entered the room, carrying bowls of thick, steaming stew.

"I'll bring the corn bread," Leslie said, hurrying back out of the room.

"I'll get the tea pitcher." Kim was right on Leslie's heels.

Zach leaned back in his chair and smiled. "A guy could get spoiled by this."

"Yeah, well, don't become too used to it. As soon as Leslie and Kim get over their scare, they'll probably start chewing us out."

Zach winced. "Oh, yeah. They'll get around to that—at least, Kim will."

Tom remembered the look in Leslie's eyes when she'd arrived at the hospital. "Trust me. So will Leslie."

The doorbell rang and Zach started to rise, but Leslie called out, "I'll get it."

A few moments later, they heard new voices from the living room.

Tom sighed. "There's another woman who'll pet us and then punch us. My mother."

"Could be worse," Zach said in commiseration. "My mom and sisters could be here, as well."

Nina rushed into the dining room and immediately pounced on her son. "Tommy, are you all right? Oh, your face! And your hand. Did you hurt your back?"

"I'm fine, Mom. Really."

Nina cupped his face in her small, soft hands, looked him over closely, then kissed his cheek. "I love you."

"Love you, too, Mom."

She smiled at him, then moved to Zach. She tipped his head back, examined the bandage plastered picturesquely to his forehead, touched the bruise darkening at his temple. "You're all right?"

"I'm fine, Nina."

"Thank God." Nina kissed him almost as tenderly as she had her son.

And then she whirled on Tom. "What were you thinking, running into a burning house like that?" she scolded. "When I heard what you did, I was sure my heart would stop."

"I was thinking that there was a little girl in that burning house who needed help," he answered her patiently. "Zach was still winded from bringing out her brother and someone had to go in. That left me."

"I was all right," Zach argued immediately, never willing to admit a weakness. "I just had to catch my breath for a minute. I was right behind you."

Kim rolled her eyes. "Give it up, Super Zach. No one's accusing you of being a mere mortal."

Tom was looking at the man who'd followed his mother into the room. He nodded a bit stiffly. "Hello, Steve."

"Tom." Steve's greeting was only slightly more affable. "I hear you and your friend are quite the heroes."

"We only did what we're trained to do," Tom replied, suddenly self-conscious in a way he hadn't been before. He nodded toward Zach. "Zach McCain, this is Steve Pendleton. Kenny's uncle."

He'd be damned, he thought, if he would add that the guy was also his mother's new boyfriend. Zach could figure that out for himself.

Nina was already back at Tom's side, smoothing his hair, running tender fingertips over his injured cheek. "I'm so glad you're okay."

Tom knew exactly how to distract her from her maternal flutterings. "Here," he said. "Hold your grandson."

Nina melted. "Come here, Kenny," she crooned, gathering the willing baby close and snuggling against his cheek. "What a beautiful little boy you are."

"Nina, you and Steve must stay and have lunch with us," Leslie said. "It's only stew, but there's plenty."

Kim hurried back to the kitchen for dishes and flatware. Nina needed no further persuasion to stay awhile longer.

Kim and Zach didn't linger long after lunch. Kim left in her car. Tom and Zach stood by Zach's truck, with the boat trailer still hooked to the back, and watched her drive away. And then Zach opened the driver's door.

"Maybe next fishing trip, we'll actually get to put the boat in the water," he said before he climbed behind the wheel.

Tom smiled wryly. "I don't know. You and I seem to get into trouble without even trying."

"Quite a team, aren't we?"

"Always have been," Tom answered simply.

Zach nodded, unspoken messages sent and received, no further elaboration necessary in either of their opinions.

Zach had just started his truck, when he suddenly rolled down the window and leaned out. "Hey, Tom."

Tom had already turned toward the house. He looked over his shoulder. "Yeah?"

"What's going on with your mom and the pretty boy?" Zach asked with typical disregard for tact and diplomacy.

Scowling, Tom muttered, "I'm afraid to ask."

Zach laughed. "Hey, I think it's great. She's all starry-eyed and he is definitely moonstruck."

Starry-eyed and moonstruck. The words didn't do a thing to erase Tom's frown. He muttered something incoherent and pointedly turned his back on Zach, who was grinning like an idiot, in Tom's opinion.

As he limped back to the house, his entire body aching, Tom reflected that it was nice to be back on a comfortable basis with Zach. Had he known that Zach had blamed himself all this time for the accident, or that Zach had felt guilty that it was Tom who'd been most seriously injured, he'd have set him straight long ago. But he supposed he'd had to work through his own problems before he'd been up to tackling anyone else's.

Everything was so easy between guys, he mused. A few

words, a couple of insults, maybe a punch or two, and problems were solved. He reached for the front doorknob, thinking of the two women who waited inside for him. His mother and his wife. His relationships with both of them were definitely complex at the moment, and he doubted that punching either one of them in the arm would settle things with them.

The muscle relaxers he'd been given were wearing off fast. He felt as though a mule had kicked him squarely in the back and then stomped on his leg for good measure. The little girl hadn't been all that heavy, though Tom knew he'd strained his back when he'd swung her off the floor and over his shoulder. He suspected he'd done the most damage when he'd half dragged the children's stout mother out of the house, with her resisting him every step of the way.

Tom entered his living room to find his mother and Steve sitting on the couch. Steve had his arm around Nina's shoulder, and his mouth a half inch from her left ear. Leslie was nowhere to be seen.

Okay, so he couldn't punch his mother, not even in fun. But that didn't apply to Steve Pendleton—and if Tom punched him, it would *not* be in fun.

Chapter Fifteen

Nina scooted away from Steve, her cheeks flushing. "Um, Leslie's changing the baby," she said hastily.

Tom nodded and moved to sit down in one of the recliners, making a massive effort to downplay his pronounced limp and general stiffness. It was with relief that he sank onto the soft cushions and extended the footrest, taking some of the strain off his leg.

Steve drew a deep breath, then spoke quickly. "Tom, I think you should know that I've asked your mother to marry me. I want her to move to Little Rock and live with me. I make enough to support us both comfortably, and I've reached a point in my career where I can take time off to be with her. Travel with her. Have fun with her."

Nina gave a squeak of protest and turned to stare at the man beside her with huge, panicked eyes. "Steve!"

He looked steadily back at her. "You're the one who was so worried about your son's reaction. This is the only way I know to find out what that is."

"You shouldn't have just blurted it out like that without warning me," she scolded. "I haven't even given you an answer yet, and here you are—"

"I didn't see any reason to dance around and pretend I haven't brought it up," Steve cut in to argue. "We—"

Tom cleared his throat. Loudly. He'd been sitting motionlessly since Steve had spoken, trying to examine his feelings, trying to decide what to say. And then he'd looked at his mother's face and realized there was only one response he could give.

Steve and Nina fell silent and turned to him, waiting for him to speak, Steve's expression rather belligerent, Nina's somewhat pleading. As if he were a crime-family "godfather," with the power to bless or forbid their union, Tom thought in mingled exasperation and dark amusement.

"Mom," he said, "this decision is entirely up to you. I didn't ask your permission before I married Leslie. You don't have to ask mine if you want to marry Steve."

Nina wrung her hands in her lap. "Obviously, your opinion matters to me. As for making a decision, it's entirely too soon for anything like that…as I told Steve this morning when he brought it up," she added with a frown. "We've known each other only two weeks. There's the age difference between us, and I'd have to do something about my business and move to Little Rock. I don't know if I—" Her voice faded, her expression grew troubled.

"None of that is really important, is it?" Tom asked with a faint, crooked smile. "So what if you've known each other only two weeks? Leslie and I were married two days after she came back to town. How long does it take for you to know whether something's right for you or not?"

He watched as Nina and Steve exchanged a meaningful glance, as if Tom had unwittingly repeated something one of them had said earlier.

He went on. "As for the slight age difference, that's completely between the two of you. If it doesn't bother either of you—and frankly, I can't imagine why it would—then don't worry about what anyone else will think. Selling your business? Moving to Little Rock? Again, it's up to you. You've got a lot of years invested in that shop, but maybe it's time for you to take some time off. Relax a little. Enjoy yourself. You worked so hard to raise me. Well, I'm raised now, and on my own. It's time for you to take care of yourself.''

"It really doesn't bother you?" Nina asked, searching his face with eyes that saw him more clearly than anyone else ever had.

He grimaced. "It'll take some adjusting," he admitted. "I'm pretty spoiled to being the most important man in your life. But what really matters is what you want to do. Do you love this guy, Mom?"

Nina looked slowly from Tom to Steve. Her green eyes were luminous with tears that Tom sincerely hoped would remain unshed.

"Yes," she said. "I do. It just feels…right."

With hardly a pang, Tom smiled. "Then follow your heart," he told her.

He glanced at Steve, who was looking back at him with quizzical approval. "Of course, if you hurt her," Tom said pleasantly, "I'll have to kill you."

"Tom!" Nina protested with a scandalized laugh. "Steve doesn't know you well enough yet to realize that you're joking."

"That's okay, Nina. I took it the way it was intended."

Which meant, Tom interpreted from the rueful look in the other man's eyes, that Steve knew Tom had *not* been joking. Tom was satisfied that Steve was getting to know him well enough.

Leslie cleared her throat. Tom didn't know how long she'd been standing in the doorway, holding a sleepy-looking Kenny in her arms. "Does this mean," she asked, "that we'll be having another wedding soon?"

"Not too soon," Nina answered cautiously. "I don't want to rush into this. I'll have to decide what to do about my shop and my apartment, and I have a dozen other decisions to make before we actually set a date or commit to solid plans or anything.''

Steve put his arm around Nina again and said, ''Yes, Leslie. There will be another wedding soon. Very soon.''

Nina rolled her eyes, but Tom suspected that she wouldn't resist very long on this issue. Steve didn't seem to be the patient type, and he would probably have little trouble convincing Nina that there was no need to waste time. They certainly hadn't wasted any time so far, he thought with a mental wince, suspecting that he knew exactly where Steve had spent the night.

Leslie kissed Nina, then turned to Steve, her expression more guarded. ''I hope you'll be very happy,'' she said to him.

Standing in front of her, looking down at her and his nephew, Steve nodded slowly. ''I guess this means we're going to be part of the same family again. Quite a coincidence, hmm?''

Leslie nodded.

Steve smiled. ''This time we'll make sure it's a happier family, shall we?''

She returned the smile. ''Sounds good to me.''

Steve leaned over to kiss her cheek. ''Thank you,'' he murmured to her. ''For being such a good friend to Crystal, and such a loving mother to her son. And for giving me another chance.''

Kenny knuckled his eyes and blew a noisy raspberry, breaking the emotional intensity of the moment.

The adults laughed, Tom with some relief. He didn't want to be ungracious, but he was ready for his guests to leave. He wanted to take a pill and lie down. He was even to the point where he would welcome a bit of pampering from his wife.

This hero business could be exhausting at times.

As if they'd read his thoughts, Nina and Steve left almost immediately. They refused to allow Tom to get up to see them off. He didn't argue.

His mother kissed him as she passed. "I love you, Tommy."

"Love you, too, Mom. Be happy."

"I've been happy since I was blessed with you," she returned mistily.

He only smiled and waved her gently away.

Leslie put the baby to bed for his nap and then stood for several long moments just looking down at him as he settled in to sleep. He was hers now, she thought with a sigh of relief. Steve had made it clear that he would cause her no further problems. Once the adoption was final—and she foresaw no problems on that count—no one could take this baby away from her again. He would belong to her...

And to Tom.

If Tom's name was included on the adoption papers, as he'd requested, he would be Kenny's father, as legally and as bindingly as Leslie would be the baby's mother. Leslie had been resistant at first to sharing the child she'd fought so hard to keep to herself. But she'd had time to get used to the idea now, and she knew she could have chosen no better father for this child than Tom Lowery.

Kenny would have a mother, a father, a loving grandmother. An uncle. Everything Crystal had wanted for the baby for whom she'd given her life. Leslie could almost feel Crystal's approval in the air around her. She hugged the sensation to herself, refusing to write it off as a silly fancy.

She found herself wondering suddenly, unexpectedly, if Kenny would ever have a brother or a sister.

The question staggered her. She hadn't allowed herself to think that far ahead before. The move here, her impulsive proposal to Tom, the wedding, even her impetuous decision to take the first step toward his bed—those had been choices made on the spur-of-the-moment, prompted by necessity. Now there was no more urgency, no outside threat compelling them to stay together. And yet she was thinking permanence. Without having any idea of how Tom felt about it.

She'd been in love with Tom Lowery for so long that she could hardly remember not loving him. And she'd been terrified of her feelings for him for just as long. So many people she'd loved had hurt her in her past. So many promises made to her had been broken. It wasn't easy for her to trust a man to keep his word.

And yet, she trusted Tom. She wouldn't have married him, wouldn't have brought Kenny to him, if she hadn't trusted him. She simply hadn't acknowledged that blind faith in him until now.

She'd once lived in fear that something would happen to Tom. That she would lose him, if not to abandonment, to cruel fate. That his reckless nature and inherent inclination to help others no matter what the personal cost would take him from her. She'd worried that losing him would mean losing a part of herself, and she'd thought herself unwilling to take that risk. So she'd run…only to learn that there was no place far enough away to escape her memories of him. Her love for him.

She could have lost him today. There was no use in being angry with him for taking the risks he'd taken; given the same circumstances, she had no doubt that he would do exactly the same thing again. He could no more walk away from someone in trouble than he could stop breathing. That was the man she'd fallen in love with from the beginning. The man she'd returned to.

She'd lulled herself into a false sense of security for a couple of weeks, thinking his injuries would keep him safe. Now she knew that nothing had really changed. Whether he realized it yet or not—and she suspected that, after this morning, he did—he was still the same man he'd always been. He would find a way to accomplish whatever he felt the need to do. And Leslie would have to find a way to deal with it, just like Kim and Sami and the other spouses of firefighters and police officers and race-car drivers and all the others who regularly put themselves into danger just because they knew no other way to live.

She was taking a huge emotional leap. She didn't want to

take it alone. She needed to know that Tom was willing to jump with her. He'd let her walk away before. She had to know that he cared enough now to ask her to stay.

Deciding that there was no time like the present to force a confrontation—and hoping to capitalize on the warmth and sweetness she had seen in Tom when he'd reassured his mother—she headed for the living room, galvanized into action.

She stopped in the doorway, her resolve melting. Tom lay back in the recliner, his eyes closed, his face pale. Lines of pain were carved around his mouth, and one hand clenched his right leg as if to massage away the ache there.

Her husband, the battered hero. He'd dealt with enough for one day, she decided. Their personal problems could wait.

She walked quietly into the room and smoothed a hand over his tousled, sandy hair. "I'll get your pain pills. Would you like water or iced tea to wash them down?"

He opened his eyes, a hint of chagrin in their bright-green depths. "I'm fine," he assured her automatically.

"I know you are. But it wouldn't hurt you to take a pill and rest awhile, would it?"

He sighed. "No. I guess it wouldn't hurt. And iced tea sounds good."

Without stopping to think about it, she leaned over to brush a kiss across his mouth. "I'll be right back," she murmured.

He caught her hand when she would have moved away. "Les?"

"Yes?"

He seemed to search for words. "I'm glad you're here," was all he finally said.

Her eyes stung. "So am I, Goose," she whispered, trying to keep her tone light for his sake. And then she turned and hurried away for the pills and iced tea, before she blew the moment by bursting into tears.

During the next week, Leslie discovered that pinning Tom Lowery down to a serious conversation was like trying to rope a tornado. Every time she thought she had him cornered, he whirled off to another subject.

They stayed busy during those days. The telephone rang constantly, friends who'd heard about Tom and Zach's rescue and wanted first to know if he was all right and then to congratulate him. Invitations poured in for dinner parties and impromptu social gatherings, all of Tom's acquaintances wanting to see him with his wife and new son.

Leslie and Tom met with Leo Weiss about starting adoption proceedings and then to talk about Leslie's new duties working for Leo's firm. If Tom had any particular feelings about Leslie's returning to work, he didn't share them.

He was very much the same Tom he'd been before, hiding now behind a steady stream of jokes and wisecracks rather than the surly self-pity he'd displayed when she'd first returned. And while she supposed that was an improvement for him, it didn't tell her any more about his feelings for her.

And she was getting more impatient with each passing day to know the truth.

Only in bed did she feel close to him. When he reached for her, there was genuine hunger in his eyes. Undeniable need in his kisses. A wealth of tenderness and warmth in his lovemaking.

They weren't enough. Hadn't been enough to keep her here before. Weren't enough now.

She needed more.

She just didn't know if Tom was capable of giving more. If he even felt more than desire.

But every time she tried to talk to him, he changed the subject. Cracked a joke. Suddenly decided to play tickle the baby. Anything to avoid letting her get too close to him.

Tom was a man of action, not words.

Apparently, it was time for her to take drastic action.

The future of their marriage depended on his reaction.

Tom came home from work Friday with a smile on his face. That, he reflected, was becoming an increasingly familiar habit.

Work was finished for the week. It was someone else's weekend to be on call. Two entire days stretched in front of him to spend enjoying his wife and kid. His life was getting better all the time.

His mom had offered to baby-sit tomorrow evening, and Tom had decided to surprise Leslie with dinner in a fancy restaurant—just the two of them, for the first time since they'd gotten married. He thought maybe she'd like that. Lately, he'd gotten the impression she wanted to talk. They could talk at the restaurant, over a candlelit dinner.

Serious talks seemed easier in public places, for some reason.

Satisfied with his planning, he entered his house. There was no aroma of dinner cooking. Maybe Leslie wanted to order takeout tonight. Or maybe she'd decided it was his turn to cook. Only fair.

"Les?" He wandered through the living room and kitchen, then checked the baby's room and found it unoccupied. He finally located his family in his bedroom. Kenny was lying on his back at the foot of the bed, playing with his toes and gurgling contentedly.

Leslie was packing a suitcase.

Tom went very still. "What are you doing?"

"Packing."

"I can see that. Why?"

She calmly rolled a sweater and slipped it into the case. "There's no reason for me to stay here any longer. I have a job again now, and Steve has dropped all threats of a custody suit. Now that everything is settled, I'm giving you your freedom back."

Tom could think of nothing he wanted less than his freedom. "Where are you planning to go?"

"My old apartment is available. It turns out that the last tenant moved out just last week. I always liked the landlady there."

He stared at her as though she'd lost her mind. "So you're just going to move out of here? Tonight?"

She smiled too brightly. "No reason to waste time, is there? It's not all that late. Barely six. And I still haven't gotten all my things from Chicago, so there's not that much to move. I'll take what I need tonight, then pick up the rest this weekend."

A spark of anger ignited somewhere deep inside him. It almost overpowered the pain. Not quite. "You didn't think we should discuss this?"

She shrugged. "I've been trying to bring it up all week. You haven't been in the mood for discussions, apparently. Besides, I knew you wouldn't mind. It's not as if you actually *wanted* to marry me."

"Of course I wanted to marry you," he snapped. "I did, didn't I?"

Why couldn't she see how obvious that was?

"You very kindly did me a favor in answer to my request," she corrected him, reaching for another sweater. "I came to you, remember? I practically begged you to marry me. You would have had every right to toss me out on my ear, but I knew you wouldn't. You're a very nice man, Tom Lowery. A good friend."

A good friend. Some might have considered it a compliment. But as far as Tom was concerned, that was the second worst thing she'd said tonight—right behind that bit about giving him his freedom.

He looked at the baby, who was lying so contentedly on the bed, talking to his toes. He looked at Leslie, so calmly stripping Tom's room of all signs of her brief residence there. They'd been a family for only three weeks, and already he couldn't imagine his life without them. Didn't want to imagine it.

Why was Leslie doing this to them?

"Did I do something wrong?" he asked, bewilderment mingling with the hurt and anger. "Did I say something to hurt you?"

"You've done nothing wrong," she answered in a flat, almost accusatory tone that only confused him more. "You've said nothing to hurt me. You've hardly said anything at all, for that matter."

"Then why the hell are you walking out on me again?" The words exploded out of him, just short of a shout. They were loud enough and forceful enough to cause Kenny to look at him in surprise.

Leslie stood beside the open suitcase, a blouse in her hands, hugged to her breasts like a shield. All of a sudden her expression was vulnerable; she looked much less serene and confident than when he'd come in. "I'm leaving this time," she said quietly, "for the same reason I left last time."

Tom's hands clenched into fists at his side. She was about to answer a question that had haunted him for more than a year. And he suddenly wasn't at all sure he wanted to hear the answer. "Why?" he asked, his voice hoarse.

"You haven't asked me to stay," she answered simply.

Leslie watched her words hit Tom like a slap in the face. He stared at her, a frown carved between his eyebrows, disbelief the predominant expression in his piercing green eyes.

Whatever he'd expected her to say, it obviously hadn't been that.

He shook his head. "That's not why you left before," he refuted flatly. "You left because you wanted to. Because you couldn't turn down the offer you got from that firm in Chicago. Your career was more important to you than I was. You chose to leave."

She set the blouse on the suitcase. "You didn't ask me to stay," she repeated. "Not once. Not the day I told you I'd had a job offer. Not the day I left. You never even said you wished I wouldn't go."

And it had broken her heart that he didn't even seem to care whether she stayed or left.

"Leslie, that's ridiculous. I had no right to ask you to pass up a career opportunity like that. It was entirely up to you whether to accept it or decline.''

"We were lovers, Tom. We'd been together for months. Yet never once did you tell me what you felt about me, other than desire. When I told you that I was considering moving hundreds of miles away, all you did was shrug and say, 'I'll miss ya, kid. Have a good life.'''

"I never said that.''

"Maybe not in so many words. But that was the message I received from you.''

"You wanted me to forbid you to take the job?'' he asked, his tone heavily sarcastic.

"I wanted to know you cared,'' she shot back. "I needed to know I mattered to you.''

"Of course you mattered to me.'' He sounded utterly baffled that they were even having this conversation. He reached out a hand to support himself against the doorjamb; he hadn't even come all the way into the bedroom with her, she realized. He'd seen that she was leaving, and he'd reacted the same way he had before. He'd drawn back, out of her way.

"How was I to know that?'' she challenged him. "Was I supposed to read your mind?''

"Leslie, we were lovers. We'd been together for months. I hadn't even looked at another woman the whole time we were together. You practically lived here—your things hung in my closet, your books and papers and stuff were scattered all through my house. But you weren't a prisoner here. You were always free to leave if you wanted to. And obviously, you did.''

She shook her head, saddened by his deliberate obtuseness. "You just don't get it, do you? I needed to know the commitment went both ways. I needed to believe that you wouldn't be the one to simply walk out one day because there was nothing holding us together. I couldn't be the one to take all the emotional risks.''

"Does this have something to do with your father?'' he asked suddenly.

Oh, Lord, the male mind, Leslie thought with a shake of her head.

"Of course it has to do with my father," she answered in exasperation. "All my life, I watched him live with women—marry women—without ever really committing himself to any of them. It was always so easy for him to move on, because he never really cared enough to stay. He's funny and charming and romantic and dashing—like you—but his philosophy has always been to love the one he's with at the time. Permanence isn't even a part of his vocabulary. How was I to believe you were any different, when you never seemed to be interested in talking about the future? When you never seemed to look past a day at a time? For all I knew, you found someone else a week after I left. For all I knew, I was no more special than any of the women who proceeded me, as easily replaced and as briefly lamented."

He scowled. "You make it sound as though there was a whole string of women before you. There wasn't. I'd dated, of course, but I'd never lived with anyone before you."

"We weren't living together, Tom. We simply had a long series of sleepovers. Living together implies that a decision was made, a question asked and answered. That never happened between us. Not until I came back into your life and asked you to marry me."

He sighed loudly. "What ever happened to that old saying about actions speaking louder than words? Not everyone is comfortable talking about his feelings, Leslie. I married you because I wanted to, not just because you asked me to. I've told you I want to adopt Kenny—and that's most definitely a permanent commitment. Everything I have is yours as much as mine now. Doesn't that say anything to you?"

"It tells me that you're a very kind and generous man. It doesn't tell me how you feel about me."

"Damn it, Leslie, you're my *wife!*"

"Yeah, well, my father's had a bunch of those," she replied bitterly. "And he never seemed to have any trouble walking away from them. None of them really mattered to him."

"I'm not your father," Tom said between gritted teeth. "And I'm not the one walking away. You are."

"Physically, maybe. You do it emotionally, every time you hold your feelings inside yourself."

"I'm not comfortable with flowery speeches. You know that."

She sighed. "You can say anything you want whenever you want. I've heard you charm little old ladies and schmooze at a party like a career politician. People come to you with their problems because they know you'll listen and give advice and encouragement. I knew when I came to you for help that you wouldn't turn me away, because that's the kind of guy you are. You're always there for everyone else. Always the rescuer, the hero, the one with all the answers. But you never seek advice for yourself. You never ask for anything from anyone. You can't—or won't—admit weakness or vulnerability."

She pushed a hand through her hair wearily. "You're always there when someone needs you, Tom. But I refuse to be the only one with weaknesses and vulnerabilities. I need to be needed, just as much as you do. I need to know that I matter."

"Leslie—"

His face was blurred, and she realized that she was seeing him through a film of tears. She'd been so determined to play this scene calmly. Rationally. It was how things had always been between them. How they'd both wanted it before. But somewhere along the way, Leslie had changed. She'd chosen to throw away the fears of her past and face the risk of making a permanent commitment. Of opening herself to heartbreak and disappointment for the sake of love.

But she couldn't do it alone.

"I don't know why you need to be so strong. Why you have to always be the rescuer. Maybe it's because you grew up as the man of your household, feeling some responsibility to take care of your mother, despite her obvious ability to take care of herself...and of you. Or maybe it's something else, I don't know. I'm no psychologist. But it's so strong in you that when you thought of yourself as damaged and weak—it changed you. You weren't even the same man. You couldn't deal with it. And then Kenny and I came along, and we needed you. And a house burned, and you found that you could still save people, no matter what the cost to yourself. This past week, you've almost been your old self again. The joker. The golden boy. The local hero. You don't need me. You don't need anyone.''

She turned to pick up the baby, hugging his warm, chubby little body close to her. ''We'll be fine now,'' she said in a near whisper. ''We'll get out of your way so you can find someone else to rescue.''

Tom stood very stiffly in the doorway, his fingers clenched so tightly on the doorjamb that his knuckles were bone-white. ''I don't want you to go.''

He'd spoken in a mutter, barely audible. Leslie cradled the baby and blinked back a new wave of tears. ''I have to go,'' she whispered. ''I can't stay in a relationship that isn't equal.''

''Leslie, I need you. Please don't leave me again.''

She closed her eyes, feeling a few tears escape to roll slowly down her cheeks. ''I would have given anything to hear you say those words before. But not like this. Not just because I've asked you to say them. It isn't just the words I want from you, Tom. I need to believe them.''

''Then tell me what I have to do to convince you. Because, God help me, I can't go through this again. It almost ripped my heart out when you walked out on me before. There wasn't one day you were gone that I didn't miss you and want you back.''

She was frozen in place by the look in his eyes, the raw edge to his voice. He sounded so sincere. Yet she was so afraid to believe…

''Why didn't you say anything?'' she asked, making no effort to hide her doubt.

''I thought I was being noble,'' he said, his mouth twisting. ''I thought I was doing what was best for you.''

''You could have asked me.''

"And would you have stayed?" he demanded. "Would you have turned down a job that was everything you'd always trained for and hoped for?"

She'd asked herself that same question many times. She'd wondered what she would have said if given a choice between advancing her career or staying with Tom. She'd tried to decide if she would have been able to overcome her mistrust of a man's promises, her old fears of abandonment. If she would have stayed. And she always came up with the same answer.

"I would have stayed," she whispered. "I loved you."

A muscle spasmed in his jaw, tightening his mouth, narrowing his eyes. "Oddly enough, I loved *you* enough to let you go. I wasn't the only one who didn't share my feelings, was I?"

"No," she admitted. "I was afraid of rejection."

"I guess I was, too. I'd never really failed at anything before. I didn't think I could handle failing with you."

"Did you marry me only to rescue me?" She held her breath as she waited for his answer.

"No. I married you because I wanted you to be my wife." He searched her face. "Did you marry me only because you needed to be rescued?"

"Asking you to marry me took every ounce of courage I had," she replied. "It was a way for me keep Kenny, but mostly it was an excuse for me to come back into your life. I wanted another chance to show you how good we are together. How much we need each other."

"I love you, Leslie. And I need you." The words came easier this time. He dropped his hand and moved toward her, his slight limp doing nothing to diminish the overall effect of solid, strong, virile male. "Please don't leave me."

Holding Kenny in one arm, she reached out to him, the tears streaming unchecked down her cheeks. "All you had to do was ask," she managed to say. "Oh, Tom—"

He kissed her roughly. Deeply. Thoroughly. "I love you," he muttered against her lips. "I always will."

"I love you, too. Always." She pressed her mouth to his again.

Kenny made a gleeful grab for Tom's hair and spewed a noisy, wet raspberry, which effectively interrupted the most romantic moment of Leslie's lifetime.

Faces still close together, Tom and Leslie broke into laughter.

Wincing as Kenny tugged firmly on his hair, Tom shook himself free, then leaned over to kiss the baby's forehead. "Give me a break, Ken. I'm baring my soul here."

"P-b-b-b-t." Pleased with the attention he'd gotten the first time, Kenny had decided to try it again.

"I love you, Son." Tom kissed the baby again. And then he kissed Leslie. "I love you, Wife. I'll try to remember to say it often, okay?"

Still misty-eyed, she smiled and nodded. "So will I."

"Great. Now, why don't you unpack this suitcase while I make dinner? I'm starving."

Leslie sighed. So much for romantic moments.

She thought of what Tom had said earlier. In his case, actions really did speak louder than words. He'd given her so much—his name, his home and now his heart. She would be content from now on to know that everything he did for her and for Kenny was based on love.

But she would also insist that he say the words at times. They were so very nice to hear.

Tom took Kenny out of her arms. "C'mon, kid," he said, moving toward the doorway. "I'll let you sit in your seat and watch me make chili. I don't want to brag, but I make the best chili this side of the Texas border."

Leslie watched her husband and son with a heart so full of love she thought it might burst. "Hey, Goose—" she said, forcing the words past the sentimental lump in her throat.

Tom glanced over his shoulder. "Yeah?"

"Easy on the peppers, okay? Last time you made chili for me, you nearly set my mouth on fire."

His grin was broad, beautiful, unshadowed. "That's okay. I happen to have a lot of training in putting out fires."

Leslie fanned her face with her hand when she was alone. Her husband was also very good at starting fires, she mused, feeling the heat rise inside her in response to that sexy grin of his. Her own smile felt wicked. As soon as Kenny was in bed, she planned to ignite a few fires of her own.

Wiping the remains of tears from her cheek with the back of one hand, she turned back to the suitcase and began to unpack. She was home. And this time, she was here to stay.

Tom needed her.

* * * * *

Silhouette Romance is proud to present
Virgin Brides, a brand-new monthly
promotional series by some of the bestselling
and most beloved authors in the romance genre.

In March '98, look for the very first
Virgin Brides novel,

THE PRINCESS BRIDE by Diana Palmer.

Just turn the page for an exciting preview of
Diana Palmer's thrilling new tale...

Chapter One

Tiffany saw him in the distance, riding the big black stallion. It was spring, and that meant roundup. It was not unusual to see the owner of the Lariat ranch in the saddle at dawn lending a hand to rope a stray calf or help work the branding. Kingman Marshall kept fit with ranch work, and despite the fact that he shared an office and a business partnership with Tiffany's father in land and cattle, his staff didn't see a lot of him.

This year, they were using helicopters to mass the far-flung cattle, and they had a corral set up on a wide, flat stretch of land where they could dip the cattle, check them, cut out the calves for branding and separate them from their mothers. It was physically demanding work, and no job for a tenderfoot. King wouldn't let Tiffany near it, but it wasn't a front row seat at the corral that she wanted. If she could just get his attention away from the milling cattle on the wide, rolling plain that led to the Guadalupe River, if he'd just look her way...

Tiffany stood up on a rickety lower rung of the gray wood fence, avoiding the sticky barbed wire, and waved her Stetson at him. She was a picture of young elegance in her tan jodh-

purs and sexy pink silk blouse and high black boots. She was
a debutante. Her father, Harrison Blair, was King's business
partner and friend, and if she chased King, her father encouraged her. It would be a marriage made in heaven. That is, if
she could find some way to convince King of it. He was elu-
sive and quite abrasively masculine. It might take more than
a young lady of almost twenty-one with a sheltered, monied
background to land him. But, then, Tiffany had confidence in
herself; she was beautiful and intelligent.

Her long black hair hung to her waist in back, and she
refused to have it cut. It suited her tall, slender figure and made
an elegant frame for her soft, oval face and wide green eyes
and creamy complexion. She had a sunny smile, and it never
faded. Tiffany was always full of fire, burning with a love of
life that her father often said had been reflected in her long-
dead mother.

"King!" she called, her voice clear, and it carried in the
early-morning air.

He looked toward her. Even at that distance, she could see
that cold expression in his pale blue eyes, on his lean, hard
face with its finely chiseled features. He was a rich man. He
worked hard, and he played hard. He had women, Tiffany
knew so, but he was nothing if not discreet. He was a man's
man, and he lived like one. There was no playful boy in that
tall, fit body. He'd grown up years ago, the boyishness driven
out of him by a rich, alcoholic father who demanded blind
obedience from the only child of his shallow, runaway wife.

She watched him ride toward her, easy elegance in the saddle. He reined in at the fence, smiling down at her with faint
arrogance.

"You're out early, tidbit," he remarked in a deep, velvety
voice with just a hint of Texas drawl.

"I'm going to be twenty-one tomorrow," she said pertly.
"I'm having a big bash to celebrate, and you have to come.
Black tie, and don't you dare bring anyone. You're mine, for
the whole evening. It's my birthday and on my birthday I want
presents—and you're it. My big present."

His dark eyebrows lifted with amused indulgence. "You might have told me sooner that I was going to be a birthday present," he said. "I have to be in Omaha early Saturday."

"You have your own plane," she reminded him. "You can fly."

"I have to sleep sometimes," he murmured.

"I wouldn't touch that line with a ten-foot pole," she drawled, peeking at him behind her long lashes. "Will you come?"

He lit a cigarette, took a long draw and blew it out with slight impatience. "Little girls and their little whims," he mused. "All right, I'll whirl you around the floor and toast your coming-of-age, but I won't stay. I can't spare the time."

"You'll work yourself to death," she complained, and then became solemn. "You're only thirty-four and you look forty."

"Times are hard, honey," he mused, smiling at the intensity in that glowering young face. "We've had low prices and drought. It's all I can do to keep my financial head above water."

"You could take the occasional break," she advised. "And I don't mean a night on the town. You could get away from it all and just rest."

"They're full up at the Home," he murmured, grinning at her exasperated look. "Honey, I can't afford vacations, not with times so hard. What are you wearing for this coming-of-age party?" he asked to divert her.

"A dream of a dress. White silk, very low in front, with diamanté straps and a white gardenia in my hair." She laughed.

He pursed his lips. He might as well humor her. "That sounds dangerous," he said softly.

"It will be," she promised, teasing him with her eyes. "You might even notice that I've grown up."

He frowned a little. That flirting wasn't new, but it was disturbing lately. He found himself avoiding little Miss Blair, without really understanding why. His body stirred even as he looked at her, and he moved restlessly in the saddle. She was years too young for him, and a virgin to boot, according to her doting, sheltering father. All those years of obsessive parental protection had led to a very immature and unavailable girl. It wouldn't do to let her too close. Not that anyone ever got close to Kingman Marshall, not even his infrequent lovers. He had good reason to keep women at a distance. His upbringing had taught him too well that women were untrustworthy and treacherous.

"What time?" he asked on a resigned note.

"About seven?"

He paused thoughtfully for a minute. "Okay." He tilted his wide-brimmed hat over his eyes. "But only for an hour or so."

"Great!"

He didn't say goodbye. Of course, he never did. He wheeled the stallion and rode off, man and horse so damn arrogant that she felt like flinging something at his tall head. He was delicious, she thought, and her body felt hot all over just looking at him. On the ground he towered over her, lean and hard-muscled and sexy as all hell. She loved watching him.

With a long, unsteady sigh, she finally turned away and remounted her mare. She wondered sometimes why she bothered hero-worshiping such a man. One of these days he'd get married and she'd just die. God forbid that he'd marry anybody but her!

That was when the first shock of reality hit her squarely between the eyes. Why, she had to ask herself, would a man like that, a mature man with all the worldly advantages, want a young and inexperienced woman like herself at his side? The question worried her so badly that she almost lost control of her mount.

The truth of her situation was unpalatable and a little frightening. She'd never even considered a life without King. What if she had to?

She rode home slowly, a little depressed because she'd had to work so hard just to get King to agree to come to her party.

And still haunting her was that unpleasant speculation about a future without King…

But she perked up when she thought of the evening ahead. King didn't come to the house often, only when her father wanted to talk business away from work, or occasionally for drinks with some of her father's acquaintances. To have him come to a party was new and stimulating. Especially if it ended the way she planned. She had her sights well and truly set on the big rancher. Now all she had to do was take aim!

* * * * *

Return to the Towers!

In March
New York Times bestselling author

NORA ROBERTS

brings us to the Calhouns' fabulous
Maine coast mansion and reveals the
tragic secrets hidden there for generations.

For all his degrees, Professor Max Quartermain has a
lot to learn about love—and luscious Lilah Calhoun is
just the woman to teach him. Ex-cop Holt Bradford is
as prickly as a thornbush—until Suzanna Calhoun's
special touch makes love blossom in his heart.
And all of them are caught in the race to solve
the generations-old mystery of a priceless
lost necklace...and a timeless love.

Lilah and Suzanna
THE
Calhoun Women

**A special 2-in-1 edition containing
FOR THE LOVE OF LILAH and
SUZANNA'S SURRENDER**

Available at your favorite retail outlet.

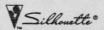

Look us up on-line at: http://www.romance.net

CWVOL2

Take 4 bestselling love stories FREE

Plus get a FREE surprise gift!

Special Limited-time Offer

Mail to Silhouette Reader Service™

3010 Walden Avenue
P.O. Box 1867
Buffalo, N.Y. 14240-1867

YES! Please send me 4 free Silhouette Special Edition® novels and my free surprise gift. Then send me 6 brand-new novels every month, which I will receive months before they appear in bookstores. Bill me at the low price of $3.57 each plus 25¢ delivery and applicable sales tax, if any.* That's the complete price and a savings of over 10% off the cover prices—quite a bargain! I understand that accepting the books and gift places me under no obligation ever to buy any books. I can always return a shipment and cancel at any time. Even if I never buy another book from Silhouette, the 4 free books and the surprise gift are mine to keep forever.

235 SEN CF2T

Name	(PLEASE PRINT)	
Address	Apt. No.	
City	State	Zip

This offer is limited to one order per household and not valid to present Silhouette Special Edition® subscribers. *Terms and prices are subject to change without notice. Sales tax applicable in N.Y.

USPED-696

©1990 Harlequin Enterprises Limited

DIANA PALMER
ANN MAJOR
SUSAN MALLERY

In **April 1998** get ready to catch the bouquet. Join in the excitement as these bestselling authors lead us down the aisle with three heartwarming tales of love and matrimony in Big Sky country.

RETURN TO WHITEHORN

A very engaged lady is having second thoughts about her intended; a pregnant librarian is wooed by the town bad boy; a cowgirl meets up with her first love. Which Maverick will be the next one to get hitched?

Available in April 1998.

Silhouette's beloved **MONTANA MAVERICKS** returns in Special Edition and Harlequin Historicals starting in February 1998, with brand-new stories from your favorite authors.

Round up these great new stories at your favorite retail outlet.

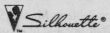